The Cinelli Vases

A Thornton King Adventure

The Cinelli Vases

By

GLYN IDRIS JONES

DCG
Publications

First Published in Greece 2011
© Glyn Jones 2009

ISBN 978-960-99470-3-9

Typeset by
DCG Publications
www.dcgmediagroup.com

www.glynjones.net

1

Ming, Tang, Qing, any of the Chinese Imperial Dynasties noted for their art, their poetry, their silk, their exquisite porcelain, might have produced the pair of vases standing behind the not too clean window of what appeared to be an antique dealer's establishment in the Westbourne Grove and at which Thornton King, London based private eye and for once feeling rather flushed in at least two senses of the word – he really ought to do something about his blood pressure - was now bending forward with hands on knees, gazing in rapt admiration and growing a little red in the face; too much so for one so young.

The reason he had a healthy bank balance for once, rather than being in hock up to his eyebrows and in constant fear of his bank manager, he of the sallow complexion, rimless spectacles and the gimlet eyes and who never suffered from blood pressure, was because he had recently been quite handsomely paid by one, Aurora Pemberton for a job well done in solving the mystery of her uncle's strange, one might even say bizarre, death by crossbow bolt. Not a pleasant way to go as Saint Sebastian would confirm if he were in a position so to do. Admittedly he, Thornton that is, not Saint Sebastian, had the assistance of his friend Miss Holly Day in solving the case and they both came within an inch of losing it all at the hands of a sex mad lunatic by the name of Mike Ayliff, a thorn in Holly's bonnet at the hush hush ministry for many years but, fortunately in the nick of time, as the old saying has it, that despicable human being had come to a deservedly sticky end and Holly had a brief fling with her rescuer which was lovely for a time but, also as the old saying goes, all good things must come to an end, especially if they become boring and, although it might have been a marriage of two bodies, it did not include a marriage of true minds which quite shortly became a distinct impediment.

As far as Thornton was concerned he had not yet thought of a suitable reward for Miss Day, having only got as far as "I owe you, Holly," but no doubt he would think of something sooner or later. "Oh, yes, Thornton," she would no doubt reply, "like the next time you need me." "I have never needed you, Holly," he would answer in jest, "only your expertise" which, in a way, was perfectly true. Holly seemed to have almost a supernatural knack of pressing the right button at the right time.

At the moment though, Thornton was so absorbed he was impervious both to thoughts of Holly, to his blood pressure, and to the pedestrians passing by or the noise and stench of the heavy traffic: diesel fumes and leaded petrol; red double decker London Transport buses, cars, taxis, bikes, lorries, delivery vans, back and forth they went, all belching out their poisonous life-threatening fumes.

Once upon a time in British cities, only a few years back

in fact, well within living memory and before the clean air act was brought in, it was the smoke from coal fires and thousands upon thousands of chimneys that led to that blinding almost impenetrable choking phenomenon known as smog when, at times, a person literally could not see a hand in front of his or her face. You walked the streets breathing through a handkerchief you held to mask your mouth and nose and when you removed it it was speckled with soot. You didn't have to actually go down the mine then to encounter any of the health hazards suffered by miners to lungs and bronchi. Now it was the internal combustion engine and the by-product of burning oil that tortured the lungs as it made Sheiks and Middle Eastern princes rich beyond belief and, as the years would go by with the inevitable increase in motorised traffic, it could only get a whole lot worse. London at the start of the nineteen seventies might be grinding almost to a standstill but there would come a time, in a few short years perhaps, when something really drastic would have to be done about it before the city ground to a complete stop.

The Imperial Chinese Dynasties, as well as their artistic output, were of course also noted for their barbaric wars and their own even more barbaric methods of torture, their cruelty was no fable – the death of a thousand cuts for instance; or runaway slaves, when recaptured, having the soles of their feet opened up, stuffed with sharp pebbles and sewn up again, making it impossible to put a foot down without the most unbearable pain, as anyone who has suffered from gout will know, when the agony of the foot touching the ground is excruciating and even more excruciating when lifting it off, as though a high voltage jolt of electricity is sent shooting from the toes up the full length of the leg.

On the whole Thornton, who according to a grateful and

generous Miss Aurora Pemberton, his first and only genuine client in the months since his dismissal from Her Majesty's government's hush-hush department, was simply the best private eye on the block, had never really been that enamoured of Chinese art. He had always felt there was something, warlords not withstanding, rather feminine, maybe even effeminate about it. Japanese was much more to his liking, though here again the extraordinary extremes of cruelty and the appreciation of beauty going hand in hand as it were, seemed to be so much a part of the Oriental mindset, in particular the Japanese: think of the haiku, think of cherry blossom, beautiful calligraphy, delicate landscape painting and the wonderful decoration of a Samurai sword, the blade forged to a razor sharp edge but of course for one single purpose. It has to be simply a part of the Oriental psyche. Cruel occidentals, of whom of course there has never been any shortage, don't display this dichotomy. When Nazi thugs and, let's face it, they were nothing more than that, a bunch of brutal murdering thugs, collected works of art from Jewish ex-citizens of The Third Reich and from conquered territories it was not because of a love of beauty but simple rapacity, a masterpiece put aside for a rainy day and a possible quick exit to Argentina or any other welcoming country should a turn of events so dictate, which of course it eventually did. Was it not Herr Goebbels who said he wanted to reach for his gun every time culture was mentioned? It couldn't have been that flabby-arsed Goering. He really did have an appreciation of the works of art he acquired, a positive treasure trove, to grace Carinhalle, the house so named in honour of his first wife. These included some exquisite carved ivory horses from Japan, objects d'art Thornton would have loved.

Once though, despite this preference for the Japanese,

4

Thornton had fallen in love with a pair of Chinese vases that he could never have afforded in a month of Sundays; probably not even now, despite Rory's generosity. They were a shiny black glaze decorated with a myriad small stylised flowers in pastel colours. They stood a good two and a half feet tall; about eight inches in diameter at the top and their beauty had him captivated. He gazed at them for minutes on end every time he passed the rather chi-chi looking antique shop in Mayfair from where they were being sold and never had the courage to go in and enquire as to the cost. It was after all Mayfair and therefore hardly likely to be in his price range. Eventually the owner of the shop, as chi-chi as his establishment, who would probably only refer to his business as "the shop" in a sort of self deprecating way and with a wry smile, seemed to grow a trifle suspicious and stood just inside looking out with the same kind of expression Thornton usually encountered on the face of his bank manager. The man's immaculate clobber was obviously Saville Row and Jermyn Street and probably cost as much as Thornton earned in a year when he was still with Her Majesty's secret service.

Then one day inevitably the vases were gone and the proprietor looking out at Thornton looking in gave one of his wry little smiles to which Thornton responded with a delicate little wave of his fingers before moving on.

And now here he was gazing at another pair which, except for height and shape, were so different but which he found equally as alluring as his earlier fancy. The difference was in both the glaze and the decoration, the glaze being the palest grey celadon-ware with a thousand hairline cracks and the decoration, consisting on one side of each vase in a darker shade of grey, almost a matt black, large dragons in bas-relief (a good luck symbol?) and, on the opposite side, also in bas-relief, the dragon could be seen flying over hanging tassels (symbolising monetary good fortune perhaps). Not being an expert he didn't know it but they were actually not made for any Emperor. At the most they were probably early nineteenth century and manufactured for the house of a top grade Mandarin whose seal no doubt would be found stamped into the base, so really Ming, Tang and Qing had nothing to do with it and this pair might just be within his reach.

Thornton heaved a sigh and wondered if it was worth his while on this occasion to pluck up courage, enter the shop and make enquiries as to the price. Possibly he could always get them on a down payment followed by affordable instalments if the owner of the shop was willing to negotiate. The peeling blistered green paint on the exterior woodwork that could be removed with a fingernail, the dirty glass, the air of sad dilapidation, all would indicate the business needed an injection of the readies to get it back on its feet. Deciding it was a case of nothing ventured nothing gained, and for once not having a bank account forever in the red and a smarmy bank manager bruising his vulnerable ego in no uncertain terms, Thornton opened the door and winced visibly at the loud jangling of the overhead bell. Activated by the opening of the door and his entry into the rather dingy premises it bounced madly overhead on its sturdy looking spring as if pleased to be welcoming a visitor. It must have been a feature of the shop since its opening in the nineteenth century or possibly even earlier.

The vases standing on a long very low shelf just behind the window appeared to be the only antiques in the place; the rest of the stock being pictures of all sizes, framed and unframed, hanging on or stacked against the walls. They were mostly covered in the dust of months if not years and, it would appear, were of no particular merit. Obviously the shop did not attract too much custom as far as sales went though to one side a lengthy, hacked about, heavy workbench and various tools showing signs of much use, panes of glass, empty frames and cardboard hangings on which were glued picture frame samples in different woods, styles and plaster, indicated some work in that direction which no doubt kept the business afloat.

As he waited for someone to appear Thornton wondered if he might find amongst the daubs an old master the shop owner was unaware of, perhaps a van Dyke or a Titian, a small Rembrandt sketch maybe. Chance would be a fine thing. Like winning the pools or a big prize on the Premium Bonds of which the odds evidently are trillions to one, these sort of things always happened to other, usually the most undeserving people, never to him.

Still, at the moment, thanks to Rory Pemberton he kept on reminding himself, he was more flush than he had been in many a long day, so much so that he had moved out of the decaying rat's nest he used to call his office and into one more befitting his being the best private eye on the block. The office was only a couple of doors up from his previous one just off the Tottenham Court Road but at least it wasn't in a virtually condemned building about to tumble down around his ears and the move, being no more than a matter of yards, he didn't have the expense of having to hire a removal company. There wasn't that much to move anyway and three of Harold Norris's strong lads, a borrowed trolley, a couple of quid and a few convivial rounds in the pub afterwards did the trick. "Anytime, Thornton, old lad, anytime. You scratch my back, I'll scratch yours." Thornton wasn't too sure how he could scratch Harold's back but was pretty certain that Harold would come up sooner or later with an itch that required the necessary scratch.

He decided to linger a little longer (Thornton's thought processes were sometimes a bit like popular song) for someone to appear in response to the jangling bell and, after quite a few minutes, a dead ringer for a Dickensian apparition stepped out from behind a raggedy rep curtain at the back of the shop. For a moment though Thornton wondered if Bela Lagusi hadn't come back from the dead to make another movie as the man advanced, staring at him almost pop-eyed, his mouth still moving and crumbs of something or other peppering his unshaven chin together with what looked like a sliver of ham with a slight greenish tinge dangling from the corner of his mouth, all of which explained the tardiness in answering the bell. Despite the clemency of an early summer day he was wearing a heavy greasy old-fashioned grey cardigan fraying here and there and that gave the appearance of having been slept in all winter. On his head there was what looked suspiciously like an ancient hand knitted much used tea cosy with a pom pom that had seen better days.

'Yes?' His furry tongue appeared to lick the ham back into his mouth.

'The vases in the window.'

'What about them?' The voice had been made harsh from years of cigarette smoke and he tended every now and again to gently clear his throat of some real or imaginary obstacle.

'How much…?'

'Not for sale.'

'Oh!'

That, it would seem, was to be the end of the conversation but Thornton was not to be put off quite so easily.

'If they're not for sale,' he asked, smiling in order he hoped to disarm the antagonism blowing his way, 'may I enquire as to what they are doing in the window?'

'Decoration. They're there for decoration. All right? Satisfied? As you can see, I am an art gallery. I don't go in for vases, Chinese or otherwise. Decoration, that's all. Now, if you're interested in pictures...'

'No, I'm not inter...' He paused. 'I don't know though...'

Thornton had a sudden mental picture of the pictureless walls of his new office, not even a Pirelli calendar, or any other calendar for that matter and, should he now show even the slightest interest in any of the daubs in oil, water colour, gouache, tempura, impasto or whatever that passed for works of art in this musty room, he might get around to persuading the old geyser to sell the vases, depending on the price of course. Looking a bit closer, Thornton decided the shopkeeper wasn't that old. He just looked old. Some people look old even when they're young. Some babies even look old. On the other hand some geriatrics look like infants. All in the genes he supposed.

Watched by the not so old man he pulled a large nondescript canvas away from the wall to see what was underneath and immediately let it go, wiping the dust from his fingers before moving on to a second stack. It would appear most of these attempts at painting were badly executed copies of various styles. Pointillism with a lot of blue in various shades seemed a hot favourite though there were a couple of Klees, a Chagall or two; and could that possibly be a Walter Sickert? It was certainly his chiaroscuro, dark, dingy and disturbing, a distinct aura of evil. Was it at all possible, as some believed, that this man was Jack the Ripper? A number of works were more than likely final projects from various art schools. If framed, the frames were worth more than the pictures. Thornton almost jumped out of his skin when he heard an accusing voice immediately behind him.

'You don't know chickenshit from paintings, do you, so what do you think you're looking at?'

Thornton had turned around and was disconcerted to have the not quite so old guy redolent of stale cigarette smoke, raw garlic, and a strong body odour standing quite so close. The cardigan, let alone the trousers, had obviously not seen the inside of a washing machine for a very long time. Thornton seemed to spend a great deal of his time in close proximity to the great unwashed which he assumed was pretty inevitable in a city like London; something one learnt to live with. He had a momentary vision of that hippy guitarist with the black toenails and the tar-stained fingers who used to strum his instrument in his favourite pub. Whatever happened to him? The guv'nor must have finally put in his hearing aid, heard what was being produced, and given the poor lad the push. So it was probably back to Tottenham Court Road underground, chilblains, and the onset of piles from sitting on the cold hard cement even with a sheet of cardboard betwixt and between. Now, endeavouring to avoid any contact with the shop's owner, Thornton couldn't back away without barging into canvasses and creating chaos so he stepped sideways and around in order, should it prove necessary, to have a clear escape route across the fairly wide dirty but uncluttered floor.

'I may not know much about art but I know what I like, to quote a million people.'

'But what you like is not in my shop, huh?' He had been followed to his new position.

'You haven't given me much time to actually look, have you? Mister... er... Mister... '

'Riccoboni, Bruno Riccoboni.'

'Mister Riccoroni.'

Bruno wondered for the briefest moment whether or not to put the man straight on his name and decided it wasn't worth the bother. It was hardly likely he would ever see the idiot again and he never knew how true this would turn out to be.

Thornton's peregrination had taken him passed the full length of the workbench so that he was now back at the window and facing the street, as busy as ever. A young girl, probably on her way home from school, paused in front of the window and they exchanged smiles and, from Thornton, a wink before she moved on. A mother with a much younger girl stopped, ostensibly to wipe the child's dribbling nose. This having been done and the handkerchief put away, the child glared at Thornton and stuck out her tongue. Thornton retaliated in similar fashion but very fast, a quick flip in and out rather like a lizard or a chameleon catching a fly so that, when the child responded in turn by sticking out her tongue again and making a big deal of it, the mother saw it and gave her daughter a whack across the ear. This set up a bawling that made passers by turn to look and Thornton to feel slightly guilty, especially as the mother mouthed an abject apology through the glass and hauled her infant away still bawling and the nose running again as well as the eyes. Thornton waggled an apologetic four fingers the child didn't see, then lowered his arm and, holding one of the vases by the rim, started to tilt it towards his chest. The stink warned him even before the sound of the voice that Bruno Riccoboni was once more at his shoulder. In fact, the voice was so thunderous, had the smell not alerted him, he could have, as he was always so fond of saying, leapt in twenty directions at once and sent the vase, possibly both of them, flying.

'What are you doing?' Bruno shrieked, his guttural voice suddenly turning falsetto, 'Put that down! Put it down and leave it alone! You could break it! That is an expensive artefact!'

'It is certainly a fact,' Thornton said, 'and arty to boot. And I wouldn't dream of damaging it. All I was doing… '

'You've no right to touch it!' Bruno was still at screaming pitch. 'That's private property, that is!'

Thornton was still holding the vase. The art dealer's complexion had gone from pasty to puce and his cheeks were quivering to such an extent the crumbs had fallen from his unshaven chin and now nestled in the wool of his cardie. Thornton decided he had better let go the vase before the man suffered a heart attack. In a slightly childish display he carefully placed his free hand on the vase's shoulder and ever so slowly and gently set it upright once more before leaning forward to take a peek inside.

'Now what are you doing?' Bruno yelled.

'It felt very heavy,' Thornton said, 'I was wondering what's inside it.'

'Sand.'

'Sand?'

'That's what I said. Sand. Don't you know about putting sand in the bottom of a vase? It's to stop it toppling over if it's accidentally bumped or some bloody idiot knocks it over.'

'Oh,' Thornton said, realising he was the bloody idiot being referred to, and he took another peek, this time without touching the vase. It was an unwise move. With his face almost horizontal to the floor he heard rather than felt the crick in his neck and knew he was in trouble. He slowly straightened up as Bruno put the flat of his hand across the vase's mouth.

'Now, if you're not going to buy anything and you've quite

finished...'

Bruno, keeping his bloodshot eyes on his obviously unwelcome visitor, stepped back, opened the door and held it open as the bell jangled. He raised one hand to grab and stop it.

'...snooping, get out of my shop,' he finished.

Thornton gave him a fairly wide berth in passing but, before leaving, turned back and said, 'What part of Italy are you from? I mean, with your name, how come you don't talk with an Italian accent, not a trace?'

'You expect me to put a vowel at the end of every word do you? Well sorry to disappoint you. Good day. Or would you rather have buongiorno?' With which he shut the door and slouched back into his shop, probably to finish his ham sandwich before the rats or the roaches got to it.

Thornton stood for a while gazing longingly at the vases, his head in doggy fashion tilted slightly to one side, before he turned away.

The next day when he passed by they had disappeared, obviously no longer needed for decoration and, with the judicious application of a bag of frozen peas the previous evening he had managed to straighten out his neck and no longer resembled a puzzled retriever, though he was still a very puzzled private eye.

2

The Swiss in their tiny democratic, peaceful, hygienic, pristine clean and healthy mountainous retreat have had to put up with any number of jibes by those envious folk unfortunate enough not to have been Swiss born or resident there. For example there is Harry Lime's much quoted jest – via Orson Welles and The Third Man – regarding democracy and the cuckoo clock; and the little Englander financiers' disparaging remarks about "The Gnomes of Zurich". There are also schoolboy jokes like, "How do you make a Swiss roll?" The answer to which is, "Throw him down the mountainside." And it would appear somebody, or more than likely some bodies, had taken that last jest to heart because that is exactly what had happened to the quite elderly mouse-like Herr Professor Ernst von Sachfelde, chief chemist at the Laboratoire Gautier when his bruised battered and broken body was discovered at the foot of a high cliff a fair distance from home in his and Calvin's native city of Geneva, and nobody, when police enquiries were naturally instigated, could think of any logical reason for it being there. In fact it took a while for the body to be identified, there being nothing on it in the way of identity card, driving licence, passport, utility bill, income tax demand or any other official type of form; no small address book, not even a restaurant bill or receipt from a shopping centre, in fact nothing. It wasn't until the good professor, after a number of days, was reported by his colleagues as missing from work and was not responding to calls, a photograph was submitted and some necessary minor reconstruction on the face had taken place, that two and two were put together. Although summer was approaching, in the high altitude where the body was found there had not been that much in the way of decomposition.

The professor, small of stature, wrinkled, and rather scrawny, balding and slightly myopic, according to those few in number who knew him, virtually all working colleagues, had never given any indication of being remotely interested, winter or summer, in mountains or the countryside in general, presumably not even when young, let alone being anything of a sportsman in advancing years when organs were beginning to deteriorate and the body was showing distinct signs of falling apart. He was without doubt what is disparagingly known as an egghead and his lifestyle was pretty sedentary. If he wasn't seated in front of a workbench in the laboratory, he was sitting at home listening to music; the nineteenth century romantics being his particular favourites.

Apart from the sedentary aspect, the process of disintegration was not due to any over-indulgence during his lifetime unless one could count, from an early age, a daily call on Mrs Palmer and her five children; that solitary vice Victorian schoolboys were severely warned against which led irrevocably to blindness, deafness, paralysis, madness and premature death and which the religiously inclined semi-educated refer to mistakenly as the sin of Onan. The professor lived an abstemious life and his needs were apparently remarkably few. He ate out a great deal at one particular favourite restaurant, not too expensive, so made an easy target for anyone wanting to abduct him which presumably is what happened.

His milieu for the past forty odd years had always been the city, his laboratory – he always thought of it as his laboratory – and his small, warm in winter cool in summer, cosy bachelor apartment where he could relax in his favourite chair and listen to those composers he was most fond of; Brahms and Mendelssohn top of the list followed closely by Tschaikowsky. He especially liked the *Pathetique* and the song *None But The Lonely Heart*. About the only person to visit his flat recently was his cleaning lady, to all intents and purposes a plump and rosy cheeked Rumanian seeker of political asylum.

Admittedly rolling down a mountainside or flying through the air to crash land at the bottom would create some pretty ghastly injuries including any number of splintered bones, shattered cranium, punctured lungs, torn liver, mashed kidneys, but a post-mortem revealed a few that weren't quite consistent with the supposed accident – such as, amongst others, burns between and under the toes – something Ming, Tang and Qing didn't think of, or maybe they did, who knows? The Spaniards certainly thought of it with the Maya and the Inca as illustrations of the Conquistador period reveal showing the poor trussed up wretches with their feet in the fire. Why do human beings by sketch or camera feel they have to record and proudly parade their cruel unspeakable horrors to history and the world?

Maybe the Herr Professor was a masochistic foot fetishist Inspector of Police Franz Lichti thought as he stood in the mortuary and regarded with narrowed eyes the skinless, barbecued, in languages that don't have a word for toes, fingers of the feet, as bad as calling gloves hand shoes really. Anything is possible no matter how unlikely or bizarre but somehow the policeman didn't think this one was on the cards. No, to even the dumbest cop, and Lichti was very far from dumb, the whole thing reeked quite naturally of the most suspicious circumstances and, following up on this elementary conclusion, the professor's colleagues (he didn't seem to have any immediately traceable friends or family) all came under suspicion of something or other and questioned in as much depth as possible which really wasn't very much and with absolutely nothing positive achieved. Lichti came up against that proverbial brick wall and, being the man he was, he was not about to bash his head against it in a futile attempt to get to the bottom of the mystery in a hurry even if it is the theory in a murder investigation that the longer it takes the colder grows the trail until it peters out. It would all sort itself out in its own good time; that was his philosophy and his modus operandi and it hadn't failed him yet. He was not a religious man but amongst all the tribal admonishments and bad natured ranting from those ancient Middle Eastern Bronze Age prophets and the like there were some quite sensible pieces of advice in the Bible to be picked out and taken to heart. For one thing it told him that's just the way things are, all that sowing and reaping, time to be born, time to die stuff so, if it's in the Good Book, why try and fight it?

Questioning of the Rumanian refugee, whose name was Sofia

and who walked with a decided limp having been shot at by border guards and hit in the rump, or that was her story, (she was prepared to show the scars to any interested body and was usually disappointed when the interest wasn't there) elicited nothing. Yes, she had been working for the Herr Professor for she didn't know exactly how long but it was no more than a month or so and, no, she never was in the apartment but for mornings and, no, she didn't know of any visitors. What about his mail? Don't domestics always take an inquisitive peep at their employer's mail? in case there was the chance of a bit of blackmail maybe. Yes, there were utility bills, all paid, and he seemed to be in correspondence with a certain countess who lived in Italy as Sofia remembered, Rome she thought, or was it Florence? Maybe Milan. She couldn't be sure. But there was no evidence of this correspondence in the apartment or in his workplace. Did Sofia remember the countess's name? Sofia shook her head. No, she did not remember the countess's name. Still, there couldn't be that many countesses in Rome or even Florence or Milan could there? So she shouldn't be too difficult to trace, starting with the laboratory's and the professor's telephone bills. But a blank was drawn on both. Obviously the mail was their only form of correspondence unless discreet calls were made from public telephones. But what was their relationship and why would they be that secretive and why had the correspondence with this countess disappeared? Not one letter remained to be examined and to give a clue as to who she was. The apartment was as clean as a whistle and Lichti didn't think it was all down to the Rumanian cleaning lady. Never mind, he would procure a list of Italian countesses and go through them in due course which would no doubt lead to something.

How did Sofia come to be employed by the Herr Professor?

Wheels within wheels as the saying goes: a very kind doctor in the hospital who had contacts, this one also a political refugee, in his case from East Germany, recommended her when her wound had healed and she was about to be discharged. It wasn't too long after his questioning her that Lichti was informed Sofia's body had been dragged from the lake and the autopsy showed a cocktail of drugs that would have killed a bull elephant let alone a human being; an interesting development. She must have died a happy girl, that is if she knew anything about it. It wasn't long after that before the good doctor from East Germany also disappeared without trace, an even more interesting development. Could it be he had slipped back into the communist block and, if so, why? Could he have gone somewhere else? Or could it be the third homicide with possibly more to follow? Lichti felt quite sure there were more to come.

*   *   *

The Patisserie Valerie in Old Compton Street just off Piccadilly and Shaftesbury Avenue is well established, long and narrow with a small serving counter on one side and tables down the length of the other, with a couple more at right angles at the far end just before and to the side of the curtained doorway leading to the busy heart of the establishment and through which waitresses, balancing trays and avoiding any standing bodies, with great dexterity enter and exit at speed, though it would appear there isn't really enough room for two bodies to pass each other down the aisle.

The tempting delicacies are seductively displayed on the counter and glass shelves behind the window inviting death by chocolate, sugar, double cream or a combination of all three.

Like the French pub a short distance away, and a little basement club called Jerry's on the Avenue where actors could drink out of hours, the Patisserie is a crowded but charming favourite haunt of theatricals and other habitués of Soho including Holly but, on this particular day, though she would have liked to have been there, at the invitation of her friend, the Countess Cinelli, she was enjoying instead a delicate tea in Fortnum and Mason's, an entirely different establishment on Piccadilly. Here ladies of fashion liked to show off their hats and it was known to that flamboyant photographer of high fashion, Adrian Spangle, and his coterie as Fanny's and Mary's and it was convenient to The Ritz where the countess was staying. It could have been tea at The Ritz of course or even The Savoy but the countess just adored F's and M's and its special blend and made a habit of taking afternoon tea there every time she was in London.

The Countess Cinelli in fact was a creature of habit and did not appreciate her routine ever being rearranged or interfered with. A person did not, for example, drink tea of a morning except for a refreshing cup first thing on waking. The morning itself, mid-morning that is, was reserved for coffee, possibly accompanied by a dry biscuit or two such as Lanques de Chat. A little light wine chilled was allowed with luncheon, not too much, and after six a cocktail, an aperitif, and of course a more robust wine with dinner, the choice depending on the menu. The meal might be rounded off with a sorbet to cleanse the palate, Viennese or Belgian chocolates or perhaps a marzipan fruit from Lubeck and finally a vintage cognac and a cigar. The countess was particularly partial to *Romeo y Julietta* and had been indulging in them a good many years which unfortunately left her with slightly stained teeth necessitating the application of a whitener. She would blithely inform friends that it was Sir Winston himself who had got her hooked on them when he was a visitor at the palazzo in Rome. Nobody knew whether this was true or a fabrication but no one thought to question it or, if they did, they kept the questioning to themselves.

The Countess Cinelli, logging her years somewhere in the middle fifties, though she would only ever admit to the early forties, was a richly and expensively perfumed lady of solid build that seemed to move like well-oiled machinery all of a piece, the solidity reinforced by her old-fashioned whalebone corsetry, her expensive but sensible shoes and her preference for dress materials in varying shades of grey. Her make-up was not exactly plastered on but was thick enough to be noticeable and the cheeks really were just that tiny bit too obviously rouged and the lips a bit too pronounced though not quite a Cupid's bow. They had to be slightly embellished; they were diminishing with each passing year. She was also a woman of formidable intellect, education, and was fluent in English, German, French, Italian, Spanish and Greek which meant she could order her meals, converse with and, where applicable and wherever she was staying, bed any number of attractive waiters and hotel employees, provided they were middle or southern European and appreciative of her largesse which most were. Money talks and obliterates the fading of youthful beauty; the onset of liver spots and tissue paper wrinkles. Any who resisted her blandishments were immediately assumed to be gay and dismissed out of hand. Obviously this did not apply to Scandinavians, not the gay bit but the language, as they all seemed to speak excellent English anyway. Oriental waiters where simply not in the frame. She wasn't particularly fond of Oriental food nor was she too taken with Oriental bodies so that didn't really matter. The lack of body hair was what tended to put her off. If God had intended Adam to be a smoothie he wouldn't have given him a beard and hairy legs, though she drew the line at hairy fingers and even more at hairy toes.

Her husband had shuffled off this mortal coil a number of years back when quite young. She usually referred to him, past or present, dead or alive, as "The" and without the O in his title. He had left her with a very large and expensive to run eighteenth century palazzo in the Prati district of Rome and a number of bank accounts, legitimate and illegitimate in various countries and tax havens though each one at his death appeared to be all but depleted.

The count, whose name was Francesco had at least six or seven other Christian names to follow, two of which were Sebastian. This was an accident, although the first Sebastian was by choice as his father who, like all the Cinellis was a bit on the morbid side, spending far too much of his time in gloomy side chapels reeking of incense, neurosis, possibly old bones in glass caskets, and penitence, and sometimes echoing to the distant sound of Plain or Gregorian chant from another part of the church. When it comes to theatricality and stage management you have to admit the Catholic Church is well and truly ahead of anybody else. The relic of a saint's fingernail can be turned into a three act drama. The count was particularly attracted for some reason to paintings of that sorrowful looking saint pierced with arrows, in particular that by Guido Reni. The count's wife, Rosa Angelica, was highly suspicious of the way her husband gazed with such adoration at any depiction of the saint he came across, so young, so beautiful and so erotic both in face and body, and in his dying agony gazing mournfully towards heaven where he soon hoped to be. The count had absolutely no doubt the emperor's centurion's wish was granted and that one day he, the count, would join him there, which he prematurely did.

There were times when Francesco couldn't always remember his names or, if he did remember them, in what order they came. He was baptised by Archbishop Angelo Paino of Messina who had to have them written down on a slip of paper but even so, as he was a little short sighted and wasn't wearing his glasses, someone had to stand by and whisper them in his ear. He was also a trifle hard of hearing though he would never admit to that. It was quite bad enough being practically blind and a certain name had to be repeated, in consequence of which the count became Francesco Sebastian Sebastian which pleased his father mightily and was forever a talking point at cocktail parties. The names that followed, even though of ancient lineage, seemed tame and instantly forgettable in comparison, even those with a Borgia connection.

Without legitimate issue Francesco was the last of the Cinellis which was a shame really because his family could be traced back at least as far as those selfsame Borgias and it was sometimes believed or put about anyway that they were originally Etruscan and related in some obscure way to the Emperor Claudius. If that failed to impress it was sometimes whispered that the naughty naughty Pope Alexander was actually the start of the line which would explain the countess's "Spanish eyes" though how this could be when she was only a Cinelli by marriage and not born to the name, again nobody thought to question.

Francesco died, according to his death certificate, of cirrhosis of the liver which, considering his relatively tender age and the fact he was virtually abstemious as far as alcohol was concerned was a trifle baffling to say the least. It was assumed he might have been a secret drinker. The cause of death was witnessed by the ancient family physician who was himself a little the worse for wear that evening after an excellent dinner of lobster in a turbot sauce, venison somewhat high with truffles, peaches in brandy and an over indulgence in grappa; and the servants at the time, who were still employed, still loyal, despite an absence of recent wages, whispered among themselves that perhaps Lucrezia was still alive and prowling the corridors, influencing the course of events, most particularly where death was concerned. They crossed themselves religiously whenever the subject was mooted and a couple, even more religious than the rest, if that was possible, went to church every morning to light a candle to their favourite saints in order to keep away the evil spirit lest her vindictiveness descended on them. It wasn't known whether Sebastian was one of the saints they favoured. Where the money was found with which to purchase all those candles was another matter for speculation. More recently though, as their wages had caught up and were being regularly paid, with increments, the whispers and the innuendo and the prayers to the favourite saints ceased, the church's coffers were slightly depleted of candle money and the ghost of Lucrezia Borgia no longer stalked the corridors of the Palazzo Cinelli.

Rich Americans as paying guests in the palazzo were reputed to be the source of the Countess's more recent healthier bank balances, one of which was with Holly's father hence the current tea party. Business and pleasure can mix and the countess was particularly fond of Holly, having known her since she was a mere slip of a thing and Holly, having visited her in Italy on more than one occasion both with her parents and on her own, riding a Vespa passed the Trevi Fountain, being constantly ogled and whistled at by young Italians and feeling very grown-up though not in the least bit sophisticated or even having her bum pinched, delectable as it was. With the rise of feminism the authorities would clamp down on that sort of thing as being bad for tourism though young Italians, like their Spanish counterparts still strutted around bantam fashion keeping a hold on their bits and pieces, making sure they were still there in working order and ready for immediate action at any given moment.

The countess laid a hand of heavily bejewelled fingers on one of Holly's and gave it a couple of light pats. It was to indicate that this was going to be a moment of great intimacy. Having made the gesture the hand was withdrawn and the handle of a teacup was gripped between forefinger and thumb though the cup was not immediately lifted from its saucer.

'Holly, my dear, I must talk frankly to you about something, something I wish to keep a secret.'

'Ye-es?' It was a slightly guarded reply. What dark secret did the countess wish to impart and, if she imparted it, it would no longer be a secret, would it? More than likely some indiscreet love affair that could lead to something like blackmail, financial loss, ostracism from the best circles and total disaster, and what, if anything, was Holly supposed to do about it? The countess had a very weird idea of what Holly's position was in Her Majesty's secret service. It was quite likely that, should the current paramour if he was making waves, needed to be eliminated, then Holly would be requested for old time's sake to perform the necessary deed. Surely if you're in her line of work you carry a gun or at least know half a dozen ways or more of eliminating someone. This registered rapidly in Holly's mind and couldn't the countess, she thought, just turn to one of her Italian friends who might be used to that sort of thing?

'Exactly what is it you wish to ask?' Holly's voice took on a nervous edge as she looked around to see who could be within hearing range and might one day be in a position to blackmail her. The tea room at Fanny's and Mary's was not all that large. Fortunately it happened at this particular moment to be fairly quiet but the countess, anyway, leaned in closer to Holly's right ear.

'I need the services of a very special man,' she whispered.

'In what...?' Holly realised her voice sounded ultra-loud so she started again. 'In what respect special?' she whispered, the mind boggling as her imagination went overboard exploring somewhere between this special man's navel and his knees.

'Well, in the first place, he has to be exceptionally brave.'

Holly's mind was now a riot of speculation. In the boudoir, she was still in the countess's boudoir; a man had to be exceptionally brave? Well maybe, if the countess uncorseted turned out to be, as was a fact, not exactly the seductive alluring figure she was in her youth.

'Astute.'

'Astute.'

'Nimble footed and quick on the ball.'

Good grief, what on earth was the woman up to? Had she invented some new bizarre kind of sexual game that encompassed unknown hazards? Was she playing at being some kind of occidental Turandot? Was it a guessing game and ultimately a sharp blade was involved here if the guess was incorrect? Holly looked around, her gaze taking in the respectable looking matrons around them, none of whom could imagine for a moment what this tête-à-tête was all about and probably just as well.

'He must be perspicacious,' the countess continued, 'tight-lipped, I don't mean merely discreet, I mean absolutely tight-lipped, and capable of recognising and outsmarting possible opposition from at least three, if not four or even five different directions.' She finally lifted her cup and took a sip of tea. This really had been a terrific effort on her part and the tea was now luke warm.

'Contessa,' Holly almost gasped, 'just tell me, what are you talking about?'

'I'm talking about a private detective. Do you know such a man?'

*   *   *

Which was how Thornton happened to find himself the following afternoon standing in the countess's suite at The Ritz waiting for her to put in an appearance and at the same time, to his utter astonishment, staring at the Chinese vases he had so coveted in the window of Signor Riccoboni's grotty shop in the Westbourne Grove. They now stood on a marble topped side table looking as alluringly beautiful as when he first saw them. 'Well fancy seeing you again,' he said, 'and so soon.' It was as if he was addressing a couple of old acquaintances.

Without that smelly gentleman hovering over him and breathing down his neck like a vulture that had recently consumed something long since dead and still had bits of it rotting around its beak, he conjured up a memory of what looked like a sliver of ham, he took a peep inside one of the vases, tilting it towards him. Now balanced precariously on a small section of the rim at its base it rolled to one side and he caught it with a one arm hug an instant before it would have gone crashing to the floor, at the same time grabbing the top of its fellow in danger of being knocked off by contact with his sudden lurch. Blowing out hard with relief, Thornton released the one gently, righted the other and took his peep inside, just as an inner door opened and the countess sailed in, as Joyce Grenfell would have sung, stately as a galleon doing the military two-step as in days of yore though, in her steel grey outfit, probably looking more like an old-fashioned battleship, what used to be called a man of war, emerging from Scapa Flow.

'Thornton King I presume?' The voice was a mellow contralto with a certain vibrato as befits a nation of natural singers.

'Countess?' This voice on the contrary was something of a squeak, having been taken by surprise and his heart still thumping at the too recent near disaster. Thornton cleared his throat to return it to normal.

'You are admiring my vases I see.' She advanced across the room. Obviously she hadn't seen how close to destruction they had been. 'Beautiful, aren't they? Are you a connoisseur?'

'Not really, Countess, though I must admit to having a great admiration for this particular pair. So much so in fact that I could wish they were mine.'

'Really?'

'In fact, when I saw them in Mister... Mister...'

'Riccoboni.'

'Yes, in his shop, I offered to purchase them but he said they were not for sale.'

'Because they obviously were not his to sell,' she waved a hand in their direction, 'as you can see. So I am sorry you were disappointed Mister King. Perhaps you will find another pair to your liking. Anyway, I am pleased to meet you and I thank you for coming to see me.'

Thornton didn't know whether or not in this day and age he was supposed to bow but decided it wouldn't come amiss so executed a sort of half-hearted half bend from the waist before straightening up and looking the countess in the eye.

She was close to him now; hand extended, and now came a further question in social protocol. Did he kiss that hand or did he not? He decided he might as well, hoping he wouldn't prove to be allergic to any perfume she may be wearing.

If Thornton could have afforded the exorbitant fees of a Harley Street psychiatrist he would more than likely be told that his recently acquired allergies were all down to the fact that in the not too distant past he had at least two attractive women pull a gun on him, once before intimacy even started and once when it was all over, and his allergies were a defence against any possible future threat from an armed female. A violent sneeze or series of sneezes can be very off-putting to an intending assailant, especially if they feel they have to stop and say gesundheit or something similar before pulling the trigger. So what was the form on the continong as far as hand-kissing was concerned in these days of bra-less ladies and female lib? He decided it was more than likely still the thing to do, the Continentals being so much more romantic than the Brits who would probably consider it sexual harassment, so he dutifully kissed the hand, well hardly a kiss, more a sort of quick breathing over it, noting at the same time the inevitable formation of those liver spots that, despite protests, gave away the lady's age. Then he stood upright once more, refocusing to face his prospective employer, he had gone slightly cross-eyed, who was appraising him with her Spanish ones.

'Charmed,' he said, sincerely hoping he sounded both sincere and charmed. He couldn't help mentally speculating as to what this meeting was all about and only hoped she wasn't at some point going to pull a gun on him as well though, as yet, there didn't seem to be any reason for it. You could never tell with Italians though. She might be nursing a vendetta against someone and it could be a case of mistaken identity. He let go her hand so she used it with an imperious gesture to indicate a nearby chair.

'Please, Mr King, do be seated.'

'I notice the vases have lost their sand,' Thornton said to open the conversation, in his turn flicking a finger in their direction.

'Sand? Sand?' She appeared quite bemused by his remark.

'Yes, you know, the ballast, to stop them toppling over. Or so Mister... Thingamabob informed me.'

'Oh, the sand!' The countess laughed loudly and for quite a long moment.

Thornton, poker faced, wondered what the joke was that could make for so much hilarity.

'Well, they're being shipped back to Rome, Thornton. May I call you Thornton?' She had recovered from her laughter. 'So there is no need for ballast is there? It would be just dead weight to add to the expense. They will be most carefully packaged. I use a specialist firm naturally, accustomed to handling works of art, antiques and fine objects. They are even engaged by auction houses and the British Museum I am led to believe so that shows you how expert they are. Now, can I offer you some refreshment?

Holly informs me your favourite whisky is the *Famous Grouse*. Am I correct?'

'Indeed you are, Countess, indeed you are. Did you enquire about that or did Holly simply volunteer the information?'

'I enquired, not only about that but about many other things besides. I needed to know as much about you as possible.'

'And why would that be, pray?' He frowned at his stilted syntax.

'Because the man I wish to hire...' it was her turn to take a chair '...must be all things to all men if he is to succeed in the business I want him for.'

'A pretty tall order, Princess, I mean Contessa. Renaissance man died out with the Renaissance. These days specialist fields are all the rage and all extremely narrow, focused as it were.'

'It may indeed be a tall order but exceptionally well rewarded if you pull it off.'

'You mean you have already decided this supermensch is going to be me.'

'You do come highly recommended.'

'Holly again.'

The countess nodded. 'Holly. And when we get to know each other better you may call me Paullina.'

'You're too kind.'

*   *   *

'I could kill you Holly, I really could.'

'Kill me?' She queried with a butter wouldn't melt in her mouth smile, 'Now really, Thornton, why on earth would you want to do that?'

'You've landed me right in it, haven't you? Right up to here.' He ran a finger across his throat.

'Have I? Do tell.' Still smiling she handed him his glass of *Famous Grouse* before joining him on the settee. It had become a little grubbier since the time she stained it by dropping sweet and sour pork from her chopsticks so it really wouldn't matter if he spilled his drink. He looked at the glass in his hand as if, like Socrates, it were hemlock he was being invited to swallow.

'You're not having one?' He raised his right eyebrow. It was the only one of the pair he could raise and he tended to overuse it, rather like a bad actor telegraphing to the audience that he was suspicious about something, though he was more than likely wondering what on earth he was doing allowing himself to be talked into playing such a lousy part in such a lousy play. He was doing it only for the money of course and because, as always, jobs were scarce, in fact virtually non-existent and there could be real food on stage to ease the ache of an empty stomach.

'Not right at the mo,' she answered. 'Just thought after your ordeal you needed a quick pick me up.'

'Ordeal? What ordeal? What are you talking about? The ordeal, my dear, whatever it is going to be, is yet to come. According to the countess what I may have to go through is the equivalent of being chained to a rock and having my liver pecked out every day only for it to grow again at night. Mind you, she could be exaggerating just a little, but I suspect not much. Call it half a liver.'

'So tell me, what is it all about? And, before you say you're going to need my help, I am here to tell you here and now I do not have any leave pending nor am I able to take any time off from the department. I hope that is clearly understood. We're absolutely snowed under, Thornton, particularly since that monster Mike you-know-who snuffed it and hasn't been replaced.'

'Maybe I could get my old job back.' Thornton's face momentarily lit up.

'I wouldn't hold out any hope there, Thornton. We might be short staffed but we're also, by we I should have said the department or the government rather, are distinctly short of the readies. Tax receipts evidently haven't been up to snuff this last year and that, I'm afraid, is that. Nothing to do with your ability to fill the post. So tell me all about your new job.'

'Sorry, old chum, strictly hush hush and you know what that means.'

'Between friends, Thornton.'

Thornton got to his feet and wandered over to the picture window from where he got a magnificent view over half of London.

'Why can't I afford a flat in the Barbican?' he moaned.

'Because you're a lazy sod, Thornton who never gets off his fat arse...'

'I resent that, Miss Holly Day! I truly resent that. My arse is not fat. There's not an ounce of fat on it. Gluteus and maximus though it may be, for your edification, my arse is what is known as petite. A number of people have thought to remark flatteringly on it. Praxiteles could not have sculptured a finer arse with more loving care. Maybe I ought to make that Rodin instead. Praxiteles sculptured ancient Greek arses and they tended to be a little bit on the bulky side, national characteristic. Not that I am a connoisseur on arses you realise but, as one goes through life, one can't help noticing these things.'

'Have you finished? As I was saying, who never goes out to

look for clients but expects them all to come to him and for the work to miraculously materialise. Well that's not the way it happens, Thornton, so be grateful there are friends like me who are happy to steer clients in your direction. You're not such a shit hot detective anyway so be grateful.'

Thornton turned back from the window and for the second time that day executed a little bow, he almost felt like clicking his heels, and then swallowed his whisky, almost choking on it. He cleared his throat and regained his breath but resisted raising his eyebrow a second time. These things can be overdone and lose their efficacy through constant use. For a while he stood silently gazing at his empty glass, twisting it in his fingers first one way then the next. Finally he looked up.

'Actually you're bang to rights there, Holly, though there's really no need to throw it in my face. I am a lousy detective which is why I can't understand why you said all those marvellous things about me to the countess. I mean, I know why Mike Ayliff recommended me to Aurora Pemberton for that last job. It was because he thought I'd make such a complete hash of it she would give me the boot before the truth came out about her uncle's death. Well, thanks to us both, he was wrong wasn't he? But note, Holly, I said thanks to us both, and now you tell me this time you're completely out of the picture? Thanks a lot. That's what friends are for. Recommend you for some death defying course of action and then desert you. I'm going to end up in a Gulag or its equivalent I just know it.'

'Don't sound so melodramatic, Thornton. I am quite sure this time you will perform your duty one hundred percent and come out of it with flying colours. What is it by the way? You still haven't told me?'

'That's because it's a secret and my lips are sealed.'

'A secret is a secret when only one person knows what it is. Right now three people happen to be in on this particular secret.'

'Three?'

'Of course three: you, me, and the countess.'

'Well if you know what it is, why are you asking me?'

'Testing you.'

Thornton's answer to that was a grunt as he waggled his glass to hint at a refill.

3

This is how it had gone. Having provided him with his scotch and seated herself close to her visitor, the countess leaned forward conspiratorially and said in a low dramatic voice, 'A very very dear friend of mine… do you smoke, Thornton?'

'No I don't.'

'Pity. I was going to offer you one of these.' She had got up and was sailing across to an escritoire on which lay a cigar box. Opening it, she selected one, closed the box, walked back to her chair with the cigar in one hand, matches in the other and sat down again.

'As I was saying, a very very very dear friend…'

She stopped and, not having her cutter handy, bit off the end of the cigar and then didn't know what to do with it as she removed it from her mouth and held it twixt forefinger and thumb. Eventually she realised it necessitated a walk back to the escritoire on which lay an ashtray. Whilst there she lit her cigar, dropped the matches, took a couple of quick puffs and moved back to where Thornton was watching all this with growing amazement. He took a quick sip of his drink and warily watched her approach.

'You were saying, Countess.'

'What was I saying? Oh yes, I asked you if you smoked. I agree with Lady Bracknell you know that a young man should have an occupation even if it is only to smoke.' She made it sound as if Lady Bracknell had confided this to her as a personal friend. 'But I do so hate cigarettes. They're so effete don't you think? Sissy would be the word for it, unless it's something like a Balkan Sobranie of course which has a faux air of class about it, or maybe Turkish which tend to be rather strong. Gauloise and Gitane are strong as well but in quite the wrong way. You looked surprised when you first saw my cigar...'

As a matter of fact Thornton still looked like a startled rabbit caught in a car's headlamps as she continued.

'... but there are women all over the world, Thornton, my dear, who delight in the occasional cigar you know, or even smoke a pipe. Women in... where now? Peru for instance, or is it Chile? Somewhere in South America where they wear those peculiar rather masculine looking hats.' She waved a hand meaning it didn't really matter which country it was. 'I've seen photographs in National Geographic. And women in Basutoland, or is it Bechuanaland? I always mix those two up they sound so alike. They wear strange hats there too, straw ones. Somewhere in Southern Africa anyway, one or other of those far away places. And they stretch their earlobes in the most extraordinary fashion. Have you seen that? Or is it their lips? I forget but National Geographic is truly a mine of information, don't you think?'

There was a second wave of the hand as she blew out another cloud of smoke and ash fell on the carpet. She regarded it for a moment like a Druid reading the runes and then looked up at Thornton. 'Now then, the question is, who was it?'

Thornton waited.

The silence grew longer.

Eventually he coughed.

'Oh! Is your glass empty? How remiss of me. Here, let me give you a refill.'

She had got up and was reaching for his glass with her free hand. He pulled the glass towards him.

'No, Countess, it's not empty and I really do not need another. What I do need is to know why you have asked me to come here and what it is I can do for you, that is if it is in my power to do... whatever it is,' he finished lamely.

'Yes, of course. This very...'

'Very very dear friend...'

The countess glared at him. She was not accustomed to being interrupted and her glare was quite dramatic. Friends called it her devil's eyes as opposed to her Spanish ones.

'I do apologise, Countess, please go on.' He didn't really sound all that apologetic. He sounded impatient. Had he been a small boy it would have sounded petulant.

She took another drag at her cigar, blew out a positive cumulus nimbus of smoke and went on, '... has been murdered.' This was stated without emotion but followed by the deepest of meaningful deep sighs.

There was another silence. This time Thornton decided to patiently wait. Eventually she would get around to finishing whatever she had to say. Giving up on the patience routine he looked at his watch, pretending to be discreet but making sure she noticed. She did.

'Yes?'

'How?'

Sometimes it may be convenient to carry on a conversation in monosyllables; gets to the nub of the matter more quickly. Unfortunately it can't be sustained for long. In fact in this instance it was over almost the moment it started.

'He was allegedly thrown off a mountain.'

'A mountain?' There was no disguising the disbelief in Thornton's voice. Had the countess said he was thrown from a high building or out of an aeroplane maybe that would have been a horse of a different colour as Feydeau might have remarked, but a mountain? People are known to fall off mountains, but not pushed, or so he thought. 'Where did this happen?'

'In Switzerland where he lives… lived.'

'And what have the Swiss police come up with? I presume they are on the case.'

'Nothing so far. They've come up with nothing except for the fact that they have evidence of his being…' there was a dramatic pause as the countess obviously found it for a brief moment difficult to continue, but bravely continue she must '… most hideously tortured before he was killed.' There was no need to make a melodramatic meal out of the professor's fate; it was quite horrendous enough, but the countess could never resist exaggeration and embellishment whenever possible. It was part and parcel of her Mediterranean temperament. Then, unable to control the emotion this had evoked, she stood up and paced for a while. 'Such a dear man… Such a dear dear man.' Thornton gave her time before...

'How do you know this?'

'Know what?' She frowned, her dear dear man having caused her to lose track slightly.

'That he was tortured before being killed.'

'Oh, I know that information was not released to the press, not generally known to the public but I do have friends in high places, or friends of friends, and that's how I got the information. It was quite a talking point for a while.'

'And you know why I take it.'

'Why what?'

'You know why he was tortured and killed.'

'Yes, I do, and I think I may be in line for the same treatment.'

'So what you want is a bodyguard, not a private detective.'

'What I want is a private detective, not a bodyguard. You see there is a by-product to the work my friend was doing and it has to be recovered, must be recovered, before it can fall into the wrong hands.'

'And what kind of work might it have been, that your friend was doing?'

'He is… was… I find it so difficult to believe he has gone, I really do… he was a chemist.'

'I see.'

'Do you?'

*   *   *

'Holly, your friend the countess is a smuggler, a drug runner. Did you know that?' Thornton sounded mightily indignant which didn't impress Holly one bit. She was used to his riding a high horse when he felt justified in doing so and he would probably flog the poor thing to death along the way.

'No, I didn't,' she said. 'Well I never! Who would have thought it?' If she had been Betty Boop she would have fluttered her eyelashes.

Thornton wasn't quite sure whether Holly really meant it or was being a consummate actress. 'Is that all you can say? Well I never? Who would have thought it? You would have thought it is the answer to that. She uses those vases as a cover. I have no idea how many times they've gone back and forth between Rome and London, maybe not the same ones all the time, customs might have grown a wee bit suspicious, maybe different ones, but take my word for it, that wasn't sand in them or, at least, if that was sand there was also definitely something else underneath and I have a shrewd suspicion of what it was. Now her chemist friend, deceased, quite horribly evidently according to the countess, has come up with something simply mind blowing, please!' He held up a hand palm outward as he saw the smile on her face, 'This is extremely serious and no pun was intended, that certain very undesirable people, too many undesirable people for that matter, know about and want because she thought she would get the highest price by injudiciously spreading the word and having something like a Dutch auction and has realised too late how stupid she's been. I ask you! How naïve can you be? She didn't know the kind of people she was dealing with and what it could lead to? Expect to be torn to pieces if you go swimming in a tank full of sharks or, if it's piranhas in the tank, eaten alive. So that is where I am supposed to come in. Fend off the sharks while I recover something potentially mind blowing, and this time the pun is intended.'

Holly shrugged. 'So what are you going to do?'

'When someone offers you ten thousand nicker and all expenses, half the fee in advance, for finding and securing in a safe place a specimen of something, even if you have no idea what that specimen is but can hazard a shrewd guess, then who am I to pass? The job market isn't exactly overflowing with promise at the moment. '

'I didn't think you would turn it down, Thornton. I didn't think you would. Bully for you.' She gave the air in front of her a little punch and tried, albeit not too successfully, to hide her smile. Thornton used the eyebrow once more.

'There is an old proverb, Holly, of which I am sure you are familiar, "If you are going to sup with the devil you need a long spoon". I have a feeling the spoon I am going to need can be measured in feet, yards even, let alone inches.'

*   *   *

'Now, Thornton, as I see it, this is what you will do.' The countess was pacing. She obviously thought more clearly on her feet but there was a lengthy pause before she continued. 'Now I don't wish to teach my granny how to suck eggs, isn't that the quaintest expression? And I am sure you know your business but on arriving in Rome you will naturally stay in the Palazzo Cinelli. They will be expecting you and of course a car will pick you up at the airport. Nobody there, by the way, knows anything of this business. For them you are no more than another paying guest. I suppose you could of course fly straight to Geneva but… no… no I don't think so. No, on second thoughts, that would never do. Rome it is.'

Thornton wondered if the countess had thought this through

with the thoroughness it required or was she winging it like an actress too lazy to learn her lines or incapable of remembering them?

'Yes, Rome it is and then, from there, to Geneva and, when you return to Rome with the... er... parcel, you will not stay at the palazzo, that would be inviting trouble I fear, but in a hotel. Yes, that would be the safest course to take. Now all my instructions must be learnt by heart. In the end absolutely nothing must be written down, is that understood?'

Thornton nodded. 'I'll chew the paper thirty times and swallow it.'

For a long moment the countess gave him her devil's eyes. 'I am being absolutely serious, Thornton. And you had better be as well. Your life is on the line here. That's what I am paying you for.'

Thornton thought his life was worth a lot more than ten grand and expenses but decided to let it pass. Maybe it wasn't and another snide remark could cost him the job altogether. Also there was no doubt her life was on the line as well which was why he was there in the first place, though there were other private detectives who could take his place, would happily take his place for that sort of money, even if they didn't complete the mission.

'The problem that immediately comes to mind of course is that you will need my letter of authorisation for the bank in Geneva to allow you access to the safety deposit box. How do we overcome that if nothing is to be written down? Well?' She seemed to think that, as he was the detective, he should have an answer to all the problems even before they occurred.

'All I can say, Countess, is that you will have to trust me to guard the letter with my life.' Thornton hoped he wasn't being too melodramatic.

'Very well. The first thing then,' she continued, 'is for you to have your photograph taken so there can be absolutely no mistake as to who the letter is for. I've made an appointment for you to see a very famous photographer you may even have heard of. This is his address; it's a mews in Mayfair.' She handed over an embossed card.

'Adrian? You want Adrian to photograph me?'

'You know him?'

'I certainly do.'

'Wonderful. Absolutely wonderful.'

'What's wonderful about it?'

'About what?'

'About my knowing Adrian?'

'I didn't say that. What I meant was he is simply the most wonderful photographer in the world, that's what I meant.'

'Oh, I see. If I see him I'll tell him you said that. He would appreciate it.'

'Appreciate what?'

'That you think he's so wonderful.'

'Yes, I do, I do! All that amazing talent, artistry,' she enthused. 'Of course you have to overlook his predilections but that's the artistic temperament for you, from the greatest to the humblest and there have been many great artists that way inclined. I take it you have no trouble with that? I firmly believe, Thornton that you can be a great artist but if you want to be a truly great artist, among the giants of the artistic world, you must at least once in your life have fallen in love with a member of your own sex. It needn't necessarily go as far as you know, actual physical contact, apart that is from the odd embrace or kiss on the cheek, but how else can you travel and appreciate the whole gamut of human emotions?'

'A very wise thought, Countess. But would it not apply the other way around?'

'Just think of the Michelangelos and the Leonardos of this world. And Shakespeare! Have you read Shakespeare's sonnets?'

'I have.'

'What else can master mistress of my hearts passion mean do you suppose?'

'What else indeed?'

'He did my portrait a couple of years ago and I'm in his book. Have you seen it?'

Thornton was tempted to ask if she was referring to Shakespeare but thought better of it. There were times, not often mind you, when he did put a bridle on his tongue and didn't let it run away from him. He seemed to remember seeing a stack of Adrian's books on a remainder table in a Charing Cross Road bookshop, the top copy pretty soiled and well thumbed through, but thought it wisest not to mention that either.

'Can't say that I have, Countess.' He scratched the side of his neck. A hive like itch always started there when he was lying.

'I am surprised.' She got up and disappeared into the bedroom to return a moment later with a rather large volume in a white slip cover with black lettering. It obviously travelled with her wherever she went and made good bedtime looking at last thing before turning out the light. She passed it over and Thornton took it with both hands, it was quite alarmingly heavy, and laying it on his lap, he gazed at it with apparent reverence.

FAMOUS FACES –
A BOOK OF PORTRAITS BY ADRIAN SPANGLE
STAR PHOTOGRAPHER TO THE STARS.

Only Adrian could have come up with that one. Star photographer to the stars forsooth! How kitsch can a body get?

'I'm on pages seventeen and eighteen,' the countess said trying not to sound smug.

Thornton duly turned to pages seventeen and eighteen, studied the portraits for a moment; they were actually very good if a little on the flattering side and then, closing the book, he handed it back. On the back cover he noticed there was a portrait of Adrian holding his dog Tiddlywinks in one hand and a camera in the other. Tiddly was wearing his woolly jumpsuit and cap with the bobbles for riding in the car.

'Very nice,' Thornton said, apropos the countess's pictures which was hardly what one might call enthusiastic, 'but if I have to have my picture taken for identification purposes then there is a perfectly good photographer not two hundred yards from here who does excellent passport photographs. Why don't I just toddle off to him? Adrian will cost you an arm and a leg.'

'Thank you for your concern but I'd rather you did as I have requested and went to Adrian Spangle. No arguments if you please.'

Thornton shrugged and gave in. Adrian it would be.

'Now, in Geneva you will not stay in a hotel,' she continued as though there had been no digression. 'There is a quite splendid and very comfortable little pension I know of very close to the bank' – Thornton winced but then thought maybe it wouldn't be too bad, after all the Garibaldi in Nice had really turned out to be a bit like home from home – 'where the you know what is deposited.' The "you know what" was whispered: walls have ears. 'I think that would be much safer than a hotel although, as soon as you've picked up the parcel, you might think it safest to head straight back to Rome, on the spot as it were. As soon as I know you have completed your mission I will return to Rome and will be waiting for you. The bank by the way is a small private bank called Celine & Cie and have no fear I will have made all the arrangements necessary for you to have access to the box. All you need is your identification, my letter of introduction, and this.'

And she slipped him the key to the safety deposit box.

*   *   *

There was a bout of hysterical soprano barking from behind the door the instant Thornton's thumb pressed the bell and a small shadowy four footed figure could be seen behind the glass panels doing the high jump like a spring loaded toy. Only a few seconds passed before the door was flung open and Adrian stood there ready to offer his hand in greeting as Tiddlywinks, in his excitement at seeing Thornton (maybe he remembered the taste of Thornton's blood), immediately peed all over the man's shoes. That is he would have done had Thornton not without some alacrity leapt hastily backwards. Adrian's costume this day consisted of a silk cravat in a paisley design of pink and apple green, loosely but carefully positioned, an ecru coloured shirt with ruffles all down the front, the cuffs fastened with Blue John links, and the tightest around the top but down below the widest flares he could get his tailor to make without the man having a coronary and Adrian being arrested on a charge of indecency in public. Adrian did not buy his clothes from any old Carnaby Street outlet. He had the money to splash out so splash out he did on handmade shirts, custom made footwear and bespoke tailoring.

'Thornton, my dear! How bona to varda your old eek once more. Enter my humble abode, enter. Tiddlywinks, you naughty boy. If you want a pee that badly go and pee against that nasty man's jardinière next door but just don't let him see you or he'll call the police and it will be the dog's home for you. Well come on, Thornton, what are you standing there for?'

'I was waiting for Tiddly to have his pee.'

'Oh, he doesn't want one really. It's all pretence. Just wants attention that's all. You know what a preening little queen he is. Can't take him anywhere but he's flirting like mad with anything that moves, just like his daddy. Come on, Tiddly, stop sniffing around and come inside.'

Tiddly dutifully obeyed and Thornton followed, the door closing behind him.

'You're looking well, Adrian, and tres chic if I may say so.'

'Why, thank you, kind sir. How nice of you to say so. Actually I'm a little under the weather today. Had a very late night. Bona but exhausting if you know what I mean.' He touched up the hair on the side of his head. 'But there you go, as the body ages so the ability to fully function goes with it. But enough about me. Would you care for some refreshment?'

'Thank you, no. I'm fine.'

'I know that. As dishy as ever, my dear, if you don't mind my saying so. You don't age a day with the passing of old father time. What's your secret?'

'It's all in the genes I suppose.'

'But you're not wearing any!' and Adrian broke into peals of laughter. 'Anyway, Thornton,' when he had recovered, 'long time no see and now here you are at the instigation of the Countess Cinelli of all people. I could hardly credit it when she called.

Are you being a wicked toy-boy then? Don't tell me she wants your photograph to perve over, your image treasured in a golden Baroque frame on her bedside cabinet, last thing she lovingly gazes upon before she turns out the light?'

'Something like that, Adrian, only the pictures she really likes to look at last thing at night are the ones you took of her that are in your book.'

'Oh, that book! That book! Such a disappointment, Thornton, I can't tell you. Ghastly! Are you sure you wouldn't like a cup of tea?'

'No thank you.'

'Something stronger maybe?'

'No thank you.'

'I know I'm not exactly short of the readies, Thornton. A society photographer of my stature, the equivalent of the Beatons, the David Baileys and Armstrong Joneses of this world but I am not as yet universal if you know what I mean and I had hoped the book would simply fly off the shelves and make me trillions and trillions.'

'Sorry, Adrian. You will be happy to know the countess thinks you're the most talented photographer in the entire world.'

'Yes? Oh, well, hopefully next time.' Obviously the countess's opinion didn't count for much because he went right off. 'I should have been on talk shows, radio and television. I should have done book signings all over the place. Tiddly stop chewing that slipper, it's disgusting. He's a foot fetishist you know. There's nothing he likes more than licking toes, the jammy the better, then he washes his mouth out with soap and water when you're in the bath. He stands at the side of the bath and you scoop up a handful of water and hold it over the edge of the bath for him to lick. He particularly likes blowing bubbles and the flavour of Camay. Mild Green Fairy's a bit of a favourite as well but that's only natural I suppose considering whose dog he is. Talk about being a perve! My word! But my publishers were totally hopeless, Thornton, hopeless! What I needed was my own PR but why should I pay for one when the publishers should have taken the selling completely out of my hands? Well then, my dear, how do you see yourself?'

'Pardon?'

'What kind of portrait are you envisaging? Naked down to the pubes perhaps. Low slung jeans, if you're wearing them, open of course, top button undone, zipper half way down showing your bug path? Shirt open wide to reveal your rugged six pack and a sexy brown nipple?'

'Adrian, you're fantasising,' Thornton laughed, 'and you'll bring yourself on if you're not more careful. What makes you think I've even got a six pack, let alone, what did you call it? A bug path? For your information my torso is like finely polished marble. There's not a hair on it. Front or back. Totally devoid.'

'How distressing. But you could always wear a chest wig if push came to shove. There are ways, know what I mean?'

'No, what do you mean?'

'Simply some people like their beasts to be hairy, ruff ruff! Meaning little old me for starters. A forest of hair drives me simply wild. Well, what's it to be then? Gazing into the distance dreaming of your far away love?'

'Adrian. All that is needed is a straightforward mug shot for identification purposes and that is all.'

'If that is all...' his tone indicated he was truly put out '...what on earth did the old cow send you to me for? You could have gone around the corner and had the job done for sixpence or thereabouts. The equivalent of sixpence anyway.' He was rubbing his thumb and forefinger together, a sure sign of his irritation.

'I did tell her that but she insisted because of her admiration for you. Although it is only for identification purposes, she did want it to be artistic, always artistic with the countess, and in her opinion you were the only man for the job. Think of it this way, Adrian, she could have chosen any of those other photographers you mentioned but, no, she chose you. I do believe from what she most enthusiastically said, she considers you a photographer without equal.'

'Am I not blessed indeed?' From his tone it was obvious Adrian felt exactly the opposite. 'Oh well, let's get on with it then,' he was only slightly mollified, 'but I warn you, Thornton, if I am not into it heart and soul I take a truly lousy picture. Can't be helped. That is the problem of having such a sensitive artistic temperament. I am sure Leonardo and Michelangelo were exactly the same.'

'Funny, that's two names the countess mentioned as well.'

'We'll do it here, take the photograph I means, no point in going up to the studio just for a mug shot.'

He set up a tripod and whilst loading his camera chirrupt snatches of popular songs from musicals, but with his own scatological lyrics. Then, once he was ready, 'Sit!' He said.

And Tiddly sat, the slipper hanging out the corner of his mouth.

*　　　　　　*　　　　　　*

The smell was nauseating but mixed in with it was something a little like the smell of roast chicken which was going to put him off roast chicken for a long time to come. He got it the moment he opened the street door so, quickly closing it behind him, he went to investigate.

He was hanging from a beam in the back room and was naturally an even uglier sight than when Thornton had last seen him. His shoes and socks had been removed and there was an overturned blow lamp lying on the floor close by, its gas canister empty. Thornton wondered if Signor Riccoboni (Was he really Italian? Was that really his name?) in his agony had divulged any important information, always presuming he was somehow connected with the countess and had it in the first place. These guys, whoever they might be, were ruthless if nothing else. Thornton knew now what he could be in for and without any doubt that he should never in a million years have taken on this assignment. He had this idea that if he saw the Chinese vases in Bruno's shop and then in the countess's suite that there might be a connection and more than just a sale, which was why he had come snooping around and it would appear he was right. What on earth had Holly got him into? Ten grand was peanuts when you thought what those bastards could do to you. Was it too late to hand back the countess her up front five thousand and cry off? Oh, but when he went into his bank to deposit the cheque the look on his bank manager's face was worth every penny, even if he never ever saw that look again. The man even took off his glasses to polish them, a sure sign of being severely put out or at least for once being wrong footed. Thornton hated to think of the look he would get on the smarmy bugger's face if the money was now withdrawn.

What did it matter if the countess thought him the wimp to outwimp all wimps? What they had done to poor Bruno's toes didn't bare thinking about if they were to do the same to him.

He happened to be particularly fond of his toes, all ten of them, exactly as they were.

He looked around the workshop which seemingly had been turned upside down with broken frames and canvases scattered all over the place. He was surprised they hadn't tried to cover their traces by setting the place on fire. There was enough flammable material lying about even without chemicals. Maybe they ran out of gas. Stop it, Thornton, he thought, this is no time for sick jokes. Then, with the thought that they might still be somewhere around, he decided it would probably be best if he were to beat a hasty retreat and give his favourite cop, Detective Inspector Reg Venables a friendly call. He realised this homicide was not in Reg's manor but, should the inspector just happen to be passing by and take a sudden fancy for a picture to decorate the front room in that little house beneath the Heathrow fly path and accidentally, on entering the shop and after a few non-answered hellos, peeping into the back room discover the body, well that would put him in the frame as it were, the very centre of the investigation. Maybe the resultant publicity could lead to even more promotion for the poor old sod before his time in the force was up and he was presented with a gong or that retirement clock and spent the rest of his days pottering in his potting shed and lovingly cleaning his paint brushes and his gardening tools. Were clocks still an obligatory part of retirement ceremonies? Or like debutantes coming out at the start of the season was it past history? Remembering the affair of the Russian princess and her murderous modelling academy and Reg taking the honours for solving the case when the glory should have gone to him, and Holly of course, don't forget Holly, it wasn't as though Thornton felt he owed Reg Venables anything but you cannot carry resentment on for ever and a day. He was quite fond of Reg's lady wife, Rita, (That's how Reg always referred to her, as the lady wife but what else could she be but a lady? That's a question that shouldn't be gone into) and with the experiences he and Reg had been through together in their association with the world of crime it had grown into a sort of keep it in the family love hate relationship. Also he was absolutely certain he would not be involved in this, that in giving Reg the tip-off his own name would not pass the inspector's lips, not if he could help it.

He left the shop in the Westbourne Grove for the last time, casting a lingering look back on the shelf behind the grubby window where the Cinelli vases, as he now called them, belonging as they did to her, had once stood. Two five inch wide almost dust free rings marked the place. A last glance around and then, making sure there wasn't a copper lurking outside, policemen are never there when you want them and always there when you don't, he slipped away to find the nearest telephone kiosk. He registered the tourist with a camera standing with a girl on the opposite side of the road though all he thought was why would the man want to take pictures in the grotty Westbourne Grove? It was hardly a scenic spot to illuminate his photo album back home in Tulsa or show neighbours and work mates. It wasn't The Tower or Marble Arch, Piccadilly Circus, Trafalgar Square, Buckingham Palace, The Abbey, Windsor Castle, or any other of the sights visitors were so fond of snapping to show back home, and he moved on. Then he wondered if the man and his girl would like to have their picture taken together and turned back to offer his services only to find the pair had vanished. Thornton paused a moment then gave a shrug and continued on his way.

4

'I never dreamed I would dwell in marble halls,' Thornton said to himself as he surveyed the spacious salon in which he stood. He didn't sing it because his version wouldn't scan with the original. He would have to put it to a different tune and although Thornton was heavily into music, a mood enhancer and if nothing else a constant source of solace during his impecunious days, he was also tone deaf when it came to personal renderings. Florence Foster Jenkins had nothing on him. Thornton couldn't sing *Three Blind Mice* in tune let alone Mozart's *Queen Of The Night* for which Miss Jenkins was so rightly famous.

Marble seemed to be everywhere, not just paving the floor in an intricate design but on the numerous tables, with their enormous carved lion's claws feet, a beautiful pink-veined marble and, between the half dozen floor to ceiling double casements down either side with their faded dusty velvet drapes and heavy tasselled tie-backs there stood marble busts of previous male

Cinellis standing on their marble plinths, and one fierce looking matriarch with a beak of a nose and a large mole on her chin and what looked suspiciously like the beginnings of a moustache. Maybe the sculptor was on a bender at the time. She was a dead ringer for Savonarola or the witch in Disney's Snow White.

At the airport the man had stood holding up a large card on which was written "Signor King" so Thornton knew he was in the right car but when the ancient chauffeur driving the vintage but beautifully maintained Alfa Romeo had pulled up outside the palazzo, Thornton wasn't too sure if they had come to the right place. The chauffeur's venerable but rather lugubrious face gave the distinct impression he might just have forgotten the address and steered off the beaten track.

Although the man had made the obligatory offer, Thornton refused to let him carry his bag. It wasn't as if it was all that cumbersome or heavy. He had hardly brought anything with him in the way of personal effects, a couple of changes of lightweight clothing; it was after all summer, toiletries, his electric razor. After all the job would be over in two or three days, four at the latest, a long weekend really. The poor old guy looked so frail Thornton found himself wondering how he managed to drive in Rome's traffic. He would have thought the countess should have pensioned him off years ago.

The cracked and peeling grubby grey public façade of the building looked as if a thousand stray Roman curs had lifted their legs against it. It looked more like that of a crumbling doss house, an ultra-large doss house maybe but a doss house nevertheless; but the swift opening of the doors and the emergence of a liveried footman to collect his one valise quickly disabused and assured him he was at the correct address.

A middle aged personage of lean and noble bearing in a morning suit who turned out to be the countess's personal assistant, or so he said, a Greek by the name of Yiorgos Ilyothis who spoke impeccable English, greeted Thornton once he was through the massive door and it had been closed behind him by yet another liveried flunkey.

'Good morning, sir, I trust you had a pleasant journey and welcome to Rome. If you will kindly follow me I will show you to your room.'

It was cool in the house and as quiet as the grave. Thornton hoped that wasn't too ominous a sign. Up a wide marble staircase and along a passage lined on either side with family portraits, they eventually came to a door that George opened and through which he ushered Thornton with, 'Here you are, sir, and I hope you will be very comfortable. Should you wish for anything please ring the bell,' he indicated it beside the bed, 'and someone will see to you.' With which he closed the door leaving Thornton alone in his new quarters.

So he had explored his bedroom suite, his valise had already been deposited on one of those low slatted tables usually found in hotels and meant specifically for luggage. The bathroom, which was virtually the size of his entire Hackney flat in the vicinity of Victoria Park, looked by the newness of it as if it had been recently modernised, fitted out of course, mainly in marble. There was the inevitable Jacuzzi as a sop to modernism but he was pleased to see the taps were not gold or shaped like dolphins. At least the Cinellis, or whichever one was responsible for the update, when it came to good taste weren't that idiotic in flaunting their wealth. On the glass shelf above the wash basin was an array of toiletries: toothbrushes, naturally still in their wrappers, ivory backed hair brushes sporting in silver the Cinelli coat of arms, featuring what looked like a smiling pussy cat but which was in fact meant to be a leopard; combs, scissors, nail clippers, enough aftershaves and gentlemen's colognes to keep anyone happy for a generation, anyone capable of getting a buzz out of scent that is. Thornton unstoppered a couple just to sample. He noticed a distinct absence of his favourite, exclusive, rather expensive Knize 5 and decided to mention it to the countess when next they met, discreetly of course. He had a bottle at home that he had kept for years using it sparingly and only on very special occasions.

The towels were enormous, fleecy and white with the Cinelli monogram and an all enveloping bathrobe was provided. All in all it was the height of luxury.

And now, having come back downstairs and all but whistling with admiration, he stood in the elegant salon, redolent of a historic past, the silence suddenly broken when a raucous voice interrupted his reverie.

'Well hi there, young fella' how ya'all doin'?'

Thornton turned to be faced with a very short, no more than five four at a stretch, pot bellied, balding, suntanned, actually more mottled than tanned, gentleman. His Hawaiian floral shirt of many colours was hanging loose and open almost to the navel to reveal, not only an extremely flabby and hairy chest beginning to go grey, but in reality to show off his gold chains and medallions of which there were three; a crucifix, a Star of David and an Ankh. When it came to the supernatural the man obviously believed in hedging his bets, playing it safe as it were; Bermuda shorts in plaid didn't quite hide the wrinkly knees, and open-toe sandals with white socks completed the ensemble. A right hand of chubby hairy fingers was thrust in Thornton's direction. The chubby fingers on the left were beringed with what looked like carnelian on the third finger, a wedding band on number four and an amethyst on the pinkie. A much too large gold watch adorned the wrist. That won't last a day in Rome, Thornton thought who, having heard hair raising tales of Italian banditry in the streets and ever on the cautious side, before leaving the plane had retired to the toilet to remove his own watch and stuff his money and the countess's letter in his socks.

'Nat Berman,' the man said.

'Thornton King,' Thornton replied, taking the hand and noticing the hairs were ginger. The hairs on the chest that still had some colour also revealed that Nat was obviously once a flaming redhead before losing what in women is called their crowning glory and in men, with the possible exception of Samson, simply their hair. Obviously men's hair is not considered a sexual turn-on. The ancient Greeks as usual were quite right in their opinion that long hair enhances a handsome man and makes an ugly one uglier.

'So tell me, are you here making with the vacation then, Thornton?'

'In a way, in a way,' Thornton replied. 'Combining business with pleasure you might say.' He was endeavouring to be jovial whilst having an urge to wipe his right palm on his trouser leg but resisting it.

'Oh? Is that right? And just what kinda business would that be?'

'Well, research actually.'

'Oh, yeah? Research into what?'

'Finding lost objects,' he said. Sometimes it would no doubt be far wiser for Thornton to think before opening his mouth in order to act the smart-arse. Why did he always get himself into situations he had to squirm his way out of? He gave a wan smile as he mentally kicked himself.

'You some kinda archaeologist maybe?'

Nat had taken a leather cigar case out of his shirt pocket, a pocket large enough to take a case holding five very large cigars. He opened the case and held it out towards Thornton who shook his head in refusal. Could it be this uncouth Yank and the sophisticated Italian countess, both being avid cigar smokers were going to get along like the proverbial house on fire? Or maybe they already did. Thornton had a great many questions to ask and answers to find if he was going to keep ahead of the pack and making stupid remarks like finding lost objects which could put them on the scent wasn't the way to do it.

'I take it you're here on holiday then?' he queried. If Nat could ask so many questions, why shouldn't he?

'Too right,' Nat barked with what seemed more enthusiasm than was called for, 'too damn right, buddy. Money ain't everything in life and life is short. Know what I mean? I mean like heart attacks happen.'

'When least expected. Life is indeed short and we only have the one so we might as well make the best of it, huh? And you are I take it a philosopher from Florida.' This time Thornton's smile was broad and inviting of confidence but, for a moment, Nat returned it with a frown.

'No, Thornton, I'm not from Florida so you can't take it.' Then he guffawed as though he had just won the best quip of the day contest. Having recovered and wiped the tears from one eye with the back of his hairy hand he went on. 'Well, okay okay, in one way you're right there, Thornton, I do happen to live in Florida right at this moment in time but my home town is Chicago. You know? That town on the lake old Frankie kinda sings about? His kinda town, my kinda town? You been to the states at all. Thornton?'

Thornton shook his head.

'Don't know what you're missing, pal. You decide one day to pay us a visit you let old Nat know. We'll give you the time of your life. You'll make it your kinda town too. Say, do you suppose we can sit on one of these plush chairs? What are they do you reckon? Louis something or other I bet.' He pronounced it as is written, Louis. 'There were a lot of Lou-ees were there not?' The plural of Louis is obviously Lou-ees. 'But they were French as I seem to remember it. What would French chairs be doing in Italy? Guess old Napoleon must ha' brung them over, huh? What the hell! The loot we're paying the old bag for staying in this run down palace says yes we can sit on her Louis chairs so take a seat, Thornton, unless of course you got somethin' better to do. Look at this will ya? The seat's all frayed round the edge and the stuffing's about to come out. Needs reupholstering real bad, that's what it needs. Either that or junked an' new stuff brought in, real modern, know what I mean? Scandinavian maybe. Glass and chrome. What is this stuff? Silk? Looks like it's four hundred years old.'

'That's probably because it is four hundred years old.'

'Jeez, is that so?' He sat down rather heavily and indicated the chair next to him for Thornton to take but, before he could do so, a Hollywood vision suddenly materialised at the open doors as if to the imagined sound of a hundred Montovani violins. Her name couldn't possibly be Charmaine could it? Could it? She hesitated a moment as though unsure of her welcome, and then advanced towards them on heels that clicked on the marble, that thrust her pelvis forward and must have thrown every vertebrae in her lower back out of alignment. If she was to suffer in later years from crushed or slipped discs or arthritis as she surely would she could put it down to being a slave to the tyranny of this day's fashion.

Thornton simply couldn't help himself. It was his turn to boggle. Nat noticed the boggling with quiet satisfaction. There's nothing like being the proud owner of a trophy.

'Hi ya, Squirrel,' he greeted her, come on in and meet Thornton. Thornton's another guest in this dump so he'll be good company. Thornton, this is my wife Louise Anna. Her folk had a great sense of humour. Get it? Louise Anna?'

Thornton obviously didn't get it because his face remained a blank.

'Boy oh boy,' Nat said, 'I got a terrific admiration for you Britishers but you sure don't have no sense of humour. How about if my folk had called me Chick Argo Berman? Or the Tuckey's called their boy Ken? Or the Sotas called their daughter Minnie? Now do you get it?'

Obviously not or, if he did, he wasn't letting on. In actual fact his whole world at this moment was concentrated on this nubile young creature who, from the platinum hair to the ruby lips to the 40-D bra, despite his usual aversion to oversized mammaries, to the swaying hips, to the butt, the kind someone once described as being like jello on springs, the legs that went right up to it, to the painted toe nails, had stepped straight out of a producer's or a film director's wet dream and not necessarily one in the porno racket. He was absolutely certain this one, should push come to shove, was going to pull a gun on him and, in fact, he would more than likely be rather disappointed if she didn't. She carried a small stylish pocket book in crocodile skin that probably cost as much as a year's rent of his London office if not more, not of course that she had to pay for it. She was obviously a very expensive lady and Nat just had to have been a very generous suitor. Thornton didn't rate him highly in the scale of sexual attraction though it is often quite a puzzle as to what some people see in other people.

'Here…' Nat ordered, 'take this.' He pushed a chair towards her with his foot. It slid a short distance across the marble with hardly a protest and, still without a word, she took it; seated herself and immediately crossed those coltish legs almost giving Thornton that aforementioned heart attack.

Nat meanwhile had fished in his capacious pockets and come up with zilch.

'Anybody here got a match?'

'Sorry,' Thornton said, finally coming back down to earth and patting his pockets for no apparent reason except to prove they were devoid of matches. 'Don't smoke.'

At the sound of his voice Louise Anna seemed to register, looking at him as if seeing him for the first time. Her eyes were blue but there was nothing distinguishable about them. They weren't sparkling or shiny or enormous, or dreamy. They weren't violet or grey or green or a mixture of all. They were simply blue like billions of others. Thornton however thought they were, like the rest of her, ravishingly beautiful; beauty being, after all, in the eye or the crotch of the beholder.

'You don't see a lighter anywhere around here, do you, Squirrel?'

She turned her attention back to the would-be cigar smoker, shook her head and waggled an admonishing finger at him meaning, Thornton surmised, naughty baby you didn't really ought to be smoking that big nasty fat ole cigar that's more'n likely been rolled on the sweaty thigh of some fat ole Cuban commie lady and you don't know where she might have been or who with, in between rolling her big fat ole cigars on her big ole fat sweaty thigh in sweaty ole Cuba. Could even have been rolling cigars for that nasty ole commie dictator Fidel Castro. Louise Anna could be a girl of much thought but few words, Thornton mused, heavily influenced by writers of the Deep South as, amongst other images that popped into his head, he imaginatively made up her unspoken dialogue for her and wondered if she talked at all would she be as Deep South as he was imagining? So far she hadn't said a word out loud and dumb blonde did not mean vocally.

'Shee-it!' Nat lumbered to his feet, further loosening some of the chair's creaking joints, and headed flatfooted for the door but did not have to exit in search of his light as George the Greek, like a genie out of the lamp, magically appeared in the doorway holding out an already struck match to light the American's big fat ole Cuban cigar.

This having been accomplished, Nat returned to his chair puffing merrily away and George, with a shaking of the match to put it out, slipped silently off stage. It struck Thornton that what he had just witnessed was a mite strange to say the least. Had the man been standing behind the door the whole time listening to the conversation and, if so, why? Or was it all part of the slick silent service big money can buy? Never trust a Greek bearing gifts or suddenly appearing to hold out a lighted match, he thought. Nat on the other hand appeared, though appearances can be dangerous, to be totally oblivious to this remarkable coincidence and sat himself down again, regarding the cigar that he was now rolling between his fingers and seemingly deep in thought. Obviously it cost a pretty penny to be a guest in the

Palazzo Cinelli and someone like Nat Berman would expect all T's crossed and I's dotted and vice versa in return for his Yankee dollars. Finally he looked up. 'So, Thornton,' he said after a hefty yawn, 'you got plans for today?'

Nat wouldn't really have been surprised had he known what plans Thornton was contemplating in his vivid imagination at this moment even if bringing them to a satisfying fulfilment might be a million to one shot. As a matter of simple fact, Nat was completely aware of what was going through Thornton's head, let alone jiggling his hormones like coins in a pocket. Any man who could resist his squirrel was a hundred percent dyed in the wool faggot and that was all there was to it, but any man who made an attempt to get too close to his squirrel in the wrong kinda way, know what I mean? that is, the way Nat didn't intend, was asking for a very bad dusting up if not something far far worse. Nat didn't grow up on the wild side of Alphonse Capone's home town without learning a mean ole trick or two.

Yiorgos Ilyothis reappeared and coughed discreetly behind his hand. Nat turned to look vaguely in his direction and Thornton noticed for the first time that one eye catching the light seemed to glint somewhat unnaturally.

'Yeah?'

'Pardon the interruption but you are wanted on the telephone, sir.'

'Me or him?' The cigar jerked in Thornton's direction.

'You, sir. International call from America.'

'So okay okay, I'm coming.'

Once more Nat lumbered to his feet and, trailing smoke, followed George from the room.

Louise Anna, aka Squirrel then did something that for

Thornton was normally a gigantic turn-off. She took a stick of gum from her pocket book, unwrapped it, popped it in her mouth and started chewing ... with her mouth open! At least she didn't let the wrapper fall to the floor but held on to it. It wasn't because she was litter conscious; it was something to fiddle with while she chewed.

Thornton couldn't bear to watch. He got to his feet, prepared to leave the room. 'Excuse me...' He was going to say more by way of making an excuse but she cut him off.

'Where you goin' buster? What's the big rush?' She smiled showing a few thousand dollars worth of orthodontic work partially obscured for a moment by the gum but not for long. It was removed by the tip of a very pink tongue. Thornton thought, as he felt a tsunami in the nether regions, the coins having made a hole in the pocket were now rolling like a tidal wave across the floor in her direction, he might just be able to forgive the gum chewing or even persuade her to give it up; so long as she didn't take up smoking in lieu of, particularly, like her husband and the countess, big fat ole cigars.

So she did talk then, in the vernacular of Hollywood. Was that the correct expression? Her voice was shrill but he loved it to the point of almost giving him goose bumps and he was quite sure if she turned up the volume she could shatter a wine glass at twenty paces.

He sat down again but now it was his turn to be lost for words.

'Talk to me, Mac,' she ordered. 'I just love to hear that English accent.'

'How are you enjoying Rome?' Thornton asked, squirming at the banality of this opening.

'Not been long enough here to appreciate it... yet.' There was a short silence before she continued with, 'Our bedroom has a terrific painted ceiling though. You oughta see it sometime.' The gum was rolled from one side of the mouth to the other and the tongue tip swept across the upper lip like a wiper across a wet windshield. This lady knew exactly what she was doing. Thornton found himself wondering how many she had practiced on before Nat came on the scene and at exactly what age did she start? His fantasies were on overtime. She was a striptease artiste, a pole dancer from Las Vegas. She was a farm kid from the Middle West who started off on her horny cousins but he was suddenly brought back to earth by -

'How's yours?'

'How's my what?' He squeaked.

'Your ceiling, what else?'

'To be truthful I haven't had a chance to get a good look at it… yet.'

'Maybe sometime we oughta do something about that.'

'Maybe we oughta.' His heart was in his mouth as an author of detective novels might write.

'And mine.' She added.

It was at this point that Nat re-entered looking decidedly put out. She turned to look at him.

'Whatsa matter, hun? You look like shit.' She raised an eyebrow in Thornton's direction which meant to imply that her hubby usually looked like shit anyway.

'We gonna sit around here all day? Let's get the hell outa this dump. See something of the town.' Nat grumbled.

'Let's do that.' She got to her feet and headed towards her man and the door before stopping and turning around. 'You coming with, John?'

Thornton looked around to see who else was in the room. It took him a moment to register that he was the John referred to.

'My name is Thornton,' he said, a slight rebuke in his voice.

'Yeah, whatever. Well, Thornton, are you coming?' There was a decided accent on the Thornton.

'I think not.'

'You think?' This was from Nat, advancing into the room and not too friendly by the sound of it, in fact adopting a decidedly pugnacious attitude.

'Well… you see… I was intending to hire a car and…'

'Okay, okay, so what's the big deal? We'll hire a limmo, the bigger the better. We'll show these Romanians how to have a good time.' He turned away and started for the door.

'… motoring to Geneva.'

There was a stunned silence finally broken by Nat who had been stopped dead in his tracks, almost tripping over his own feet. He turned to look back at this weird limey.

'What do you wanna do that for, for Chrissakes? You only just got to Rome, Italy. Geneva, Switz-er-land is like over four hundred miles away.' This was a guess but a pretty good one. 'What're you gonna do there? Find a Neolithic cuckoo clock? Ha ha ha ha!'

There it is, Thornton thought – that old cuckoo clock joke again, and where on earth did someone like Nat Berman learn the word Neolithic? Maybe as a kid he visited a museum of natural history and the word stuck in his head. Strange words tend to do that. Common or garden words can be instantly forgettable. Unusual words can be instantly memorable.

'Did you know there are, so I am reliably informed, something like thirty museums, art galleries in Geneva?' It was a feeble excuse and he knew it but his mind closed down like a dynamo being switched off and he couldn't immediately think of anything else.

'Is that right? And how many museums an' art galleries do you suppose are in Rome right where you're standing at this very moment in time and a helluva lot closer than Switz-er-land? How many museums an' art galleries do you think there are in some big ole ancient *I*-talian dump like Florence where once upon a time all those faggotty men stood around wearing upside down flower pots on their heads and bum-freezer jackets and women's stockings with stripes down one leg an' had their you know whats framed in what they used to called a codpiece so you couldn't help but notice it? Know what I mean? I seen pictures, all standing around like this giving each other the eye.' Nat took on a Renaissance pose, one leg slightly bent and one hand on hip. He obviously had a big mental hang-up about faggots. 'It weren't just their swords an' daggers they was pokin' about with. Know what I mean? So how many museums an' art galleries you reckon they got within a hunert mile radius of this place?'

'Quite a few I suppose.'

'What was that?'

'I said, quite a few I suppose.'

'You suppose. Well then, for why do you want to drive four hundred miles to Geneva Switz-er-land just to visit a couple a ole museums and art galleries when you can look all you want right here?'

'I didn't say that.'

'You didn't say what?'

'That I was going to Geneva simply for the museums.'

'Then what did you say? Didn't I hear you right? Didn't I hear the man right, Squirrel?'

But Squirrel seemed to have lost interest in the argument which did look indeed as though it was going to go around in circles for a while and she had wandered off to have a one-sided conversation of her own with one of the Cinelli ancestors on his marble plinth. She thought he looked real cute with all that avalanche of hair tumbling down in great curls over his shoulders. She didn't know it would have been a wig under which he would have been bald as an egg. Had he grown his own hair the lice would have had a field day. She moved on to the next one who was a craggy looking fellow she didn't take to at all. In fact, she squinted passed him to where the two men were talking. He looked a bit like Nat she thought so she pulled a face and moved on.

'There are also any number of antique dealers there.' Thornton was trying not to pull a face.

'And that's where you're going to find your cuckoo clock.' Nat whooped with delight and nearly choked on his cigar smoke. Thornton waited for him to recover.

'No, as a matter of fact it's vases I'm particularly interested in.'

'Is that a fact?'

Thornton nodded. He couldn't be sure but he thought he detected a slight narrowing of one eye, the one that was watering. Had he put his foot in it once again?

'Any particular kind of vase?' He pronounced it vaise. 'You're a collector are you? Or maybe a dealer?'

'Neither a collector nor a dealer be, I'm only interested in studying a particular period of Chinese ceramics.' For God's sake, Thornton, he thought, back off while there's still a chance. You're getting in far too deep here.

'Is that right? And you have to go four hunert miles to Geneva to do that? Why don't you go to Beijing? Or Hong Kong while you're about it? And so what's wrong with books? You can look at the pictures. Save yourself a heap of trouble an' expense.'

Thornton realised he was getting in deeper and deeper here and was beginning to wonder either how he could get out of it or whether he should plough on regardless and see to where this might all lead.

Nat had done with his cigar, looked around for somewhere to stub it out and was now making as though to try and open one of the large casements, an obviously impossible task it had been so long since any of them were opened, probably not since some big shot stood on the balcony receiving the plaudits of the crowd, when George appeared at the door, ashtray in hand and at the ready. With raised eyebrows, a cough and a nod of the head Thornton indicated to Nat that George was standing behind him. Nat turned.

'Well hiya, buddy, where'd you spring from? Hey, what's with this guy? He's like one of those old fashioned, what do ya call 'em?'

'Jack in a box?'

'Jack in the box. He pops up just when you need him? I could do with someone like that back home in the states. You wanna come back to the states with me, buddy?'

'I think not, sir, thank you all the same.'

'You could buttle for me. Make it worth your while.'

'Much appreciated sir, for your generous offer, but I am a European at heart and have never had a fancy for visiting the New World.'

'New world huh? Well, you quaint old-fashioned thing then. There was a time when you Europeans couldn't wait to get to the states, Ellis Island notwithstanding. Well, have it your own way. Ain't nobody gonna twist your arm. What's your name by the way?'

'Yiorgos, sir. In English that is George.'

'That so? Well what're you waiting for, Yiorgos?'

'I believe you wish to dispose of your cigar, sir.'

'All part of the service,' Thornton said with a little laugh, hoping they had now got off the subject of Geneva and vases although he realised this might be too much to hope for. He had almost put his foot in it twice. Come to think of it, maybe he ought to carry on, see what the reaction is to any more hints he might let drop, deliberately this time.

Nat was still waving his cigar butt around and George was patiently waiting to have it deposited in his ashtray which it finally was. He turned and left with a sideways glance in Thornton's direction which seemed to mean what are we dealing with here? and Nat moved closer to Thornton who was wishing he had used that hiatus to get away as well but too late now as the old song goes.

'So tell me, Thorn, tell me about these particular vaises you're so interested in. Something special about them maybe? Truly valuable are they? What are they worth do you reckon?'

'I have no idea.'

'But you're the friggin' expert, no? You oughta know what they're worth.' Nat couldn't keep the astonishment out of his voice. 'Supposin' they was to be sold at auction. London, New York, Sotheby's, some place like that, millions of dollars?'

'Could be I suppose.' Thornton was growing a little irritated with this questioning but decided it would be best to keep his cool. He had a lurking suspicion that, unless carefully handled, this animal could inflict a rather nasty bite, possibly fatal.

'And you got the necessary moola to buy them?' Nat accentuated the question with a rhythmic poking of Thornton's chest with his index finger. 'Or are you working for someone who has?'

'Look, Mr Berman...'

'Nat, Thornton, Nat.'

'Nat.'

'The Contessa maybe, huh? Maybe she's got the readies which is why you're here. Is that it, Thornton? Huh? You working for the Contessa? You don't strike me as the kinda guy got the means to stay in a dump like this without a bit of help, am I right or am I right?' Nat's one eye had narrowed considerably. The other one stayed alarmingly wide open.

'If I am going to get this car and motor to Switzerland I'd like to make a start right now so, intriguing though this conversation may be, Nat old chum, I'd like to call it a day if you don't mind. Maybe we can pick it up some other time. How long are you in Rome for?' Thornton had edged, he hoped surreptitiously, a little closer to the door.

'Till my business is finished.'

This brought the Englishman to a full stop. 'Business? You're here on business? But I thought you said you were on vacation?'

'I'm never on vacation, Thorn, even when I think I am. Every day a working day wherever I happen to set down my butt, and it'll be like that till I'm kicking up the daisies. So tell me more about these vaises. I'm truly interested. What kinda vaises you particularly interested in? Maybe with my connections I could help you out a little here, so level with me, pal.' This time the pal was heavily accentuated.

Thornton had been led to believe that Americans were quick off the mark when it came to making friendships but he hadn't realised he would be a pal in such a short passage of time and he was beginning to wonder why exactly. Mind you, he had called Nat his chum so possibly he had been just as forward.

'Do you know where the word chum originates?' he asked, ready to go into a diversion with one of his explanations.

'Can't say that I do and can't say I'm that interested. The vaises, Thornton, we're talking vaises here, not chums. You might as well start talking about faggots, a subject I am totally uninterested in.'

If he's totally uninterested, Thornton wondered, why does he keep bringing it up? Out loud he said, 'Well, Nat, the vais...vases I'm particularly interested in as you put it stand about so high...' he held his hand out to indicate the height '... are nineteenth century Chinese celadon-ware manufactured for the house of a wealthy Mandarin, decorated with dragons ...' He had discovered all this thanks to the countess who knew all about them, having done her research in the Oriental section of the Victoria and Albert.

'This Mandarin has dragons? I'm not surprised if he didn't have flowers, they was all faggots.'

There he goes again. He certainly has faggotry on his mind.

'The vase has dragons and flowers and they have sand inside them.'

'The dragons have sand inside them?'

'The...' Thornton finally realised as the penny dropped that Nat might just be taking the piss and he forced a laugh as if to join in the joke. It didn't sound too convincing though Nat laughed as well and that wasn't exactly a pleasant sound. Come to think of it, neither was Thornton's.

'There you are then, Thorn, ain't that better that you lighten up a little? So friggin' serious you Britishers, the bulldog breed I am led to believe is what you're called.' With a little difficulty considering his height in comparison to Thornton's he put an arm around the younger man's shoulders. The sweat stain revealed under the armpit was not only an unedifying sight but slightly nauseating to boot. Thornton had always believed that Yanks never went a day without showering at least three times, unlike unhygienic Europeans, but this was evidently not the case with Nat. 'Now how's about us all three visiting that ole Coliseum where those gladiators used to hang out and they used to throw the Christians to the lions.'

If the lions got one whiff of you you'd be gone in one gulp or they'd run away whimpering, Thornton thought. He was seriously wishing he'd tried out a few more aftershaves while he was in the bathroom. Stale body odours and Thornton did not mix. He was far too squeamish and was desperately trying not to breathe. 'Then we can take in a few more of the sites,' Nat continued, 'and have us a bite to eat somewheres, though they more'n likely do not have proper American hamburgers in this place, and you can tell me more about these vaises that have sand in their bottoms.' Nat's arm had fortunately dropped before Thornton was asphyxiated and he thankfully took in a good lungful of fresher air. He was about to open his mouth and protest at Nat's plans when he noticed Squirrel had returned from her perambulation down the length of the salon and back and was smilingly urging him to accept the invitation. He accepted. It didn't take much urging.

He didn't let on that, apart from having money in his shoes, he had the key to a Swiss bank safe deposit box and a letter of introduction strapped to his leg.

The Countess Cinelli wasn't worried exactly. It would take a while for her to grow tired of being in London where her suite was most comfortable and, unlike Rome that had recently become much too dangerous, she felt safe and amongst friends. Holly for one was only a phone call away and she had her recently acquired giant bodyguard to keep a watchful eye on her so she sailed serenely through the days, her schedule undisturbed.

Not enough time had elapsed, she thought, for Thornton to do the business he was being paid for and, after everything she had heard about him, she had every faith in his ability. She did wonder, after talking on the telephone to George, why he was still in Rome and not already on his way to Geneva but George didn't seem unduly worried and maybe Thornton had his reasons, like making sure all those who were interested in the goods could possibly be identified before he set off and so allow him to take proper precautions. She couldn't know the real reason for the delay was his interest in a nubile young American by the name of Louise Anna who it seemed wasn't in the least bit put out by his interest despite the presence of her husband. But then the scenario changed.

'Oh, honey, do you have to?' She had wailed theatrically through her gum chewing when informed after a flurry of cross Atlantic phone calls that Nat had to leave on urgent business, destination unknown and he didn't know exactly how long he would be away, a few days at most.

'I tell you what,' he said, 'we'll get Thornton to hang around a couple a days more while I'm gone just to keep you company. I know he wants to get moving but I'll talk him into it. Make sure you don't get up to no hanky-panky though, know what I mean? Not that I don't trust my squirrel.' He pinched her cheek but the smile that went with the gesture was a false smile and menacing. 'I mean, Jeez! What's the big hurry to get to Geneva anyway? Geneva's been there a long time, it ain't gonna go away, now is it?' Nat roared with laughter. He had come to the conclusion that Thornton was pretty harmless when it came to women, obviously not because he was a faggot or anything near but because, on hearing of Nat's imminent departure, Thornton had especially confided in him that he needed to see a doctor in Rome or visit a clinic as he thought there might be something, you know, wrong with his waterworks. Terribly embarrassing, old chap. Not something the English liked to talk about. Nat was all sympathy, suggested George could point the sufferer in the right direction clinic-wise and went off a reassured man. Restoration comedy has its uses.

*   *   *

She was quite right, the Sistine Chapel it certainly wasn't and some of the brushwork a little crude but it was a very interesting ceiling nevertheless, even though the painting in some places was cracking up, flaking, or had been dulled, darkened, almost obscured; degraded by the passing of time and the accumulation of a big city's polluted atmosphere in the age of the internal combustion engine. A number of jaundiced looking putti, colour wise that is, were flying among the pink edged clouds looking mischievous with smiles that were either erotic or knowing and with wings that were ridiculously inadequate, which wouldn't have held up a fly let alone a chubby cherub; well more than just chubby, horribly obese in fact but then babies, unlike adults, always had an excuse for being fat. There were a couple of flagons, one lying on its side spilling the last of its wine, and goblets indicating a fair amount of alcohol might have been consumed which could explain the jaundiced look of the putti if they were into underage alcohol abuse.

To one side there was a voluptuous reclining nude, Venus most presumably, voluptuous hip-wise that is but ridiculously small in the mammary department, being attended to by a number of scantily clad nymphs, their diaphanous robes just enough to titillate. She was having a nipple pinched or softly caressed by the podgy fingers of one of the more adventurous of the putti hovering like a humming bird within striking distance. She didn't seem inclined to slap his hand away but had a rather dreamy expression on her face, Post coitus tristus Thornton thought which could very well have been the case because close by, reclining on a rock and looking completely shagged out, lay the figure he supposed to be Mars, armour cast aside and his sword in a position to be imagined as a somewhat after the event drooping phallic symbol.

It had been many a year since Thornton last wet the bed. In fact he couldn't have been more than a month or two out of nappies when it happened and it was because a violent thunderstorm with much too close flashes of lightning woke him up with a terrible fright in the middle of the night, but right at this moment he knew he had done it. The bedding was sopping. Of course if he were dead or wounded it could be blood, great gouts of the stuff, but he couldn't be dead because his ears were ringing painfully, his eyes smarting, his heart galloping and his nostrils felt as if someone had spurted acid up them. He simply couldn't believe it.

Once again a woman had pulled a gun on him but how on earth had she missed at point blank range? He was practically on top of her when she let rip, now here she was, half propped up in bed, still with a smoking snub nose in her right hand, returning his gaze as if nothing had happened to mar their blissful afternoon encounter. One moment they had been entwined in fond embrace, the next… it didn't even bear thinking about. He slapped the side of his head with a flat hand in an attempt to stop the ringing in his ears and the wet between and down his legs was now extremely uncomfortable and, in differing circumstances, would have also been highly embarrassing, unless she was into the golden shower and she had given no indication of that. Also bed was hardly the most appropriate or convenient place for that sort of caper, not even on rubber sheets.

Louise Anna flopped back on the bed and stretched out her arm to place the gun on the ormolu decorated bedside cabinet, then she scrabbled around in the bedding for a moment before coming up with something that made her smile. If Thornton was in a state of shock prior to this he was now going to go into overdrive with the screaming habdabs. She held up her hand, forefinger and thumb making a ring and in the centre of that ring a blue eye was staring unblinkingly at the male in her bed. If he had been able to locate his voice he would have screamed, just as he did when as a child he was woken by that clap of thunder and flash of lightning outside his little bedroom window bringing his loving parents hastening to his room to pacify him with hugs, kisses, and reassuring cooing noises.

Louise Anna concentrated on her hand and, still holding the eye, manoeuvred it backwards and forwards as if she were playing with a puppet. She gave it a couple of jerks and a twist so that the eye seemed not only to look slightly possessed but to focus on something behind him. Thornton finally caught on and turning to look over his shoulder saw Nat spreadeagled across the marble floor. He threw back the covers and hopped out of bed, moved across to where Nat lay and stared down at the body. There was a neat little hole in the man's forehead. Louise Anna, like the legendary Annie Oakley, was obviously a dead shot. One eye stared back at Thornton; the other one was still between Louise Anna's fingers. It was totally macabre. There wasn't much blood, only a slight trickle, but a fair amount of wormy brain lay scattered about. Thornton dragged his attention away from the corpse to look back at Louise and finally he found a remnant of his voice, rather hoarse.

'What … What did you do that for?'

As Nat still had a gun in his right hand it seemed a totally superfluous question but she answered it all the same.

'He was going to kill us both, honey, make no mistake about that, even though that would have been a big mistake. He was supposed to keep an eye on you all the way.'

'Why?'

'Come off it, Thornton, don't play dumb. You know very well why.'

Thornton looked down again at the recumbent Nat, the late Nat Berman, and then up again at Louise Anna. Where, he wondered did she fit in the frame?

'All very well, my dear,' he said with voice still trembling from the shock, 'but what are we going to do now?' He took a deep breath and his voice became clearer, more the ringing tenor he knew so well rather than the frog in the throat, and he really felt he needed to get this episode over and done with so he could retire to the bathroom and clean himself up before getting dressed. He would be able to think more clearly with his pants back on. What the housekeeper was going to make of the sodden bed he had no idea but no doubt the resourceful Louise Anna he hoped would be able to squirm her way out of that one. In the meantime, and more importantly, in fact crucially, there was the question of the late Nat Berman to consider. Calling the police was out of the question. A crime of passion might get the beautiful Louise Anna in front of a sympathetic and horny judge acquitted in France or at least given a minimal sentence, if the French still believed in that sort of thing, but he wasn't too sure about Italy and, anyway, that would be a long way down the line and in the meantime there was a job to finish and the intrusion of the police would not only hamper it but well and truly put the kybosh on it if they were both languishing in a Roman jail.

'Well?' He demanded.

'Ring for Yiorgos.'

'What?'

'George, Thornton, ring for George. Oh, here, he can still keep an eye on you.' She tossed the false eye to him which he caught one-handed and immediately felt like dropping with revulsion as she stretched out for the bedside phone, lifted the receiver and waited, as did he, after he had carefully placed the eye on Nat's chest. He didn't think he would be able to fit it back into its socket without heaving. Sometimes, as Holly would no doubt have pointed out, Thornton could be the complete wimp.

After a while the phone was obviously answered.

'Oh, Yiorgos,' she purred, 'there's been a little accident and I need your help. Can you come up here please? Thank you.'

She replaced the receiver and hopped out of bed. In order to avoid treading on the bits of brain which would have squelched like turkey shit between the toes, Louise Anna was brought up on a farm as Thornton had suspected, she took a wide detour, loping across to where he was standing like a mesmerised chicken with its beak in a line on the sand. She took his hand and they both stood gazing down at Nat. She cocked her head to one side as though examining a specimen of something which in a way was exactly what she was doing.

'He was your husband,' Thornton managed to whisper.

'Yeah, I know that, Thornton. It was a drive-by quickie wedding in Reno. Don't mean a thing really. Three minutes, pay up an' it's all over, 'cept I guess I got a bundle coming to me if the lawyers back home don't screw things up. I'm not too sure we were legally hitched anyway. Number one I divorced okay but number two never did show up. We think he got eaten by a shark in the Caribbean but it weren't certain. This one was number three. Guess if he disappears as well there cain't ever be a number four. What'cha reckon, Thorn?' She was still regarding the prostrate Nat as though seeing him for the first time. 'I had an Australian lover once,' she said, 'who called all small animals like those bears they got in that country...'

'Koalas.'

'Cola's a drink, Thornton.'

'Not cola. Koala.'

'Whatever. He called all critters like that furry little buggers. I suppose you could call Nat a furry little bugger, wouldn't you say?' She turned her head to favour him with the sweetest expression.

Thornton did tend to agree. In death Nat seemed to have shrunk in size, perhaps no more than five now, and there was no doubt as to his overall hairiness. He wondered if it were true that hair continues to grow after death. Nat could end up in his coffin looking like an orang-utan, a very dead one but a hairy one-eyed orang-utan nevertheless and as for the cross, Star of David and Ankh, who knew what afterlife he was facing, if any?

Louise Anna kissed her most recent lover on his shoulder and he shivered.

'Shall we take that shower?' She asked, running her tongue down his arm.

He agreed to that as well, almost comatose allowing himself to be led by the hand. He had decided she knew exactly what she was doing and Yiorgos, if and when he arrived, would be no trouble. He was thoroughly confused by events and relationships but no doubt there would be a handsome pay off somewhere down the line. In Greece they call it the *fakelos,* the envelope, and it is a part of life, as ubiquitous as olive oil. They disappeared into the bathroom just as there was a discreet knock on the bedroom door, which after a proper interval was silently opened by the oily Greek.

Thornton's surmise had been correct. When they finally exited the shower, Thornton still somewhat wobbly on his pins, he found the bed stripped to its base, no sign of the late Nat Berman, no trace of blood, brains, or even one artificial eye. Louise Anna's gun though was still on the bedside cabinet. Thornton decided if he and she were going to make with a repeat performance of pre-kill dilly-dallying, he would ensure the gun was empty or far out of reach elsewhere. Accidents can too easily happen and ninety percent of them happen in the home.

5

Thornton had located Hertz on the Viale del Galoppatoio, decided with never a second thought on an open top tourer as befitted his new lifestyle, went through all the necessary paperwork, paid with his Barclaycard, now having sufficient funds for it not to be rejected, and was now studying the map he picked up with his car, pondering on which was the best way to go and also wondering if it wouldn't have been a much better idea to let the train take the strain. After all Italian railways had a terrific reputation for comfort, good food, and punctuality ever since the fascists made Mussolini's boast come true that the trains would run on time. Maybe it was all that punishing castor oil that made the wheels go around. Not another sick joke, Thornton, he silently admonished himself.

Eventually, after some consideration, he decided he would take the via Aurelia coast road as far as Genoa and then cut inland to Turin and Milan, continue north passed Lake Maggiore, up to and over the Simplon Pass and so on to Geneva, a piece of cake really, once out of Rome. The original road over the pass he learned from the traveller's guide book he had purchased was evidently built by Napoleon to ease the passage into Italy of his grand army which, on army rations probably needed easing, and Wordsworth crossed over in the opposite direction to Thornton when on a walking tour in 1790, so he read amongst other pieces of information.

Alternatively he could drive via Aostra and the Grand Saint Bernard Pass to Martigny and along the north shore of the lake. Whichever way, he was really looking forward to it. It would be his very first view of the Alps from the ground up rather than from an aeroplane down but before then he would stop off at Pisa and see that fabulous leaning tower - an ambition since early childhood, only in childhood he had hopes of it actually toppling over, hapless people falling off it and others on the ground running for their lives before they were crushed to death. As a schoolboy he had made a drawing of it in art class with matchstick men and women dropping by the dozen much to his teacher's disgust who thought him a very strange little boy which in some ways no doubt he was. Too often in class far away in daydream land he had to be slapped back to reality. Small boys just shouldn't fantasize to the extent of which Thornton at a tender age was capable.

He could spend the night in Pisa and move leisurely along the next day. After all, what was the hurry? An extra day here and there was not going to make any difference to the outcome although he had already, as tradition demanded, tossed his coin into the Trevi Fountain to ensure his return to Rome so that was a foregone conclusion and it wasn't until he had passed the Vatican and caught sight of the shimmering silver sea that he realised he was without two important, if not absolutely vital, pieces of equipment for his deadly mission – sunglasses and a hat.

*　　　　　　　　　　*　　　　　　　　　　*

The memory of the recently deceased Nat lying grotesquely, almost brainless and one-eyed not more than a yard or so from the foot of the bed was proving an insurmountable barrier to any further erotic activity contemplated, at least as far as Thornton was concerned. He was not only as limp as a sardine but about the same size as well, a very small sardine at that, and no amount of encouragement from Louise Anna was going to make the slightest bit of difference. Had Thornton been a smoker he would have preferred a comforting cup of tea and a soothing cigarette. As it was, his mind wondering, he gazed at the ceiling, noticing all its imperfections. It was that kind of a situation. All right, so Nat might not have been everything a decent man ought to be and more than likely responsible himself for some pretty gruesome episodes but did he really deserve to be murdered in hot blood?

Louise Anna sighed and leaning on one elbow looked down at her silent partner who eventually turned from the ceiling to focus on her face. She smiled.

'What do you call a horny Eskimo?' She asked.

'I don't know,' he said, 'what do you call a horny Eskimo?'

'Frigid midget with a rigid digit.' She shrieked with laughter. He was totally unimpressed. She thought she would try again.

'What do you call a eunuch in a harem?' She asked.

Thornton frowned. 'I don't know,' he said. 'What do you call a eunuch in a harem?'

'A massive vassal with a passive tassel' and once more Louise

Anna shrieked with mirth. 'Which is what you are at the moment,' she added when she had recovered, 'though not quite so massive.' She gave it a playful waggle between finger and thumb.

'Yes,' he agreed. 'Sorry about that.'

'So then, Thorny not so horny…' Thornton winced '…what are we going to do now? I tell you what, lover boy, let's get freshened up and then you and I will go out for a delicious meal and a night on the town. How does that suit? I'll get George to recommend some dinky little place for us to eat after which we can get romantic all over again. Whatja say?' She had already hopped out of bed and was padding her way to the bathroom. Even the sight of her naked, delectable as it was, failed to raise a thing.

*   *   *

Thornton was remembering this episode and his humiliation as he drove out of Rome a second time. Not a happy thought to dwell on but like an itchy sore it insisted upon being scratched. Apart from a slight deviation inland for Grosseto, the road travelled the full distance to Pisa next to the sea and Thornton reckoned the journey would take about four hours without hurrying. In fact it would more than likely take longer because he might just stop off at Grosseto for a lunch of wild boar and the famous local wine, Morellino de Scansano, the fruity red cousin to Chianti. Life is too short for a bad wine, as Thornton once heard a Cretan say, and never a truer word was said. It could be the basic philosophy for a complete life. Could be it was originally said by a Minoan three thousand years or so ago living it up in Knossos, but who knows?

It was Yiorgos who had suggested this detour. Yiorgos and

Squirrel between them seemed to have gone out of their way to make life easy for him. He was beginning to wonder if this was a good thing but he didn't brood on it. He hadn't, for example, enquired as to what had happened to the body of the late Nat Berman. Cesare Borgia knew what to do with bodies. He merely had them dropped into the Tiber. Could that have been the case with Nat and was he already washed out to sea to sink, be nibbled by fish or wash up on land again well salted?

But back to thoughts of lunch. He remembered the delicious wild boar he had tasted late one night in that remote (well it seemed remote) French farmhouse the time Holly was abducted by a pair of hoodlums, one of them being the son of the farmer and his wife. Kidnapped was too strong a word for what those morons got up to and memory of the episode brought Luigi to mind. He wondered how that little Sicilian rapscallion was getting on in an Italian jail. Thornton sincerely hoped he had found a protector who, even though he might be using that beautiful young Sicilian body himself, would at least prevent it's being ravaged by a prison full of frustrated horny convicts. On the other hand Luigi was probably cute enough to look after himself come what may.

He hadn't sought out Louise Anna before leaving, thinking it best to just quietly slip away. He still wasn't sure what game she was playing. Come to that, what was George's position that, at Squirrel's request, he was capable of disposing of unwanted goods in the blink of an eyelid and seemingly without question? Where had he disposed of the remains and what assistance did he call up? That was another decidedly smelly kettle of fish. He couldn't have managed it on his own. He was a middle-aged man probably not as fit as he could be and a dead weight is a dead weight even if it is only five feet tall. Then to quite calmly, as though the violence hadn't even taken place, give Thornton and Squirrel advice on the best place to eat and for Thornton's trip north as though he were some sort of travel guide. No, there was definitely something going on that Thornton didn't know about and he wished he could concentrate on his upcoming lunch rather than keep on going around in mental circles playing at being a detective. There would be a time for that. He thought back on their last night. He had the creepy feeling that throughout dinner in that little trattoria Yiorgos had recommended he and Squirrel were being watched but he couldn't make out if it was real or merely, particularly after the Nat Berman episode, his overwrought imagination.

Leaving Rome for the second time, now well armoured in hat and glasses against the sun and the diamond sparkling sea, Thornton had kept a wary eye out for anything that could be interpreted as untoward but, apart from a number of open shirted medallion wearing Italian boy racers who probably imagined they were in a Fellini film, some of them apparently well into their sixties and seventies, all seemed fairly free of a dangerous encounter.

The lunch was every bit as he imagined it would be and he had decided to be careful not to take too much wine. Couldn't tell what it would do to him in this hot sun. Eventually, deciding he had lingered long enough, having paid the bill and surprised to find the wine had nearly all gone, he sipped the last, put down his glass and looked around to make sure there were still no suspicious characters around who could upset his day as he continued on his way towards Pisa. The problem in Italy though, he thought as he rose to leave, is how do you tell who is suspicious and who isn't?

The car was as and where he had left it. No sign of vandalism, no sign of any tampering which was not surprising really as, if anyone had been following him, they would need to know his destination and where he was expected to pick up the goods. To put him in any danger by tampering with the car would be more than foolhardy; it would be downright stupid to say the least. In fact they might even have protected it from mindless vandals so Thornton hopped in, whistling tunelessly to himself, inserted the key in the ignition and switched on. The car purred into life as he expected and he smiled at a couple of comely young ladies on the sidewalk as he pulled away. Next stop Pisa. He hadn't gone very far when he wondered if he hadn't detected something a little strange about the comely young ladies who had returned his smile so warmly. In the first place they were both ash blonde and didn't look in the least Italian but then so what? Neither did he for that matter. Italy was awash with tourists and holiday makers and not all Italians look like Italians. Nevertheless there was something about the girls that worried him. Oh, well, he gave a shrug, deciding not to think about it any more but just take in the scenery and enjoy the ride and it wasn't until he had travelled a goodly distance that he suddenly asked himself the question, why would two obviously attractive young ladies be wearing heavy belted full length leather coats in the middle of a hot summer's day?

*   *   *

The short journey, seventy five miles, from Grosseto to Pisa was uneventful. A couple of near misses with suicidal truck drivers but otherwise all clear. He decided on the Grand Hotel Bonnano as being a ten minute walk from that famous leaning tower and the centre of things and in a moment had settled in nicely. There was still no sign of anyone showing an untoward interest in him as he set out to explore.

It didn't take long for Thornton to realise Pisa was a gourmet's paradise and he found himself wandering away from the famous tower and the Campo dei Miracoli and heading for the river. He didn't actually know where he was going but Thornton was always a great one for following his nose and there were lira courtesy of the Contessa burning a hole in his pocket and it had been a long time since lunch.

Thornton sat in his hire car, the kind of car he fantasized he would one day be in a position to own if ever he thought of owning a car once more. The countess Cinelli's largesse unfortunately did not extend to that possibility and it would be a dream for a long while yet he felt sure. Maybe he could get it second-hand through Harold who would give him a good price and let him pay on the never-never. Though, come to think of it, owning such a car in London was really asking for trouble. If it weren't mindlessly trashed by brain-dead idiots it would no doubt be stolen to be redesigned or for spare parts so maybe it wasn't such a good idea after all; but one could always dream, could one not? He was studying his AA map and deciding on his route. He thought he would give Milan and the Simplon Pass a miss this time and take what seemed the easier and quicker route as originally planned, to Genoa, Turin, and up to the border at Mont Blanc and so into Switzerland. How many white mountains are there in the world, he mused? Crete has its White Mountains, the Lefka Ori; Kilimanjaro in Kenya simply translates as White Mountain. He wondered about Mount Fuji, did that translate as White Mountain as well? His Japanese didn't extend beyond sayonara. America must surely have at least one White Mountain. America has everything. He also wondered if there was anything worth seeing in Genoa while he was about it. He believed the cemetery was worth looking at. Thornton had heard people actually took their picnic lunches to sit and munch and knock back their vino among the gravestones of the dear departed. Maybe some of them were not all that loved, quite the reverse in fact and sitting on their tombstones noshing away was a means of giving them a metaphorical twos-up as it were. You're in there; I'm still here, ha ha! Genoa being surrounded by hills had little room for cemetery expansion so a body was allowed its rest for a period before the bones were removed to the charnel house to make room for a new occupant, and there was evidently a mass of interesting sculpture to be admired including the Capulet family mausoleum, or was it the Montagues'? Thornton had once played the part of Mercutio in a school production of *Romeo and Juliet* and he had a soft spot for that particular Shakespearian play. Even though he felt he should have been cast as Romeo and sulked for a while, he supposed Mercutio was a good second best with a highly dramatic death scene he milked for all it was worth and it does include one of the most famous speeches in the entire canon, "Ah than I see Queen Mab has been with you." Did Shakespeare get it all wrong? Was Genoa and not Verona the playground of the feuding families? He smiled at the memory of his one moment of theatrical triumph but decided the mausoleum would be given a miss this trip. He really had wasted too much time already. He turned the key in the ignition, slipped the car into gear and set off for the via Aurelia. Thornton loved driving and this car was a joy to handle. It wasn't long before he turned on the radio, hoping for some opera, preferably his favourite Puccini or, failing that at least some Neapolitan song or something like Leoncavallo's *Mattinata* maybe. What he got was *Volare*, not the Dean Martin version but sung in Italian. He could accompany the first two lines, "*Volare oh oh, Cantare oh oh oh oh*" after which he was lost. The song came to an end and was followed by a gabble of quick fire Italian so he switched off and sung out off key, "*When the moon hits your eye, like a big pizza pie, that's amore,*" and that was as far as he could get with that one. He remembered Adrian's risqué lyrics to popular song and chuckled to himself. The trouble with driving any distance on your own is, as much as you might admire the scenery, after a while it does tend to get a bit lonely, having no one to share it with. He would have picked up a hitch-hiker just for the company had he passed one though he could have picked up danger at the same time so it was as well one didn't appear and, anyway, he knew that would be quite the wrong thing to do. He always felt bad though about passing hitch-hikers and not stopping for them when he had an empty car. Usually he gave a sort of hand signal indicating left or right as though he was going to turn off, but when the turn-off was a long way ahead that didn't always work. Pity he couldn't have brought the squirrel with him. He found himself wondering about her and what game she could be playing. The fact that she was what might be called a cold-blooded killer hadn't as yet impinged on his conscience. He thought of Holly. Holly would have been on the ball right from the beginning but what was she doing right at this moment? Sitting in an office in Whitehall having tea and biscuits no doubt. At least she no longer had to fend off the attentions of that sex maniac Mike Aliff.

It wasn't until he was well out of Pisa that he came out of his day dreaming (he had never outgrown his boyhood habit) to suspect he was being followed. Every now and again he glanced in his rear view mirror to see the same car still there despite both it and he being passed by a number of other vehicles. He sussed it to be a Russian car but he couldn't see who was driving it. He decided instead of speeding up, because the Russian would surely follow suit, he would slow down and indicate he was allowing the car to pass. He couldn't be certain but surely the car, a big black monster of a car, was a Zil, the Russian equivalent of a Daimler or a Cadillac. Here? On the road to Genoa? Was some VIP in the Politburo spending his roubles doing the tourist bit? Or, more likely, was it the KGB? Despite his indicating three or four times for it to pass there was no sign the driver was going to accept his invitation. The car sat firmly on his tail. He slowed down further. It wasn't too long before there was a positive convoy of impatient drivers behind, some hooting away, all desperate to get by the slow coaches up front whenever an opportunity presented itself, sometimes when there really wasn't one. The tail grew longer and longer until a police car came screaming up, siren blaring and Thornton was waved to the side of the road. This gave the diver of the Zil no alternative but to finally pass him as well as the others in the stream, all waved on by one of the two policemen directing them while the other set about quizzing Thornton. Because of where the second policeman stood directing the traffic Thornton couldn't see who was in the Zil as it passed. Its tinted windows would not have allowed him to see in anyway.

Thornton turned on all the charm he could muster up but was careful to include the fact that he was not all that au fait with either French or Italian. All his documents were in order so reluctantly the cops had to let him continue on his way but not before in extremely broken English he had received a severe dressing down and instructions on how to drive properly, properly meaning recklessly and at high speed like everybody else. Slow drivers are the cause of many an accident. Promising to take their advice on board he set off once more feeling a lot happier now that the Zil (he was now convinced it was KGB) was no longer on his tail. Looking in his mirror he saw the two cops watching him go and shaking their heads in disbelief. The English are all crazy.

He reached and passed Turin without further incident and it wasn't until he was in the mountains and thoroughly enjoying the drive and the scenery when turning a bend he spotted the Zil parked in a viewing lay-by a short distance ahead and presumably waiting for him. Thornton's heart, as the old cliché goes, was suddenly in his mouth as visions of abduction and the Lubyanka, if not Siberia and a Gulag, materialised only too vividly in his mind's eye. If he drove passed it would no doubt sit on his tail again and there was no chance of speeding up on these mountain bends so instead, he pulled up close behind it, kept the engine running and waited, and it wouldn't matter how long the wait might be, he was prepared to sit it out.

He didn't have too long a wait. After a few minutes the driver's door opened and an irate young lady in a heavy leather coat stepped out. She removed the coat to reveal an extremely shapely form but stepping out of the car and carelessly tossing the heavy coat back in where it half landed over the steering wheel was definitely a big mistake.

Knowing the countess would pay for any damage done, Thornton slipped the car into gear, moved slowly forward the last yard or two and gave the Zil a none too friendly bump forcing it a few inches towards the edge. The young lady who had started to approach Thornton's car hurriedly returned to hers. The leather coat ripped off the steering wheel came flying out but before she could go any further Thornton gave the Zil another nudge and she was too late to prevent the offside front wheel going over the edge. The car tilted crazily and it would be some time before the girls were extricated. Thornton slammed his own car into reverse, then forward and drove away giving the Russians a cheery wave as he passed. Presumably if the police now pulled the girls in for any reason they would quote diplomatic immunity though that might not save them from their own spell in the Lubyanka if not something worse.

*   *   *

Thornton sat on a slatted iron framed seat in the Jardin Anglais and, just as he had wondered about how many countries had white mountains he was now wondering how many continental cities boasted parks called English gardens. He knew there was one in Munich. Adrian Spangle had told him at great length all about the joys of that one late at night and in the early hours so he felt quite sure there must be others, not necessarily providing the same amenities.

He had admired the lake, the tall trees, the statuary and the fountains, the flower beds and the floral clock and really felt, if he was going to get anywhere, he ought to make a move, pleasant though his current position was. He glanced to his right where an Oriental gentleman was seated on one of the benches seemingly absorbed in his guide book, and a glance to the left revealed a second Oriental gentleman similarly engaged only this one was standing, a stocky figure, legs slightly apart, far too muscular and sinister looking in Thornton's opinion and he suddenly had that prickly suspicious feeling that all was not well in this particular English Garden. The stocky one held a slender document case, the seated one a quite heavy brief case. These were not what first came to mind when thinking of these gentlemen as tourists or holiday makers. It was time to leave while there were still other people around who could give him cover, possibly protection if needed.

Thornton had no doubt whatsoever that, after his brush on the highway with the two Russians, he would be followed everywhere he went until the moment the Neolithic cuckoo clock, as he now liked to call whatever it was he was going to find in that safe deposit box, was safely in his keeping and before it would be whipped off him, swiftly, with no further ado, and possibly a fair amount of pain. So his plan, quite simple really should he be able to carry it to a proper conclusion, was to go in and out of as many banks as he could before closing time in an endeavour to throw the bloodhounds off the scent by leading them as merry a dance as possible before losing them, entering the correct bank, grabbing the loot and, like a magician performing a hasty disappearing act haring it back to Rome. From Rome he would return to London and safety and another cheque for five grand. He might even be able to wring a few extra quid from his expense account. Fortunately there seemed to be no damage to the front fender of the car. On the other hand, if things didn't go as planned... he could be dead. There's an old song that goes, you are nearer to God in a garden than anywhere else on earth and, if he didn't get out of there fast, it could unfortunately prove only too true.

6

Lichti simply could not believe it. Two more bodies had turned up. That is two most unnatural deaths, both Oriental, had been discovered on his patch. Discovered? Hardly! They were lying there on the sidewalk of the Rue D'Italie for the entire world to see and he had any number of passer-by witnesses as to what happened none of whom could remember a single thing except that they heard a shot and, with the women, had more than likely started screaming. One or two of the men probably screamed as well and there was the added complication of a heart attack.

He stood in the mortuary looking down at the first corpse on its slab. There was a bullet hole to the right side of the chest, black and difficult to see at first because of all the tattoos. The entire body was covered in tattoos, from the neck down, front and back and the little finger of the left hand was missing. There was no doubt this was a member of the Yakusa, but what was he doing in Switzerland? That was the big question and why had he decapitated the Chinaman? The remains of the Chinaman lay on another slab. Well, the answer to that was pretty obvious as the Chinaman when found was still holding the Makarov in his right hand. So the questions here were what was the Chinaman doing in Switzerland killing a member of the Yakusa and having his head sliced off in return by something closely resembling the blade of a circular saw. It could even have been the blade of a circular saw, necessity being the mother of invention. And why was he using a Russian gun, something he would never have got through customs, so where did it come from? The answer to that was more than likely the Soviet Embassy, a present from one communist lot to another, so did that mean the KGB was involved here? Thinking of the two on the highway who it had been reported claimed diplomatic immunity when they were rescued from their predicament and who had subsequently disappeared it seemed pretty self-evident this was the case. Being called back to the Kremlin was not the same as being invited to a picnic. Where were they now? Possibly in a Gulag or... well at least their corpses hadn't shown up on his patch, hopefully never would. The whole mess was getting more and more complicated and Lichti was pretty certain it all started off with the murder of the good professor. So how many more corpses were likely to turn up? Lichti would have been surprised had he been able to see into the near future. So would Thornton King.

*   *   *

He had sat on for a long while in the English Garden musing on his options, waiting for something to happen, rather like a fisherman on a river bank waiting for the bite that never comes and in the dusk trudges his weary way home. "No luck?" his wife would ask with a cheery smile, to which he would grunt, yell at the kids, and pour himself a stiff scotch before falling asleep in his favourite chair.

Apart from occasional individuals, strolling couples, and the odd threesome, the park seemed currently almost devoid of humans except for patient Thornton and two just as patient inscrutable Orientals who obviously weren't going to make a move until he did, and the first mass entry to pass by turned out to be totally useless as far as providing possible cover was concerned consisting, as it did, of a couple of priests, one tall and cadaverous, the other a veritable Friar Tuck, and a crocodile of nuns. Garibaldi might have hidden in a nunnery on Sicily, the Trapp family might have hidden in a nunnery in Austria but Thornton didn't think he'd look too fetching in a habit, especially as his five o'clock shadow was becoming obvious, and there was no way he could get into one anyway in broad daylight in the middle of a park. He doubted any of the nuns, one or two of whom smiled sweetly discreetly at him as they passed, would be carrying a spare set with them.

The second crocodile, a few minutes later and going in the opposite direction, was, for his purpose, as useless as the first, consisting of about forty pubescent school girls of all shapes and sizes, some of them obviously early developers, in chocolate coloured gymslips, chocolate coloured blouses with chocolate coloured ties, chocolate coloured blazers with chocolate coloured badges, hats with chocolate coloured bands, chocolate coloured stockings and chocolate coloured shoes. It was a bit, Thornton thought, like watching a steady flow of chocolate being extruded from a machine at a Cadbury's plant though, as he was now in

Switzerland, maybe it should be Nestlès. Several of the brazen little hussies smiled at him, not discreetly nor sweetly as had the nuns but, without doubt, with lasciviousness written all over their little faces and Thornton actually felt himself blushing. Whoever believes tender little things don't have a sex life is ignorant in the ways of nature. Two teachers brought up the rear, from one of whom Thornton would have appreciated a smile but who simply raised an eyebrow when he invited it with a smile of his own. The other so hatchet faced it didn't matter in the least that she kept her gaze fixed on the schoolgirl's head straight in front of her. Now, had he been Nat or the male equivalent of the countess he would probably have put her down as being lesbian but as it was he thought she was merely a frustrated spinster who would more than likely remain that way. Good men are hard to find, dildoes are two a penny. Thornton heaved a deep sigh and wondered who might be along next. Time was of the essence now and, if he couldn't escape his Oriental watchers soon there would be no banking business done this day. It was the result of procrastination and wanting to play the tourist instead of getting on with the necessary. No, that wasn't quite true, to be fair he had to test the waters, or at least that is what he told himself.

Then, just as he was on the point of giving up, with no alternate plan in mind except to make a run for it and hope he was fleet enough of foot, fate produced a helping hand as at last he saw a group approaching who offered the sanctuary he sought. It appeared to consist mostly of middle-aged to elderly tourists, he guessed by their complexions and blonde locks, those who hadn't gone bald or grey, to be Scandinavian and, indeed, as they drew nearer, the sing-song in their voices as they chatted away seemed to confirm this.

Thornton slipped his guide book inside his jacket pocket and waited until the middle of the group was opposite his bench before getting up and sneaking in among them. There were maybe a couple of questioning frowns but on the whole he seems to have been accepted. At least no one openly objected and eventually at what he considered a safe enough distance he sidled sideways to make his exit from the jardin.

He had already decided as far as the banks were concerned to start with the Brits and Barclays was the closest. A dodgy crossing of the Quai du Général Guisan, a short walk up the Rue D'Italie and he was there. He stood outside and looked around. Could he have shaken off his tail? No such luck. Both Orientals were standing some distance away in opposite directions, eyeing him warily. Thornton was annoyed with himself at not having been able to shake them off but he didn't think they would make any kind of move until he came out of the bank, presumably assuming then that he had collected the goods. He grinned first at one, then at the other. There was no response. He could have been invisible except that he knew he wasn't. With their reputation for being inscrutable they seemed intent on living up to it. With a shrug he entered the bank wondering if he was wrong and they would follow. For a while he stood just inside, looking out through the glass doors but, there being no sign of them, he turned his attention to the bank itself for no other reason but that was where he happened to be at that moment, and more than likely would be for quite a few moments to come. Obviously, or so he surmised, they were going to hang around until he came out and no doubt they would then make a play for whatever he was carrying.

It was very much an interior of the sixties from the floor of patterned tiles belonging to an earlier period; to the faux marble front of the long counter that ran down one side with its Rexene covered cushioned squares where customer's knees might come into contact. The counter was topped by a row of quite ornate slender brass grilles behind which busy little bees were working no doubt Thornton thought, shovelling lots and lots of money from one financial institution to another, stoking the fires of commerce, industry, speculation and making the world go around.

The lighting was provided by a series of nineteen thirties looking fittings of squared glass panes hanging from what looked like shot steel hooks and beneath each down the centre of the hall was an octagonal veneered table with a glass top on which was placed inkwells, pens, wooden holders for stationary and bank forms, and plastic holders for leaflets and brochures. There were shelves just below and on the floor waste paper bins for people who invariably filled in their forms incorrectly and had to screw them up and start all over again. A lot of paper is wasted that way. There were no chairs. Obviously this particular bank didn't encourage customers to linger. At the moment it was not busy. In fact if the Orientals had followed him in they could have jumped him then and there as there were only a couple of customers standing at the counter who by the look of them would hardly have wanted to become involved in any kind of fracas, so he nearly jumped a mile when there was a discreet cough behind his back.

He swung around to see a prim looking middle aged lady, slender in a well tailored suit of navy blue, sensible shoes and a creamy silk blouse with ruffles and a high collar tied with a bow. She was not smiling but looked about as poker faced as the Orientals outside. Her gaze was steady and a little disconcerting.

She carried an aura of authority and the delicate scent of Eau de Cologne.

'Can I help you, sir?'

'What?'

'I said may I be of assistance, sir?'

'In what way?'

'I beg your pardon?'

'Could you be of assistance,' Thornton said. He was sometimes not quick enough mentally and this prevarication was for him to try and find, without actually having one, a reasonable excuse for being in the bank without metaphorically putting both feet in it. Physically both feet were already there of course.

'You seem to be at something of a loss, sir, if I may put it that way.'

She could put it any way she wanted, he thought, he still had to come up with a reason and he still hadn't thought of one. 'Lost?' He said, 'No, no, no. No, I'm not lost, no not at all. I was just looking.'

'Looking. I see.' She pursed her lips before continuing. 'Looking for what may I ask? This is a bank, sir. You walk around looking at things in shops, department stores, museums, art galleries, looking for something that catches your eye, takes your fancy, something you would like to purchase or admire, but that is not the case in banks. Banks are totally different if I may point that out to you. With banks you come in for the purpose of negotiating a financial transaction, or maybe you were not aware of that.' Was she being just a little bit snide, a little bit on the sarcastic side? Under any other circumstance it would have made Thornton bridle but he knew she was in the right no matter which way she chose to put it.

'Aha!' He raised a finger and a wry smile. 'There you might be in the wrong, Miss...' He leaned forward to get a closer look at the polished metal nametag on her lapel. 'Miss Harridan.'

'Harden!' Now the lady visibly bridled. 'The name is Harden.'

'Miss Hardon ...'

'And it is Mrs if you please, not Miss.'

'Mrs Hardon, the reason for my looking is...' It was here that, were a cartoonist to illustrate it, an electric light bulb would suddenly light up in a balloon above Thornton's head, a bright idea, and unfortunately he opened his mouth again before the bulb went to the next frame of the comic strip to reveal it might not be such a bright idea after all.

'The reason why I am looking around,' Thornton said, lowering his voice to conspiratorial level 'is because I am checking on your security.'

If Mrs Harden hadn't been made of sterner stuff it was at this point that her jaw, like Jacob Marley's when the bandage came off, might have descended quite alarmingly. As it was she decided she had in front of her a gentleman who was slightly off balance and the best thing to do would be to humour him, usher him slowly to the doors, talking soothingly to him all the while, simultaneously behind his back making signals for a member of staff to make a quick emergency phone call. To call for personal assistance at this moment, face to face in the middle of the floor, could lead to the balance of the mind indubitably becoming badly disturbed if not completely distorted; who knew with what disastrous consequences?

'And tell me...' She stopped to clear her throat in which a frog had suddenly materialised, '...just why you would be interested in the bank's security? Mr... Mr...'

'Berman. Nat Berman.'

Thornton had no clear idea why he said this. The name popped into his head out of nowhere.

'Mr Berman.' Maybe she thought a little light-hearted humour here would help. Another couple of customers had entered the bank who needed attending to and she really ought to put an end to this conversation as quickly as possible. 'Thinking of opening an account are we? And afraid our little pink piggy bank with the flowers on his back might get broken into?' Was she smiling or sneering, Thornton wondered. He felt himself blushing but, having started on this tack, decided he had to continue. The alternative at this point was to beat a hasty retreat and hope no alarms went off. Besides the Oriental gentlemen were probably still outside patiently waiting for him. He was most definitely between a rock and a hard place.

'As a matter of fact I am making enquiries on behalf of my employer, the Countess Cinelli,' he said, adopting what he fondly imagined was a tone of superiority, 'I have no doubt you will have heard of her?'

Mrs Harden gave an almost imperceptible shake of her head, removed a dimity handkerchief from the sleeve of her jacket, held it to her nose and sniffed. The hankie was no doubt drenched in that eau de Cologne he had got the scent of. She tucked it back beneath her sleeve.

'The countess is a woman of extreme wealth…'

'We have among our accounts any number of extremely wealthy persons, Mister…'

'Berman. Nat Berman.'

'Mister Berman.'

'So obviously security is of the utmost importance,' Thornton said with a frown. 'You need to be one step ahead of the criminal mind every second of the day. For instance, there are two extremely suspicious looking characters outside this building right at this very moment, both Oriental in looks and I really would like to know (a) what they have in their briefcases and (b) what their intentions are. Loitering with intent is a phrase that springs immediately to mind.'

Mrs Harden decided that with no further ado something had to be done with this young man and catching sight of a senior figure emerging from an inner office she excused herself and moved towards him. Menacing Orientals or no menacing Orientals, Thornton reckoned on it being time for him to make a quick move as well and made swiftly for the front doors.

Mrs Harden and the senior figure turned to look towards where he had last been seen only to find he had disappeared. It was at this moment they heard the shot, loud and clear, followed by the screams, and Mrs Harden fainted into her manager's arms, something she had dreamed of for a long time only compos mentis rather than out like a light.

*   *   *

Lichti, with his second in command standing behind him, sat in the manager's office facing both the man himself and Mrs Harden. He had high hopes of at last gleaning a few nuggets of information as far as the double homicide outside the bank was concerned but his hopes were fading fast.

'I'm sorry,' the manager said, shaking his head, 'I'm afraid I'm not all that observant at the best of times but I was in here and didn't even see the man Mrs Harden is talking about. When I came out and looked in the direction she indicated there was no one there so I simply cannot help you. The gentleman obviously left in a hurry and, from what I've been told of his behaviour...' here he gave Mrs Harden a sympathetic smile but she still hadn't recovered so disappointingly neglected to smile in return. '... he did appear to be a trifle odd.' To the manager, anyone who entered his sacred portals was indubitably a gentleman or at least should be treated as such unless it was proved to the contrary. Who was to say the young man wasn't perfectly legitimate in his intentions? Women could be quite hysterical at times and arrive at the wrong conclusion and the sound of the shot had certainly unhinged Mrs Harden for a while. She would without doubt want to take time off to recover. Despite women's lib the manager believed implicitly in the glass ceiling and the male being the superior of the species, think of stags and lions. The whole of nature led to that conclusion if you discounted husband-eating spiders and the praying mantis that bites off her husband's head before enjoying sex and satisfying her appetite at the other end by eating him and horrid abnormal creatures like that. Nature can be truly bizarre at times.

Lichti turned back to the lady in question who was quite obviously still rather distraught over the whole episode as, he thought, she had every right to be. His approach in consequence was very gentle.

'Mrs Harden, if I may come back to you. Please, take your time and try to recapture in your imagination everything that happened from the first moment you saw and approached this man standing in your bank.'

Your bank? The manager thought but decided not to say anything though he did give a discreet cough behind his soft white hand to indicate disapproval.

The dimity hankie came into play for a moment as Mrs Harden tried to gather her thoughts.

'He had his back to you I take it, when you first saw him.'

'Well … yes … I noticed him standing by one of the tables in the centre of the hall and he seemed, well he was looking, that is he appeared to be either lost, you know? Or he was deep in thought. So I coughed, ever so gently, to get his attention and my cough obviously startled him because he jumped quite visibly.' There was a pause while she gathered her thoughts. 'Yes, he definitely jumped. No doubt about that.' She gazed at Lichti with a slight frown on her face. 'He must have been very nervous about something don't you think?'

'Yes? It does sound that way and I suppose that is what aroused your suspicions, so go on, what happened then? He turned to face you I take it. Can you remember that moment? Describe him to me.'

There was a longer silence. The frown deepened. Mrs Harden looked to her manager for support and he nodded encouragingly but she only looked back at Lichti biting her lip then, 'I can't,' she said.

Lichti looked down at his highly polished toecaps and then up again at Mrs Harden who was now desperately fiddling with her hankie, twisting it between her fingers.

'Is that very strange?'

'No, not in the least,' he assured her. 'You've had a nasty shock that's all and maybe for the moment you just don't want to remember; a perfectly natural case of amnesia that will pass. Let's see if we can arrive at this young man another way, shall we? I say young without really knowing if that is the case but I take it he was young?'

'Oh, yes. In his late twenties or thereabouts I would think. Yes, definitely late twenties. Maybe early thirties. It's hard to tell isn't it?'

'Well now we know his age, approximately. There's little difference between late and early.' He smiled encouragingly. There you are you see, that's a start. At least we know he wasn't a grizzled old greybeard, huh?' He chuckled but immediately stopped and in his turn coughed behind his hand as he noticed the manager's face. The business of the bank was being seriously disrupted here and, as the man was a greybeard, this hardly seemed the right thing to have said so Lichti went hurriedly on. He was wondering whether any other members of the team questioning the staff elsewhere in the building and outside were having better luck. He decided to persist with what was probably going to be his one and only witness. So far nobody from the actual scene of the killing, that is the street outside the bank, could remember a thing.

'Did he give any indication as to why he was actually in your bank?'

Your bank, again, your bank, the manager thought, mentally tut-tutting. He was a despot when it came to accuracy especially as far as rank was concerned. If he says "your bank" again I will simply have to correct him.

'He said something about opening an account. I didn't believe him for a moment of course. The supposed account was for some countess or other I'd never heard of.'

'Countess?' Litchi's voice at that moment took on so urgent a tone Mrs Harden felt herself freeze. 'The name! What was the name?' He almost shouted it.

'What name?' She squealed in return, trying desperately not

110

to burst into tears.

'The countess! You said countess. What was her name?'

'He never gave me her name. Did he? I don't remember.'

'All right then, let's get back to the man himself, how tall was he?'

Mrs Harden looked blank.

'When you stood facing him across the table was he taller than you or shorter? In other words did you look down on him or did you have to look up? Or maybe your eyes were level.'

'I looked up.'

'By much?'

'Hmn … About three inches I'd say.'

Lichti turned to look at his sidekick who shrugged.

'That would be about seven and half centimetres,' the manager said.

'Thank you.'

'Maybe four,' she said.

'Give or take a couple of centimetres we'll leave it at that. What colour were his eyes?'

'Blue, a very bright blue.'

Lichti smiled.

'Hair?'

'Blonde, quite long, well, not quite blonde, sort of blondish if you know what I mean, and not too long, sort of longish?'

'Yes, shall we just call it fair? It was his natural hair I take it. Moustache?'

'Oh, no, clean shaven.'

'Did he say what he was doing in the bank?'

'Indeed he did. The sauce of the man! Said he was checking on our security arrangements though he wouldn't say why. I immediately suspected something nefarious was going on. He was up to no good of that I am certain.'

'Quite right. What was his nationality?'

'British. His name is Nat Berman.'

They all three stared at her.

'I just remembered that. He repeated it when I forgot it the first time.'

'Thank you. You've been a great help.'

Mrs Harden smiled at last, a weak pathetic smile but a smile nevertheless.

*   *   *

Thornton was enjoying a Viennese coffee, soaking up the sunshine and surveying the lively scene when he noticed two suspicious looking men after they had stood a short distance away for a while obviously discussing him. He was immediately wary. These guys could be up to no good though he thought he was pretty safe in the middle of such a busy scene of people enjoying their morning refreshment, waiters with laden trays bustling to and fro. What do they look like, these waiters, Thornton mused, watching their swaying bodies as they trippled around the tables? Ice skaters maybe. No, more like swallows, house martins, swooping and diving after flying insects. It was a great pity Thornton thought that London's weather didn't really allow for this sort of outdoor socialising. It really was so civilised. He made out he was looking at his guide book but kept a wary eye open for anything out of the ordinary that might suddenly materialise.

'Bonjour, monsieur.'

Wary eye or not the men were right in front of him before he knew it. Must have sneaked up on him around his back and took him unawares. He looked up from his book and smiled.

'And bonjour to you two too which is about as far as you're going to get with my French.'

'You are English?'

'I am indeed. You couldn't tell?'

'You have identification on you please?'

'Certainly, certainly. As soon as you show me yours. You show me yours and I'll show you mine.' Thornton giggled but the men were not amused. Maybe Swiss schoolboys were too Calvinistic for that sort of game. One flashed a card accompanied by the spoken word. 'Police.' Thornton immediately reached into his jacket pocket and produced his passport which he placed in an outstretched hand. Together the men looked at it and at the photograph and back to the man himself.'

'Mr King?'

'That's me.'

The passport was handed back.

'What are you doing in Switzerland if I may ask?'

'Certainly you may. I am enjoying a well earned vacation. Why do you want to know anyway?'

'Do you know this man?'

The first of the pair had suddenly produced an identikit printout and virtually shoved it under Thornton's nose. Thornton took it from him and studied it at a more reasonable distance. They waited.

'Well?'

'Ugly looking brute isn't he? What's he done?'

'Do you know him?'

'Don't think so. What's his name?'

'Look more closely.'

'Thank you, I think I have looked close enough.' He made to hand the picture back but then stopped and looked at it again.

'Hang on a mo. You know something? Without a terrific stretch of the imagination, this could be me, couldn't it?' He held it beside his head face towards them before giving it another look. 'Just hope I never look as grim as that.'

The first policeman took back the picture and looked at it, then at Thornton, then back to the picture. 'Yes, I suppose so… in a way.'

'Well I only hope you're not thinking of arresting me on suspicion of something I didn't do.' Thornton laughed, hoping the laugh sounded natural as coming from an innocent man.

The first policeman smiled. The second policeman remained stony-faced.

'Good day, sir,' the first policeman said as they turned to leave, surveying the other customers as they made a slow exit.

'What a jolly fellow,' the first policeman said when they were clear.

'What an arsehole,' the second police man said.

'Wait a bit,' the first policeman said as he stopped, causing the second policeman to stop as well. The first policeman looked again at the printout. 'Who is the arsehole here?' He asked as they turned to look back the way they had come, but Thornton had vanished.

*   *   *

Two extremely despondent soldiers of the Camorra, the brothers Fabrizio and Maurizio Pensotti, both still wet behind the ears in a manner of speaking, sat in a bar in Geneva nibbling on nuts and gazing into their glasses, bemoaning their failure and wondering helplessly what was in store for them if they continued to fail. For a start how would they ever be able to face mama again? She'd have the cast iron frying pan around their ears with a vengeance and more than likely a heap of boiling spaghetti over their heads to send them packing; bringing such shame and disgrace on the family. Why were they sent in the first place for so high-powered a mission? Two such junior mortals, hardly out of their teens, hardly out of the rookie class. It should have been a capo, a big cheese, someone with years of experience. Had the organisation gone mad? Well it was partly their own fault for swaggering around playing the big man and being so boastful about their expertise when they were really no more than a couple of pickpockets and street hoodlums, and the question now was what was to be done to mitigate any repercussions that might follow their failure? It was a future not worth thinking about or, if they did think about it, it chilled their balls something terrible.

'I hate this frigging town,' Maurizio said. 'It's too damn clean. Not like Napoli.'

'You're right,' his companion replied with a sigh, twirling the liquid in his glass as though, like a crystal ball or leaves in a teacup, it might come up with an answer to their problem and then, taking out his last cigarette and ignoring the ashtray at his fingertips, he dropped the empty packet onto the floor below his stool.

'And now it's swarming with frigging cops so you can't go take a leak but one of them's looking over your frigging shoulder.'

For a hard case soldier Maurizio was careful of the language he used. It was out of full respect for their beloved mama of course. Even though she wasn't actually present, she was forever with them in spirit. She was more than likely kneeling in church at this very moment praying for their safe return to the bosom of the family, in both senses of the word. She truly hated kneeling on that hard cold floor because, with her size and her knees, it was difficult to get back up again but it was penance she willingly paid to keep her absent sons from harm.

Fabrizio looked up from his glass and gazed adoringly at his brother. Maurizio was the younger by a couple of years but he had the brains, he was the bright spark, the one who always got them off a scrape, who knew what to do, who had a drumstick for each hand, and Fabrizio would never take that from him. He'd rather die first. When they were children they played with each other in the bed they shared but they were young men now and their thoughts were only on girls, at least Maurizio's were, and in a way Fabrizio regretted the passing of time, especially as his handsome brother was a true lady killer, a born Lothario, a Don Juan of the first order, and he knew it. His roving eye was never still for a moment. One day soon he would marry a beautiful girl his beloved mother would approve of, have lots of children and even more mistresses. That's the way it was going to be. He would also be very very rich. The thought that he might end up suffering an early and violent death or in an Italian jail never entered his head. He was far far too clever ever to be caught.

'So what're we going to do then, Maurizio?'

But Maurizio hadn't heard the question. He was eyeing up a rather svelte young lady seated at the bar toying idly with a cocktail stick, gazing pensively into space, and he wondered whether he should amble across and chat her up. She looked as though she might welcome it. So his brother repeated the question.

'What?'

'I said what are we going to do now?'

Maurizio's eyes swivelled back to the bar but he did respond, murmuring and at the same time fingering his crotch. His pants were getting a trifle uncomfortable as his very own soldier started to make itself felt. 'We're going to go back to Rome,' he said.

'Empty handed?'

'It was one big mistake to come here in the first place. I should have known better. Fabby, baby, we're against a really terrific guy here. That Contessa knew how to pick the best that's for frigging sure. How did she find him? That's what I'd like to know. It's a pity he's not one of us.' Fabrizio now had his brother's full attention. 'You got to admire him.' He shook his head almost in complete disbelief. 'The way he got rid of those Oriental guys was genius, friggin genius...' If only Maurizio knew that Thornton's genius consisted of exiting the bank in such a hurry to get away before security could be called, that he failed to notice what appeared to be an oil patch on the pavement and in consequence tripping over his own feet he landed almost flat on his face the very instant the Chinaman pressed the trigger and a nano second later had his head sliced off as Thornton, regaining the upright, disappeared into, through, and beyond the nearest screaming group of traumatised bystanders, blowing on his grazed hands as he went. '... and then gets the place swarming with frigging cops so that a guy can't breathe.'

'Or take a leak.'

'Or take a leak, and we're not going to get close to him here. So we go back to Rome and we wait for him there. He arrives with the goods and we take the goods from him. Capisch?'

Fabrizio nodded as he thought about this. 'But, Maurizio,

what about the Chicago mob?'

'What about them?'

'They'll be looking to get to him before us and we'll lose out. Then we'll be right in the shit.'

'Mind your language.'

'Sorry.'

'So where are they then, the Chicago mob? You seen any of them around?'

Maurizio looked around in search of anyone who might belong to the Chicago mob

'No.' Fabrizio shook his head. 'Doesn't mean to say they're not here though, does it?'

Maurizio gave a couldn't care less shrug. 'Listen, there were these two Russians, right? What has happened to them? They tangled with this guy on the highway and pffft! They disappear, right? Then there's this Yakusa. He's gone, and there's this Triad fellow, he's gone too. And the police... I read it all in the papers...' he waved the paper under his brother's nose '... are looking for someone they call Nat Berman. Do you want to know something, Fab, baby? This Berman guy is our Chicago gangster, if I may so use that word, no disrespect, and I will bet you whatever odds you want that Mr Thornton King has disposed of him as well. Wanna bet?'

Fabrizio shook his head.

'Right, so it's back to Rome and we wait for him there.'

'Why don't we wait for him on the way?'

'Because even if, as they say, all roads lead to Rome, we don't know which one he's going to take when he leaves, now do we?'

Fabrizio nodded and smiled approvingly. His bother had an answer for everything. Everyone should be so blessed, to have a brother like that. He allowed Maurizio to give him a hearty slap on the back as they slid off their stools.

*   *   *

Lichti sat in his office playing with a propelling pencil on his desktop and brooding over which way to move next. He still had no reliable witnesses as to what actually happened outside the bank and Mrs Harden still hadn't come up with the name of the countess. He wondered whether he should ask her to visit a hypnotist. On top of this there was absolutely no trace in the whole of Switzerland of the mysterious Mr Berman. The border police had come up with a complete blank; he was not registered in any of the hotels and, despite blanket enquiries, no trace of him had surfaced. All Lichti wanted was one tiny little lead but so far it would appear he was destined to bang his head against that proverbial brick wall. In disgust he rolled his pencil away from him and stood up, deciding on a cup of coffee in the canteen and a bit of company. Brooding wasn't going to get him anywhere. It was a wise decision. His slender lead was about to reveal itself. That is not coincidence; it is what is known as fate. As he passed a table where a number of off-duty gendarmes were listening to one of their number his ears pricked up and he stopped. So did the conversation. Everyone looked up at him including Guy Morvan, the gendarme who had been speaking, having to turn around and look over his shoulder in order to do so.

'What were you saying?' Lichti asked.

There were smiles all around the table and the speaker was laughing, 'I was telling these guys about this crazy Englishman we questioned.'

'Where was this?'

'He was having a coffee in the Bourg-de-Four.'

'What made you question him?'

'He looked so obvious.'

'Obvious what?'

'You know.'

'No, I don't know. Tell me. You're saying he looked tapette?'

'Sort of but, well, he was obviously English and you know what they say, La vice Anglais?' He flapped a limp wrist and everyone laughed.

'Could he not have been Scandinavian if his complexion was what you were going by?'

The smiles and the laughter had stopped as the table realised Lichti was for some reason being very serious and by the look on his face not at all pleased.

'Well, I said to Marc...' he nodded across the table in his partner's direction, '...this guy looks a bit like the identikit, you know? So maybe we better find out who he is.'

'That's right,' came the other's voice. Lichti turned to face the speaker who didn't look exactly like the brightest pebble on the beach and then turned back to gendarme number one who was seemingly in possession of a bit more nous.

'So you went up to him and asked him who he was.'

'Yes. Asked for identification which he was quite happy to produce. Then we showed him the fit up and do you know what he said? He said, with a bit of imagination, it could be him, that's exactly what he said, and he wouldn't like us to arrest him for something he hadn't done. Can you imagine that?' He placed a hand on his hip and wriggled his shoulders.

There was more laughter, mostly of the sniggering variety

though it was pretty obvious that at least one of the gendarmes at the table laughing the loudest was as camp as a row of tents.

'What an arsehole,' Marc said with a snigger but clammed up tight when he saws the look on Lichti's face.

'Do you remember his name?'

'Yes, it was King. Easy to remember because I said to Marc it should have been Queen.'

They all found this terribly funny but once again the laughter died away when Lichti's face expressed nothing.

Guy cleared his throat and looked down at the table-top. There was something very wrong here.

'I don't suppose you had such a neat way of remembering his first name. Obviously not. Well this is what I would like you to do, I would like you to get a complete list of all the Kings listed in London and bring it to my office and as soon as possible if you please. Starting like now.'

With which Lichti turned on his heels and walked away, all thoughts of coffee forgotten.

Guy gave a shrug, looked around the table and got slowly to his feet. 'Why not in the whole of England while I'm about it?'

'What an arsehole,' Marc said.

*   *   *

Thornton, having finished his coffee and deposited money on the table, had watched the two gendarmes leave, and slipped away to make his way towards the Rue du Rhone and the bank, Celine & Cie, finding it without difficulty, small as it was and dwarfed by its neighbours on either side. He paused on the doorstep ostensibly to scratch his leg but in fact to look around and make sure he was not being watched and to surreptitiously remove the countess's letter and the safety deposit box key, palming them into a trouser pocket. His palms were still a little on the throbbing side from where they had hit the pavement so breaking his fall and he was mighty glad to feel the circulation restored to his foot though this could just have been his vivid imagination. What to do with the tape was another problem, solved by rolling it into a tight if somewhat sticky ball and stuffing it in a jacket pocket. He then marched through the doors into a beautiful panelled banking hall that was more like someone's drawing room in a baronial mansion though all in the best of all possible taste. It was no wonder the countess was a customer here, he thought.

He was greeted by a smiling somewhat swishy underling in a morning suit. Guy and Marc would have had a field day with this one. Thornton quietly stated his business and was asked very kindly, if somewhat sibilantly, if he minded waiting just a moment. The underling with a gracious gesture indicated a chair which Thornton declined before, still smiling, the youth made his way to a glass fronted office in which a senior member of staff could be seen sitting at his desk The underling tapped on the door and was obviously invited to enter, which he did, closing the door behind him. Thornton watched with interest though he pretended to be much more interested in something elsewhere. He also kept a beady eye on the front door just in case he had missed something important outside. As a private detective on a highly dangerous mission you needed eyes in the back of your head. The few customers who were in the bank all looked pretty harmless enough, though looks could be deceptive. He smiled at a little old lady who seemed to be regarding him with some interest but she failed to return his smile and in fact, after a totally blank stare, turned her back on him. He was obviously not that interesting. The manager at his rather large and opulent desk opened a drawer and took something out; obviously one of Adrian's better efforts the countess had mailed to him, looked at it and looked at Thornton, replaced the photograph, closed the drawer and got to his feet.

The underling, bowing and scraping in true Uriah Heep fashion, hastened to open the door and stood back as the senior man came gliding through. He too was smiling and extended his hand in greeting as he approached. Thornton thought florid would be the word most apt to describe him and, as an emissary of the countess he would no doubt be in for the full red carpet treatment.

'Mister King. I am delighted to meet you, sir.'

'Thank you,' Thornton said, a little taken aback by the warmth of the greeting, but it was probably all down to the countess and her patronage and a lifetime's habit except for those whose accounts were in the red. He wondered if there could possibly be a relationship between this little man and that large woman. Anything is possible; opposites are supposed to attract. He couldn't help wondering why his own bank manager couldn't be as affable as this instead of the churl he always seemed to be. Maybe it was because Thornton so seldom in his account had anything worth talking about and was more than likely costing the bank money in maintaining what little he had. That would all change very soon he believed. In fact wasn't the bank already raking in exorbitant interest on his five grand? He airily dismissed the interest the bank was paying him which was peanuts.

'I believe you carry a letter of introduction? And, if it is no trouble, I would like to take a peek at your passport. Would that be in order do you suppose?'

'Certainly,' Thornton said producing both the letter and his passport for this rather fey gentleman to take his peek which he promptly proceeded to do, for some reason clearing his throat as he did so. Clearing of the throat it seemed so often went with business matters. Thornton smiled at the underling who smiled in return; then the passport was returned.

'You have your key with you, Mister King?'

'I do.'

'Then we will waste no more time. Mister Florien will show you the way.'

'Thank you. After you, Mister Florien, I'm all yours.'

From the response he got he wished he hadn't said that.

*   *   *

Lichti, back at his desk and waiting for the requested information, was meditating on the whys and wherefores of this most peculiar case. In view of the death of the Yakusa which brought Japan to mind he wondered if a haiku might help. He was particularly fond of this Japanese form of poetry consisting of seventeen syllables in three non rhyming lines. It had been useful before in helping to unravel a seemingly intractable case. One of these fine days if given the chance he might travel to Japan; such a fascinating colourful country he thought with its phallic worship and cherry blossom festivals, its tea ceremonies, Samurai, geishas, Kyôgen, the theatre of comedy, Noh plays, Kabuki and onnagata. He knew nothing about Shinto but he had read *Zen and the Art of Motor Cycle Maintenance* and felt he would like to study Buddhism in greater depth. He might think of a haiku in a moment. In the meantime he had gone back with the flat of his hand to rolling his pencil back and forth across his desk, stopping now and again to give it a flick with his middle finger and catching it before it rolled off the edge. It was as good a therapy as doodling. Apart from haiku, Lichti was a devotee of the romantic poets and particularly proud of their association with Lake Geneva and The Villa Diodoti. Many a happy evening he had spent at home reading their works, not aloud, he didn't think he was good enough for that, but silently pouring over the lines. They gave him so much pleasure and it was mainly because of them that he was so fluent in English. He thought it very funny that Mary Shelley's *Frankenstein*, a never ending best seller, was rejected by both her brother's and Lord Byron's publisher and didn't the same apply with publishers who were offered *Gone With The Wind* and *The Wizard of Oz?* No one was interested. He wondered if it was a true story that a Hollywood magnate when offered *Gone With The Wind* for filming said "Who's interested in the civil war?" He must have kicked himself all the way to the grave; up to that point the biggest grossing film of all time. And considering his own brother's seemingly futile attempts at interesting a publisher in what Lichti thought was a rather good thriller, (he had provided his brother with all the necessary police procedural details) he decided all publishers were egocentric conceited ignorant arseholes. He stopped pushing the pencil. He had his own Frankenstein monster here and what was he doing about it? There were four deaths that he knew of, three disappearances and no sign of this person calling himself Nat Berman; but there was a strange Englishman by the name of King who appeared possibly to have a decidedly warped sense of humour. Who was he? The name rang a distant bell or was that just his imagination? When or where had he come across it before? Maybe a haiku would help. Lichti thought he had his own poetic bent even if not an overly talented one and liked to turn a cute phrase now and again for his own amusement. He wouldn't dream of letting anyone else see his scribblings. He would be too embarrassed to show his efforts to anyone. For example right at this moment he decided to "mentally thumb through the index cards of my memory." Was that a good poetic line? Maybe, maybe not. Maybe he could appeal to Interpol for help but in the meantime, Haiku first line, starting with King of course – King... King... King... Kingfisher... Kingfisher... sits on... Second line – the holly bough and...

Holly! King! Holly! Memory was suddenly stirred and wide awake. He didn't have to go back too far, only as far as that Interpol jamboree in the south of France and only a couple of years back. There was that English policeman, famous for solving a dozen murders, or so it was said, murders committed by beautiful young models under the tutelage of a Russian princess, of all things bizarre. He was supposed to make an after dinner speech to the international gathering of law enforcement brothers. What was his name? Reg something... Reg... Var... Ven... Vera... Vena something... and his wife was kidnapped so he never got around to his speech, poor sod, because he got as pissed as a newt and totally incapable. He was put to bed and the party went on without him. The kidnapping appeared to have been an accident and the wife was rescued by a giant kilted Canadian Scot who turned out to be a member of the CIA. There was foundation for another good thriller there, Lichti thought. He would mention it to his brother, but enough musing. He mentally pictured the foyer of the hotel that evening of the dinner. There were three people standing in front of the reception desk, one was a French policeman, what was his name? Doesn't matter, doesn't matter. The others were a lady called Holly... Holly who?... Doesn't matter... and King, definitely King and his name was... Kingfisher sat on the Holly's prickly leaves... too many syllables... bush... thorny bush... Kingfisher sat on the thorny bush... thorn... Thornton... Thornton King! Lichti gave the desk such a thump with the side of his fist his pencil leapt inches into the air and, as he caught it, there was a knock at the door and Morvan appeared with a list of London based Kings. He stopped dead and stood staring stony-faced at his superior wondering what the joke was when Lichti couldn't stop laughing. Eventually the spasm subsided and Lichti wiped the tears from his eyes.

'All right,' he said, 'what have you got there?'

'What you asked for, a list of the Kings in London.'

'Good. So what's his first name then?'

Guy shrugged and looked at his piece of paper. 'How would I know? There are a few of them.' He wondered, should he say "do I stick in a pin?" but thought better of it. You never knew which way Lichti was going to jump. He could take it as a joke but then on the other hand ... no, better safe than sorry.

'Then I will tell you what his name is. It's Thornton. Is that name down there? Well go on, take another look.'

Guy took another look, looked up and nodded. 'Yes... yes it is. How did you know?' Did Lichti have extra sensory perception or whatever it was called?

'Elementary, my dear Watson, elementary, and a little Japanese magic,' Lichti said, starting to chortle again, 'I used this,' and he tapped the side of his head with a forefinger. 'All right, put it down there even though there's no more need for it.' He indicated the desk top and Guy duly laid down the paper before stepping back, presumably to make his way out. 'And next time you see someone who appears to have a bit more class, a bit more style, maybe even a bit more intelligence than you, don't jump to hasty conclusions. Judge not the book by its cover. Thornton King just happens to be ex-British secret service and currently a highly rated private detective and he obviously had your measure from the start. Got the picture?'

Guy nodded.

'Good, so then, the next thing and this is priority numero uno, my friend if you think you're up to it, is to find this private detective, Thornton King and either bring him to me or me to him. Do you understand me?' He got to his feet. 'I need to know what he is doing here and I need to know what is going on and I need to know like ten minutes ago if not sooner so get onto it.'

'Yes, sir.' He turned to go, stopped, and turned back. 'But if I find him, what excuse, I mean what reason could I have for bringing him in?'

'For once try using your imagination. That thing between your ears is called a brain; make some attempt to use it.'

'Yes, sir.' Guy turned and fled, mentally calling the inspector all the names he could think of, chief of which of course was arsehole.

Lichti sat down again and hoped he wasn't too late but he didn't feel too good about it. Maybe another haiku would be the answer.

*　　　　　　　*　　　　　　　*

Mister Florien, with an engaging come hither and follow me

smile and a well practised flick of his blonde quiff, indicated by gesture for Thornton to please keep up and shimmied his way passed a couple of curious temporarily unengaged female tellers idling the time away who gave Thornton the eye and a curious if friendly smile to which he responded most engagingly in return, even more engagingly than Mister Florien who, after ringing a bell, opened a door as its locking mechanism was released and ushered Thornton forward. He found himself in a sort of lighted vestibule, more marble, with apparently no way in or out but the door they had just come through and no windows, barred or otherwise to let light and intruders in and out either. The door had closed and locked behind them. A flight of marble steps led down to a steel grille behind which a security man in uniform sat at a desk reading a newspaper. He folded his paper, laid it on the desk, rose to his feet and advanced to open up and admit the two men before turning his back on them and retiring to his desk and his paper. Was it Thornton's imagination or did the security man surreptitiously size him up? Whatever, he was there now and had to go through with what was expected of him.

Florien, who obviously felt it below his dignity to acknowledge the security man, led the way down an aisle both walls of which were lined with the fronts of steel safety boxes until he reached the one he wanted. The countess's box was number 394 which reduced to 16, which reduced to 7, Thornton's lucky number, not that he would admit for a moment to any whiff of superstition in his make-up. He had never had his palm read, studied the tealeaves, had his fortune told via a crystal ball, not even in fun, or believed in the stars although he read his horoscope in his paper every day just out of interest, hoping the good forecast (especially with money) would come true and ignoring the bad, and knew that Venus was in the ascendant when he was born which evidently was supposed to explain a lot.

Florien inserted his key, Thornton did likewise and they both turned. Then Florien, although he was dying of curiosity, withdrew to leave Thornton to pull out and open the box in private. A narrow table in the centre ran the full length of the vault on which the boxes could be placed for examination and Thornton duly placed his there. This was the big moment. This was what the countess was paying him all that lovely lolly for, that and getting it safely back to her. This was what a lot of people, or so it would seem, were itching, in fact risking death, to get their hands on. What would he find? He could hardly believe it, being as laid back as he always thought he was, that his heart was thumping in expectation and he was finding it almost difficult to draw breath.

What he found was a small hour glass, or maybe it could be called an egg-timer. An antique? Possibly. It had a sort of art deco look about it, was made of some precious metal he guessed, silver perhaps or silver-gilt and adorned around each rim with what looked like small rubies. It was no Fabergé creation that was for sure but at a guess certainly worth a bob or two. No more than four inches high and not too large in diameter it could slip easily into a jacket pocket. It naturally held a powder that would drop from one glass section to the other when the timer was turned and Thornton didn't need to think twice as to what that powder was, though its exact composition of course was a mystery which was why criminals from three continents were angling for it. It certainly wasn't common or garden sand in there. On closer inspection Thornton discovered what looked like a chemical formula, though it could have been hieroglyphics as far as he was concerned, he never was much cop at any of the sciences, etched or maybe scratched with a sharp point around each underside of the top and bottom, or bottom and top, depending on which way the timer was standing. This then was Nat Berman's cuckoo clock. Well not exactly a cuckoo clock but as befits hidden treasure in Switzerland at least it was a time piece of sorts. There was nothing else in the box so, making sure the security man was buried in his paper, he slipped the object into a pocket, closed the box, returned it to its slot, not bothering to lock it, after all it was now empty, he doubted the countess would have any more use for it, and made to leave.

The security man, who was now starting in on his lunch, the tin lying on the desk open in front of him and he already chewing away on his first mouthful, looked up, pressed a bell on his desk, got up, and opened the door. He never gave Thornton a second glance and having relocked the door went back to his desk, his lunch, and his newspaper.

Mister Florien was waiting for him at the top of the stairs and, smilingly, ushered him out. The door automatically locked behind them.

The manager and his underling hoping everything was satisfactory and wishing him a courteous adieu, Thornton left the premises of Celine & Cie keeping an eye out for any possible danger, but all seemed well which was not too surprising considering the Japanese, the Chinese, the Italians and the Russians were now out of the way and there was still no sign of the Americans. He didn't believe the Russians would give up that easily, possibly neither would the others but it might take some time for them to send reinforcements. He felt he could breathe easy for a while but did not hold out any hopes that it would last, feeling quite sure this was the proverbial calm before the storm or, in modern parlance before the shit hit the fan.

The car was parked not too far distant and he headed straight for it. He had already taken the precaution of booking out of his comfortable pension as there really was no need for him to stay any longer. The previous evening he had been given something of a scare when he found the door to his room slightly ajar and suspected a break-in, possibly the intruder still there but the intruder it turned out was merely the maid turning down the bed. It had been a nasty heart-thumping few seconds though. Thornton, even as a schoolboy, stayed away from any hint of fisticuffs as long as he was able. The better part of valour is – discretion. Even if for nothing else, Shakespeare is always good for an apt quote.

He decided to take a different route back to Rome and this time would go via the Simplon Pass and Milan, stopping off in Italy's second city, first city to the Milanese, financial centre and once the capital. As he drove through the tunnel he mused on the fact that the greater part of Napoleon's army, as well as Wellington's and the Austrians no doubt and a great many of the civil population of the time suffered from what was then known as "the great itch", in other words, scabies, that nasty little under the skin munching parasite, for which, at the time, there was no apparent relief. Thornton was full of arcane or totally useless bits of knowledge like that and, having once been unfortunate enough to have had personal knowledge of the great itch, picked up, not in sowing a field of wild oats but quite innocently he would always maintain if ever he indiscreetly confessed to it, he wondered the whole of Europe in the eighteenth and early nineteenth century wasn't driven totally mad and thanked his lucky stars for twentieth century medicine. Imagine all those soldiers scratching their way over the Alps. On second thoughts maybe if they had stripped off and rolled naked in the snow that would have frozen the little buggers and killed them off. He smiled at the image. What would Rowlandson or Gilray have made of it? In his mind's eye he could see the cartoons quite clearly. And did Napoleon himself suffer the same? Who knows? A piece of knowledge Thornton didn't have at his fingertips. This got him musing on the myths surrounding the emperor's sex life but he wasn't too far across the border and into Italy when, rounding a sharp bend he came out of his day dreaming as he saw a car at the side of the road some distance ahead with the bonnet up and a man standing a yard or two away who, as soon as he saw Thornton's car, stepped out into the road and started waving frantically for him to stop. A second man was hunched beneath the bonnet presumably trying to trace whatever fault it was that had brought their vehicle to a standstill but Thornton quickly noticed the man wasn't looking at the engine but was surreptitiously surveying the road. For a nanosecond Thornton lifted his foot from the accelerator but immediately pressed it down again. He didn't think the man in the road had any inclination of committing suicide but to make doubly sure he flashed his headlights and headed straight for him. At the last second the man flattened himself against the side of the parked car as Thornton's sped passed.

Glancing in his rear-view mirror before flooring the accelerator, Thornton could see the bonnet was already down and the two men were scrambling into the car to give chase. Other cars meanwhile had put themselves between hunter and quarry. They obviously hadn't been waived down, supposedly for assistance, and were now preventing the pursuers from catching up unless, in passing on blind bends they really didn't worry too much about imminent death, though maybe what Thornton had in his pocket would urge them on to being totally reckless. As for him, the sooner he made the anonymity of a large city the better, and that city was of course, Milan.

7

Reg Venables, a very disgruntled growing a trifle long in the tooth police officer who hadn't shaved that morning and was looking particularly scruffy, sat in his office and looked again at the article in his morning paper as he absentmindedly scratched his incipient beard. He had searched for his name a number of times over the last few days and in a number of newspapers as well, from *The Times* to *The Telegraph* and by way of *The Guardian*, a paper to which with his right wing leanings he took an instinctive dislike, on to the tabloids, ending up with *The Sun*, but his name had hardly been mentioned. What was wrong with British journalists that they could neglect so vital a part of this truly fascinating story the entire nation was agog to hear, that is when, as far as *The Sun* readers went, they could tear themselves away from football results, the racing, and page three? He had been asked for and graciously given two brief interviews, was mentioned in passing once as the policeman who had discovered the body and then – nothing, absolutely nothing. If he could bring himself to say it, sweet F.A. Had Reg thought about it carefully though, it was probably just as well he wasn't more in the limelight as his story was full of holes, the first being over-elaboration, but then that was Reg forever blowing his own trumpet, out of tune though it invariably was; the second and more important was the question of what was he doing in Westbourne Grove in the first place? He had absolutely no reason in the world to be there. As far as the first was concerned, fortunately he was never asked to repeat himself or he might not have remembered what he said the first time around, and as for the second, nobody thought to question it, except for Rita who suspected a secret assignation, as though such a thing was possible with someone like Reg Venables brought up in the strictest Wesleyan tradition; but you never know, stranger things have happened, especially as middle age inexorably advances, the male menopause looms and there is a sad yearning for a youth that can never return, the desire to have one last great love before eternity takes over.

Rita regarded him over the breakfast table slit-eyed with silent accusation, and a too vigorous banging about of crockery, even to the extent of breaking the handle off her favourite blue and white milk jug, made her feelings obvious until he managed to convince her of his innocence. Had Reg still been interested in his matrimonial duties she could have done a Lysistrata and denied him the marriage bed but the milk jug did in lieu off and, in convincing her of his innocence as far as anything priapic was concerned, Thornton's name was brought once more into the equation for tipping him off but he didn't think it would matter with the lady wife. She was hardly likely to mention it to anyone, hopefully, and she was somewhat mollified when he promised to replace the broken jug.

Had anyone asked him what he was doing in Westbourne Grove in the first place, it was hardly in his manor or on his way home to that little house beneath the Heathrow flight path where he lived in constant fear of his cucumber frames being shattered by the breaking of the sound barrier, he would have said he wanted to surprise his wife. Oh! Was it her birthday then, Reg? They might have asked down the station. Well, no, but let that pass, it was a spur of the moment thing, buying a picture for the front parlour, not too expensive mind you, just something colourful to brighten up a wall, a nice landscape or something like that, none of your modern stuff though. After all, the inherited Pre-Raphaelite monochrome prints had hung there for a long time. *The Light of the World* wasn't lighting up anything and as for *Love Locked Out*, to begin with he never did like that one; it was far too suggestive. All very well Victorian artists painting ladies' titties but bums were quite another matter. However it's not just contempt that familiarity breeds, the pictures had in fact got rather boring.

As far as the murder was concerned, the man in the street was informed that the police were following up a number of promising leads at this time, though in actual fact it was all hot air. That number added up to precisely zilch since they didn't have a single clue. In fact the investigation, though they would have vehemently denied it, was already on the back burner. The consensus of opinion among the more experienced was that it was a hit. The hit man had entered the country, the hit man had made the hit, the hit man had left the country, and there really was little point wasting money and police time in pursuing the matter unless a remarkable and unlooked for stroke of luck put them on the right track.

The story as far as Fleet Street was concerned had run its course and died a natural death as everything eventually must. There were world tragedies enough to make headlines and fill the front pages and editorials in the better class of newspaper and plenty of hot gossip about sex and wannabees in the more lurid tabloids. But it was still a stark dark image as far as Reg was concerned and he shuddered slightly at the memory of what, thanks to Thornton's phone call, he had found in the back room of that dusty shop. He was glad Constable Roper wasn't with him at the time. The poor lad would never have recovered from a sight so grisly. But talk or, in this case, think of the devil and, as the old saying has it, he's bound to appear for at that moment Roper, after a perfunctory knock on the door, waltzed in. Reg lowered his paper and watched the young man's approach. He could never get over the child-bearing hips as Roper advanced on him and he found himself wondering if it was the ex-KLM employee, the pretty Blodwen nee Hughes, now Mrs Roper, who had given birth to the twins or if it was Roper himself. He smiled at the thought, perverse though it was. Perverse thoughts come naturally when you've spent your life as a policeman. Fancy Roper fathering twins, he thought, shaking his head, who would have believed it? Only goes to show first impressions really can be dangerous.

'Yes, lad, what is it?' He asked in avuncular fashion. He was really, though he would be the last to admit it, quite fond of young Roper despite his original misgivings about the lad, and could have wished his own son was more like him instead of being a no-good unwashed hairy layabout. As for his daughter, well the less said about that little minx the better. Rita made a big mistake bringing back that too revealing costume from the

South of France. As the child was expanding in all directions, both buttock and breast wise, the result was becoming positively obscene. He wondered if he was going to be asked to be godfather to the Roper twins, Glyn and Gareth. He would like that. They would have Welsh names wouldn't they? Of course.

'It's a message for you, sir, from Whitehall.' Roper said, laying an official looking brown envelope on Reg's desk.

From Whitehall? The corridors of Power? If Roper had said Number Ten he couldn't have been given a bigger shock. He could just picture Mister Heath standing in the open doorway, grinning from ear to ear, chortling away, shoulders heaving, waving cheerily to the gathered reporters as he always did when standing on his sea-going yacht. Nobody could accuse Reg of not having a vivid imagination. He stared at the envelope for a considerable time, or at least it seemed like a considerable time, wondering whether to pick it up or not, let alone open it. Fine chap, Mister Heath. Fine chap, all that sailing and playing with his organ. It was a shame he would never know the happiness and joy of a good marriage but there you go, marriage wasn't for everybody. There was a tingling in his groin at the thought of what promises the envelope could contain. Promotion surely. Or possibly asking his permission to place him on the honours list. He believed that was how it was done, that was the form. What would it be? A CBE? A knighthood? He could already feel Her Majesty's' sword lightly touching his shoulders as he knelt humbly before her at Buckingham palace.

'How do you know it's from Whitehall?' He asked, breaking the spell.

'Says so on the envelope doesn't it?'

'Oh. Yes. Yes, of course, of course.' He studied the envelope again, still without picking it up. Roper was waiting, all curiosity. Reg looked up. 'What now, lad? What are you waiting for?'

'Any orders, sir.'

'No, no, off you go.'

'Righto.'

Roper turned and left. Having been denied any knowledge of what the envelope might contain he headed straight for the canteen no doubt to start the inevitable Chinese whispers and like poor Yorick set the station on a roar but not with infinite jest though that might come later. Poor old Reg was always good for a laugh. Still living when chief constables were chief constables and brooked no nonsense, he believed when criminals were actually caught they received due punishment instead of a slap on the wrist and told not to do such naughty things again. The punishment should fit the crime, no? He even found himself sometimes wishing for the death penalty to be restored but this was a rare phenomenon, an emotional outburst when he was in a truly black humour or the crime perpetrated had been too revolting and vicious.

His hands were trembling as he picked up the envelope and slid a quivering finger beneath the flap to prise it open. There was a faint hint of expensive perfume which for a moment was a trifle disconcerting until he saw the signature at the bottom of the now open page. It was that of Holly Day with a request for him to meet her, should he be able to make it, that very morning in the Patisserie Valerie in Old Compton Street. She would be there from eleven o'clock and sincerely hoped he could join her there. She apologised for approaching him in this manner but didn't want to use the telephone as she mistrusted the security on hers. You never knew who from behind the iron curtain could be listening in.

Reg turned over his wrist and looked at his watch. Ten-thirty. His disappointment at not receiving an honour or a promotion was manifest but obviously Miss Day had something serious on her mind so he would meet her, if just out of curiosity. Who knew to where it might lead? He got up, collected his hat and coat and left the office.

It had been two days previously that Holly, ploughing wearily through a heap of files on her desk, wishing the day was over and seriously thinking of changing her occupation, suddenly looked up to see her boss, teacup and saucer in hand, standing in front of her desk. Why, she wondered, do these upper middle class gents of the establishment always wear striped shirts with detachable white collars? And why do they have a pinkie ring engraved with a coat of arms bought in an antique shop, probably in the Burlington Arcade, and which is patently not theirs? Pathetic really. She could just picture him strolling down the Arcade, stopping to look in a window and spotting a tray of interesting looking rings, deciding to go in and purchase one with an engraved stone, some heraldic beast or other or a piece of weaponry like a lance or a sword. Once or twice she had innocently thought of querying the authenticity but, on reflection, felt she would only get some cock and bull story about an obscure ancestor being ennobled by Henry the Fourth or some other distant king or coming over with William the Conqueror so why bother? Mike Ayliff, who seemingly had walked around with a permanent erection, wore one and he definitely had no ancestry to talk of unless it was a Bonobo monkey and everyone knew what they get up to, continuously. She was finding life so boring at the moment she perversely almost wished Mike was still with them. In retrospect she thought, at least his sexual innuendos and constant clumsy if ever hopeful forays, she could hardly call them seductive or even flirtatious they were so gauche, livened things up somewhat.

'What do you know about an Inspector Lichti of the Swiss police?' The boss asked.

'Absolutely nothing. Why?'

'Because he knows you or, rather, he knows of you, who you are, and he's been making enquiries.'

'Enquiries? About what? Have I done something what I didn't aughter?' Holly gave the chief one of her ravishing smiles but she wasn't feeling quite so cheery within. She knew as soon as Switzerland was mentioned that Thornton had more than likely got himself into some kind of a pickle and she was waiting to hear the worst.

'Evidently he feels you can help him in a murder enquiry.'

Now he had Holly really worried.

'Murder? Who has been murdered?' She had a vision of Thornton's lifeless body lying cold on a slab and was already feeling guilty as hell.

'Aha!' If the boss had had a hand free instead of keeping a hold on cup and saucer he would have raised an index finger. 'I know what you're thinking but rest easy'. He took a sip of his tea, three lumps and just a soupçon of milk. 'Evidently there have been up to four killings at least, starting off with some professor fellow being done in, in rather gruesome fashion so I gather. Then there was this Rumanian woman, at least she said she was Rumanian but she had no identification and absolutely no one from the Balkans has ever been known throughout history to tell the truth so she could have been from anywhere. Was more than likely a spy for the Stasi. Then there was a Japanese gentleman and a Chinaman so it would seem to have pretty widespread ramifications don't you think? But exactly what help this Lichti chappie thinks you can give him we will never know unless you feel like taking a trip to Switzerland.' There was a long pause, perhaps to give her superior time to draw breath. He tended to be a little verbose at times. 'Well, do you?'

'Do I what?'

'Feel like a trip to Switzerland? Geneva as a matter of fact.'

'Of course, if I have leave to go.'

'Wouldn't be asking you otherwise, old girl.' Holly hated that old girl routine. It smacked of a bye-gone age and still seemed disrespectful somehow even if not meant that way. He took a final sip of his tea and replaced the cup on the saucer before he spoke again. It was quite a fine cup and saucer, Royal Doulton in fact, Wildflowers pattern, and he stood admiring the design for a moment as if, even though he drank out of that cup every day, he had never seen it before. The boss was not a leading member of his local amateur dramatic society and a keen disciple of Stanislavski for nothing and he was all for creating some sense of drama in real life that for him, despite his occupation, seemed curiously lacking. At home he had shelves filled with books on theatre and he was well aware of the impact a dramatic pause can have, though once or twice his pause on stage had been of such an inordinate length the audience thought something had gone wrong and on one occasion the prompter, thinking the same thing, actually hissed the line very loudly from the prompt corner which was a trifle embarrassing to say the least. The boss prided himself on the fact, even if his acting wasn't in the Olivier, Gielgud or Richardson class, that he was disciplined to the nth degree, always dead letter perfect, always came in on cue and never forgot a line even if he had the habit of turning a simple piece of business into a three act melodrama all of its own. So the prompt was unappreciated. However, unlike that Victorian actor he had read about, Mackie was it? who had what he called his pause, his long pause, and his grand pause, he did not walk over to the prompt corner, haul the poor unfortunate man (in this case actually it was a lady of advanced years in a home knitted cardigan) and thump him/ her on the nose, turning to the bemused audience and uttering that famous line, "The villain prompted me in me grand pause." Why leave all drama to poxy dramatists? Well, not all poxy he supposed, there had been and were some pretty good ones really. He would have liked to have tried his hand at this play writing lark himself but felt it could wait until he retired to that dreamed of cottage in the country and had more time to turn his mind to it. His plays of course would be all about skulduggery in the world of espionage, after all he had plenty of knowledge in that department even if his job was mainly desk bound and had been for some considerable time. He turned on his heel to leave.

'See you when you get back and you can fill me in with all the details,' he said before he disappeared into the corridor. 'Expenses on the firm of course, as long as you don't overdo it.' His voice faded as he walked away. 'Anything to help a colleague, even a foreign Johnny. Never know when you might need him to return the favour.' Holly didn't hear the final bit; her mind was already halfway to Geneva.

The Patisserie Valerie was crowded, smoky, and noisy with chatter and clatter but Reg spotted her at the back of the room the moment he walked in, mainly because she was the only person wearing dark glasses, though why in the dim light he couldn't be sure, unless she was showing off he thought as they were extremely expensive high fashion glasses. She was seated in the corner furthest from the door and acknowledged his approach with a smile, making room next to her for him to sit down.

'Thank you for coming.' Her voice was so quiet he almost didn't hear her and it was obviously going to be the tone of the conversation so that neighbouring tables didn't hear either. He wondered why she had chosen the Patisserie Valerie for their meeting instead of L'eminence Grise or somewhere similar but then, remembering the circumstances of their first encounter at that famous, fashionable, if rather expensive, nosh bar, maybe she didn't think it would be politic.

'I'm sorry I approached you in this fashion, Inspector but, as I told you, I'm afraid I don't trust the security on my phone. What are you having?'

'You could have called from a public telephone box and I'll have tea and, what is that on your plate?'

'It's called a rum baba.'

'French concoction is it?'

'You are in a French café, Inspector.'

'Of course, of course. Tea then and a… and a… just tea thank you, maybe an éclair. They look delicious.'

'Delicious, as is everything else here, though you do have to watch your cholesterol level I suppose, and for some, their hips.' She gave him another smile meaning she was definitely not one to worry about the width of her hips, meanwhile looking at a couple of ladies to whom hip-width was obviously not a priority either.

'A bit famished I must say. Been a long time since breakfast.'

They both tried to catch the eye of a passing waitress but she appeared far too busy delivering a tray of fresh cream goodies to another table for the couple of middle-aged ladies to whom Holly had been referring and who looked as though they had been living on cream, single, double, clotted or iced ever since childhood and it was high time they gave it up. The waitress had obviously noticed them though out of the corner of her eye so stopped on her way back and, tray hanging down by her side, other hand on hip, she waited for Reg to place his order before she left and he turned back to Holly who had by now removed her glasses. Sunglasses don't disguise anyone. On the contrary they make them more obvious, especially fashionable ones.

'Now then, Miss Day...'

'Holly.'

'Holly. What may all this be about?'

'I can't tell you now. Too many ears about and you never know who's listening. Would you be able to visit me this evening? This is the address.' She slipped him a piece of paper.

Visit her this evening? At her apartment? Reg almost broke out in a cold sweat. If Rita ever got wind of it her eyebrows would touch her hairline. But still, he was intrigued and there was one good thing about being a policeman, an urgent case could always be an excuse for not being at home.

*   *   *

The firm might be paying expenses but there was a limit even to government coffers, especially when non-VIPs or non-celebrities were concerned and Holly Day fitted neither description so the limit meant her having to fly cattle class. She didn't mind too much, it wasn't that uncomfortable and it wasn't for the first time, though she could have done with just a little more leg room and without the aggravation of the kid behind who kept on kicking the back of her seat. If flight time had been longer no doubt she would sooner rather than later have remonstrated with the child or the child's mother; but as the mother was seemingly incapable of controlling her brat or couldn't care less which was the more likely, that would probably precipitate a row, so she let it ride. A complaint to one of the cabin staff would no doubt produce the same effect.

Holly, who was seated on the aisle, glanced sideways and noticed also in an aisle seat on the opposite side and just behind her what looked like a more than presentable young man who gave her a shrug, a raised eyebrow and a sympathetic smile. Holly returned the smile, pulling a slight face in turn implying what does one do? In reply the young man then proceeded to indulge in a short but quite elaborate mime meaning would Holly like to change places with him? She declined the offer with a shake of the head and a mouthed thank you and looked out front again. With the image of the young man's face in mind she was wishing she had thought to bring a book with her. Whoever loves who loves not at first sight? The ultra-glossy in-flight magazine had long since given up its secrets, most of which consisted of advertising, especially for what could be bought on board duty free and, as the direction in which the plane was heading was towards the Alps, Swiss watches were absolutely in evidence. The trolley would no doubt soon be wheeled along by fixed smile attendants hell bent on getting passengers to part with their cash. There was a moment's respite from the kicking as the child had turned sideways to watch the mime and momentarily forgotten its boredom. In a way Holly could forgive him she supposed. She also found flying an extremely boring experience, except sometimes there might just be a fellow passenger of interest, like now. She resisted the temptation to turn around and take another look though she was quite sure he hadn't taken his eyes off her.

She sat smiling to herself. Up to this point she had been so preoccupied she hadn't noticed the young man before and wondered how on earth (or in the sky for that matter) she could have missed him. She hadn't even noticed him at check in or on boarding. Maybe he arrived late. Then, once on the plane, why didn't she see him walk up the aisle as he was seated in the row behind her? Never mind, maybe she was stowing her bag in the overhead locker at the time and had her back to him, but aisles in aeroplanes are extremely narrow, bodies have to squeeze sideways to get passed. Very strange, though it was, not to put too fine a point on it, a case now of be still my beating heart. She hadn't seen a man as handsome as this in a long while. He was obviously friendly so she might try and precipitate a meeting once they landed. The passenger seated beside her for example, who refused adamantly to give her elbow room on the arm rest as he spread himself out, had a belly that could only have come from too many pints of lager and a virtual complete lack of exercise despite his apparently youthful face. That wouldn't last long either, Holly thought, but would quickly go the way of his physique. He had tried to start up a conversation but receiving nothing but most unfeminine non-committal grunts in return soon gave up. She must have been in another world, yes, a worried one, not to have noticed the handsome stranger before. But now she tried to put him out of her mind as she thought back on her meeting the previous evening with Reg Venables.

For a man of his age and experience the policeman sat on her sofa, knees together for all the world like a timid virgin worried about the possibility of being ravaged. With that pose and his high-pitched voice he could have been a cross-dresser. He had placed his hat on the sofa next to him and didn't remove his coat despite Holly's offering to take it. Fortunately the weather was dry but like Jewish men with silver ties – Harold Norris was a good example - or establishment men with their striped shirts, police detectives always seemed to appear in shabby raincoats, or anyway that's the impression they gave, probably because of television. It's quite amazing how tribal symbols persist even in so called civilised societies. Maybe he didn't want to take it off because he felt he wouldn't be there long enough to warrant it. Maybe he thought it would be there to protect him should Miss Day have something untoward in mind though he couldn't for the life of him think what that could be.

'Very nice apartment you have, Miss Day,' he said, looking around, 'very nice indeed. Most tasteful if I may say so.'

'Thank you, Inspector. Would you care for a drink?' She asked.

'Well, as I'm not on official duty, Miss Day, that wouldn't go amiss I must say.'

'Please call me Holly and what will it be?'

'I beg your pardon?'

'Drink wise.'

'Oh! Oh yes. Well, a very small scotch wouldn't come amiss, if you have it.'

'Of course. *Famous Grouse* suit you? It's Thornton's favourite.'

Was it her imagination or did she see Venables wince and had he suddenly developed a slight tic in his left eye?

'That will do nicely, thank you.'

'Water? Ice? Or straight?'

'Oh, just as it comes, thank you. Mustn't spoil the water must we?'

He was a bit miffed that Holly didn't respond to his humour and already wondered on what all this could be about. He had expected with all this cloak and dagger stuff, messages and secret meetings, to be involved in an exciting case of international espionage. After all the West End had hardly been all that lively recently, not as far as serious stuff is concerned, and his job for a while had been hideously desk bound so he could do with a spot of excitement to, as he would put it, liven the proceedings up a little.

He remembered his first meeting with Holly Day when he suspected her and Thornton King of murdering the colonel with a booby trap golf ball, and had her down the police station where she rang rings around one of his juniors, causing the poor fellow to almost have a nervous breakdown and threatening to emigrate if ever he was faced with her again; but now he had a shrewd suspicion this evening was all to do with Mister Thornton King. Had he twigged that earlier he wouldn't have bothered to come. If Thornton King was in a scrape, Thornton King could get out of it without the assistance of Reg Venables, thank you very much. Mrs Venables would have a litter of pink kittens and raise merry hell if she ever found out he was alone with a beautiful young woman in her apartment even if it were supposedly in the line of duty. But could it possibly be something else, something more sinister? For example, there had been cases recently of important people being caught and photographed for the purposes of blackmail, in flagrante delecto, that is to say with their pants around their ankles, snogging with, not to put too fine a point on it, ladies of the night or worse as far as Reg was concerned, with members of their own sex! He gave a little shudder thinking about it, trying desperately not to form any kind of mental image. He believed the Russians were particularly adept at this type of chicanery and entrapment by the use of hidden cameras, afterwards forcing their victims to work for the Soviet Union or be disgraced by having their misdemeanours disclosed to their superiors or worse to the newspapers, in particular the *News of the World* for all and sundry to gawk at and make fun of. The miscreants would receive perfectly innocent looking envelopes which, when opened at the breakfast table and their contents revealed made the blood run cold. Life could never be the same again. In fact for some life ended there and then, that was the sad part. Perhaps Miss Day was a double agent, playing one side off the other and making a killing off both. Reg's imagination was in overdrive.

She had poured his drink and was handing it to him in a Waterford cut glass tumbler he noticed with a twinge of jealousy. How could these whippersnappers afford apartments like this and Waterford cut glass tumblers? He'd always had a soft spot for Waterford but felt a set of six of any kind, be they sherry, wine, port, or tumbler, was an extravagance he and the lady wife could ill afford. Maybe for their fiftieth anniversary he would be able to afford a set. Maybe a set could come as a retirement present if he was sure in the most subtle way positive to make his preference known.

'Are you not having one then?' He asked as he took the glass, at the same time giving her a slit-eyed look of suspicion Rita would have been proud of.

'A bit early for me,' Holly said with a little laugh that he thought sounded rather false.

'Early?' He lifted his arm, looking at his watch to ascertain the time and, forgetting he had the drink in his hand, tipped up the glass and poured most of his scotch over the couch. He leapt to his feet spilling the remainder.

'Sorry, Miss Day, ever so sorry!'

'That's all right. Inspector, please, calm down. It's as well it wasn't boiling hot tea or you could have done yourself a nasty injury. I'll just get something from the kitchen to mop it up.'

While he stood looking as disconsolate as a bloodhound that had lost the scent, she headed for the kitchen to return presently with a bowl of hot soapy water and a sponge. What could the matter be with the man? she wondered. Instead of the loud, self-assured, domineering person he usually was in his own milieu, he was as nervous as a kitten.

'I don't believe that couch is a very lucky one.' She laughed, still trying to lighten things up; put him at his ease. 'It's not the first time it has been the recipient of the unexpected. I spilled a whole bowl of Chinese food all over it once, chicken chop suey with egg fried rice and sweet and sour pork. It was, I might add, thanks to a phone call from Thornton interrupting my enjoyment of *The Corrie*, in the very last minute as well would you believe? So I missed the tag and I hate that.' She had dipped the sponge in the basin and squeezed out the surplus water. 'He seems to have a sixth sense when it comes to phoning at the wrong time. I suppose I needn't have answered the call but one never knows how important it is, does one? It took a complete professional and expensive cleaning job to put it right but this should be a doddle. It's got a bit more stained in patches since then anyway.'

She was about to bend down in front of the couch to swab it down when, as the contrite guilty party, he decided to interfere.

'Here, let me do that,' he offered, reaching out for the bowl and spilling a bit more liquid about the place and nearly dropping his

Waterford crystal.

She held onto the bowl, he managed to hold onto the glass.

'Inspector Venables...' Holly tried not to sound too irritated '... please do sit down.' She waved an arm indicating a nearby chair. 'No, on second thoughts pour yourself another drink first, you hardly tasted that one, and then sit down while I finish this and then we will talk.'

Blushing like a chastened naughty schoolboy he did as he was told and, drink in slightly shaky hand, watched silently as she finished swabbing down the couch. He had taken his hat with him and it was now placed on his lap. Fortunately none of the whisky had spilled on it or any other part of him, despite her jocular remark regarding the tea, or she might have offered to swab him down or, alternatively, he would have gone home smelling of the stuff. People in the tube would have looked at him askance, maybe even nervously move away. That would have been extremely embarrassing, especially as he was a police officer. What if a passenger decided to put in a complaint and a lower order railway policeman tried to arrest him? The indignity of the situation wasn't worth thinking about.

'There,' she said, 'no harm done, not like sweet and sour sauce that could stain anything it touched.' She waltzed back to the kitchen to empty the bowl and deposit bowl and sponge in the sink. 'Actually now I think I will join you in that drink.'

He watched as she returned to pour herself a Bacardi and coke and then he broke the silence with, 'Would you like to tell me what all this is about, Miss Day?'

'Yes, it's about murder.'

'Hmn-hmn?'

'I mean one murder in particular, and you would know the

one I'm talking about.'

'Would I?'

'Yes, the art dealer in Westbourne Grove.'

'Hmn hmn?'

'I believe you are the person who discovered the body.'

'Hmn hmn?'

'And am I right in also believing it was a phone call from Thornton that put you on to it?'

Inspector Venables pursed his lips tight, looking for all the world as if he was expecting an immediate kissing session, and gazed into his glass before looking up again.

'There really is no need to be so tight-lipped about it, Inspector.'

'Is there not? This is police business, Miss Day.' He was obviously never going to call her Holly. 'What I wonder is your interest in the case? You could have visited me at the station any time to ask these questions. I must presume it has something to do with Thornton King. By the way where might he be at this moment?' He had thought of saying this miscreant but thought better of it. 'Are you trying to protect him from something? Some misdemeanour in which he is involved? Some case he might be investigating?' This last was said with something akin to a sneer. 'And am I correct in thinking no doubt a second person is involved both of whom you are trying to protect? Am I right in that assumption?'

'Spot on. Inspector, spot on. How jolly clever of you.'

Venables smiled for the first time that evening; in fact he positively beamed and took a sip of his whisky. She noticed, after his request for a very small one, second time around he had poured himself what looked almost like a triple. Having swilled the whisky around his teeth and felt it burn its way down his throat, it wasn't often he indulged in hard liquor, it wasn't often he could afford it, a policeman's pay even in the higher echelons being what it is, he continued. 'You realise Miss Day that if you know anything about this murder, anything at all, and are withholding vital evidence from the police in the process of making their enquiries that that is a most serious offence, very serious indeed.'

'I am fully aware of it, Inspector, but the fact is I know nothing that could be of any assistance to the police…'

'Hmn…' which meant he somehow doubted that.

'…otherwise you wouldn't be here and I wouldn't be asking you for information, would I?'

'I'm not too sure about that.' He sniffed, moving his nostrils to one side with the aid of his mouth that was no longer in kissing mode. 'You did say you were protecting someone else.' He took another sip of whisky. 'I must presume you're not going to tell me who it is and I still don't know why you are otherwise so interested.'

'All right, I will tell you. Tomorrow I am flying to Geneva to try and assist a Swiss colleague, well more a colleague of yours rather than mine. Maybe you remember him from Beaulieu.'

Reg coughed and spluttered. He never wanted to be reminded of what was for him a completely disastrous episode. 'Whisky went down the wrong way,' he said between whoops.

'It doesn't matter.'

Reg wasn't sure if she was talking about the Swiss chap or the whisky going down the wrong way but her next remark put him straight.

'Anyway, the inspector is endeavouring to solve a number of murders there and I was wondering if this one in London had any connection.'

'Why on earth would you wonder that? Why should a murder in London have anything to do with a murder in Switzerland?'

'Maybe it's just a hunch...'

'Womanly intuition.' He smiled again. Quaint old-fashioned thing, Holly thought.

'Perhaps there was something, for example when you went into the shop and found him, that could give me some information I could take to Geneva, maybe a similarity in the method of killing perhaps.'

'Maybe it was your friend Thornton King who killed him and only passed me the information to get himself off the hook, a red herring as it were.'

'That is ridiculous, Inspector and you know it is.' Holly snorted in very unladylike fashion.

'Do I? Is it? And why would that be if I may so enquire?' Reg was the kind of person who called a train driver a locomotive operative and with too many like him coming up in the world it was going to get even more ridiculous such as "audible warning instrument" for motor horn.

'What possible motive could he have?'

Obviously unable to think of a plausible reason for Thornton committing so gruesome a murder on what was an apparently inoffensive, if maybe somewhat eccentric, picture framer and dealer in artistic rubbish, Reg avoided Holly's eyes, turned down the corners of his mouth and gave a little shrug before taking another careful sip of his whisky. The last swallow was still irritating his tonsils and he was just pleased that in coughing, none of it had gone up his nose.

'Besides which,' Holly continued, 'Thornton is so squeamish, if he accidentally treads on a beetle, he has a guilty conscience for days. Thornton says please and thank you and apologises to animals. He would fill his flat with strays except that his lease forbids even the keeping of one animal. He is no more capable of killing someone in cold blood than you or I.'

'Who said it was in cold blood?'

'Wasn't it?'

'I suppose, if you consider how the man was tortured, it might have been cold blood.'

'Tortured?'

'Terrible it was, with a blow torch. Hardly any meat left on his toes at all.' Hardened policeman though he was, Reg couldn't help but shudder at the memory.

'There are only two reasons for inflicting that sort of pain on someone and that is either you are an out and out sadist who takes the greatest delight in inflicting pain or you want information and it's not forthcoming.'

'Or to teach a lesson or give out a warning?'

Holly felt she had got him, the inspector opened up at last, though it may have been the whisky helped and she gave no indication of her feelings. He seemed to have forgotten all about her protecting the countess who had in her hotel suite, as previously mentioned, taken Holly's advice and procured herself through an agency advertising in a magazine some personal security in the shape of a twenty stone zombie who did seem to know what personal protection was all about even if he knew little else. Ostensibly he was required, so she informed him, because she was afraid for her jewels. Now Holly partly salved her conscience for withholding information from Venables by thinking if she had given her away the last thing the countess needed was Mister Plod clomping into her hotel suite in his size elevens and, anyway, she was sure the old girl couldn't actually point a finger at the killer or killers.

'So what's your theory?' Holly was keeping the ball in Reg's court.

'Simple really. Obvious in fact. It was a contract killing, wasn't it? Stands to reason.'

Holly failed to see how reason came into it but it was at this point in her musings that the child interrupted her thoughts by resuming his kicking game. The slob seated next to her laid back his head and turned his face sideways facing her, his eyes never leaving her face though he was addressing the child.

'Listen, sonny boy,' he growled, 'if you don't keep your fucking feet to yourself you're going to get more than you bargained for.'

There were one or two quite audible gasps from surrounding passengers at the use of such bad language in a confined space and the implied threat of child abuse but otherwise silence, especially from the seats behind. He grinned at Holly who had the good grace to acknowledge his smile by smiling back. The child's eyes were out on stalks, the lower lip was thrust out and quite visibly trembling and the kicking, much to Holly's relief, stopped never to be started again.

8

'I think you'll find it was a hit, a contract killing.' She neglected
to say "stands to reason" but looked steadily across the desk
at Lichti seated the other side gazing back at her with equal
concentration. It was a momentary case of mutual admiration
as far as appearances were concerned, both of them being
attractively in their prime as it were, but they weren't getting
anywhere in coming up with ideas regarding the professor's
murder, the East European lady with a bullet in the buttock, or
that of Mister Riccoboni of the barbecued toes in distant London,
though it was quite obvious the modus operandi was virtually, if
not completely, the same in each case. 'So I don't think you stand
a cat's hope in hell of getting your killer,' she continued.

Lichti frowned and dropped his eyes to his desktop.

'Unless you have a spot of luck of course,' she added rather
lamely.

There was a short hiatus as Lichti thought about this. He rolled
his pencil across the desk, rolled it back again, watching it, then

looked up again.

'I'm sorry. I'm forgetting my manners,' he said, 'I haven't offered you any refreshment. Would you care…?'

'I'm fine at the moment thank you.'

'Your flight was a pleasant one I hope? Sometimes over the mountains one can get a lot of turbulence. Sensitive stomachs find it a bit hard to take.'

'It wasn't too bad except for a wretched kid sitting behind me and kicking my seat and I really hate that. And I don't think we actually flew over any mountains not to speak of anyway.'

If Lichti thought he was going to get to her by offering refreshment and small talk he was very much mistaken and he realised this.

'Well, nevertheless I have to thank you for coming all this way just to tell me that,' he said.

'Tell you what?'

'That I haven't how did you put it? A cat's …?'

'Cat's hope in hell?'

'A cat's hope in hell. Interesting expression. One that I've not heard before. Completely illogical of course.' He gazed out the window so as to avoid her reaction which, in fact, was merely a little smile. Then he looked back and his next question was straight to the point.

'What was your friend Thornton King doing in Switzerland?'

Aha, Holly thought, now we're down to the nitty-gritty. He knew all along I could really tell him nothing about the murders but Thornton's presence is another matter and the two could just be linked.

'I didn't know he was in Switzerland,' she said, which was actually true, he could have still been in Rome. 'Was he?' The innocent act was laid on a bit thick and Lichti wasn't going to be taken in by it. For answer he opened a drawer, produced the identikit and passed it over the desk. Holly studied it. The resemblance was too close for comfort. He gave her a moment before continuing.

'Is that, or is that not, Thornton King?'

Holly looked up from the likeness lying on the desk. 'Hmn... Very like him I have to admit, though the nose is maybe a little too sharp.' She looked up momentarily and then down again as if giving the drawing a closer study though in truth she wasn't even focusing on it. 'And the jaw, his jaw, well, I'd say it is much squarer than that.' She passed the paper back across the desk. 'No, I don't believe that is him. It just bears a sort of resemblance, close resemblance I have to admit. Could be a doppelganger?'

Lichti stared at her. She smiled back. He wasn't taken in.

'When did you see him last?'

Holly laughed.

'Something is funny in my asking that?'

'No, no, it's just that it brought something else to mind. There is a very famous painting, maybe you know it. It's called "When did you last see your father?" and it shows a small boy in blue standing on a sort of cushion or footstool or something in front of a desk and being questioned by a whole gang of Roundheads enquiring as to where his Cavalier father might be hiding. You know all about the civil war in England I'm sure. The boy's sister stands behind him crying and being held by some rascally looking soldier. It's a very fine painting, Victorian I think. Can't remember the name of the artist though.'

Lichti was not going to be sidetracked. 'Fascinating, Miss Day, truly fascinating. In answer to your question, yes, I do know all about the English civil war, Oliver Cromwell and all that lot, but you are not, I am very glad to say, a small boy standing on a cushion and I am not a Roundhead so I am asking you again, when did you last see Mister King?'

Holly shrugged and looked over his head as if trying to remember. 'No idea offhand. A few days ago maybe... let me see...' She lowered her gaze and refocused.

'You have no idea? The two of you are very close, are you not?'

'I am not my brother's keeper, Inspector Lichti.'

'Thornton King is your brother?' There was no denying the surprise in the inspector's voice.

'It's a saying, Inspector. Don't you know your Bible?'

'Not very well I have to admit.'

'Tut-tut, and you living in Calvin's city. You know all about the English civil war but you don't know your Bible. It comes in Genesis I believe, though I can't give you chapter and verse.'

'You were together in the South of France a couple of years back as I remember.'

'Can friends not take a holiday together? It does happen you know, frequently. I felt I deserved a break and I also felt Thornton would be good company, rather than go on my own. Are you trying to say you believe Thornton and I are an item? Because, if you are, I'm afraid you're very much mistaken. Friends, Inspector, good friends, that is all.' She didn't add that she thought she and the inspector could be an item given half a chance, or that she and the young man on the plane could be an item. "Goodness gracious, girl", she said to herself, "what's got into you? You're behaving like an alley cat on heat." She realised while her thoughts were wandering that he had said something. 'I'm sorry, what did you say?'

'I was starting to say, it would seem we have brought you all the way here to little if any purpose.' It was obvious from his tone that he thought she was not being very forthcoming. 'So may I suggest to make up a little for the inconvenience that I invite you to dine with me this evening?'

'How very kind of you, Inspector.'

'My name is Franz.'

'And mine is Holly.'

'Shall we say I pick you up at your hotel at … what time do you like to eat?'

'Fairly early if that's all right with you. I'm afraid I am not really a late bird. I remember when I was on holiday in Greece watching people eating huge meals at all hours of the night. We were finished at our table by nine o'clock and people were still arriving in a restaurant gone midnight and eating the most enormous portions. How they could go to bed and sleep on such full stomachs was beyond me. Have you been to Greece, Inspector?'

He shook his head and forbore asking her what she was still doing in the restaurant at that late hour if she had finished dining by nine.

'Shall we say seven o'clock then?'

'Lovely. I look forward to it.'

'I'll have a car take you back to your hotel now and I'll pick you up at seven.'

Holly wasn't too sure about the pick you up bit and he didn't offer to kiss her hand which she found a trifle disappointing. As she moved towards the door he came around from behind his desk.

'Are you married, Inspecteur?'

This momentarily stopped him in his tracks before he advanced again to open the door for her. 'I'm afraid not, Miss Day.'

'Holly.'

'A crusty old bachelor, that's what I am. I believe that's what the English say?'

'Hardly old, Inspecteur, hardly crusty.' She favoured him with one of her most ravishing smiles saved for special occasions. If he had been an impressionable youth he would have blushed.

'But, one more question for you before you go, who is Nat Berman?'

Holly turned back. 'Who?' It was quite obvious from her honest reaction that she had no idea who Nat Berman was.

'Never mind,' he said, 'until seven then.'

*   *   *

Thornton meanwhile was enjoying his ossobuco and Chianti in La Crota Piemunteise a snug bar restaurant, cosy with its plain tables and chairs and one wall holding a hundred or more upright bottles of wine. He wondered if any diners were ever tempted to count them. Chianti wasn't his usual tipple but he thought he would give it a try on its home ground as it were. He had booked into his charming comfortable hotel on the Corso Magenta, a hop, step, and a jump from the church of Santa Maria della Grazie housing da Vinci's famous masterpiece, *The Last Supper*. Before moving on he might inveigle himself into a group to get his few minutes of viewing; after all he might never be this way again. On the other hand he thought he might take in the Civic Gallery of Modern Art instead. Just as well to get in a little nouveau culture while he was there and the gallery is housed in the building Napoleon slept in. Great guy that Napoleon. Crowned himself king of Italy in the Duomo. Today of course there is no doubt he would be indicted as a war criminal which Thornton supposed is what in truth he was; but in that case, so his thinking went, so was Julius Caesar and Alexander the Great and that gay blade king of England, Richard the Lionheart, and the Knights Templar, and Genghis Kahn, let alone all those modern ones who were tried at Nuremburg, and African dictators; so many others throughout the centuries. Warlords and war criminals unfortunately have been thick as acorns on the ground throughout history and it is invariably the innocent and inoffensive who suffer because of them.

The Swiss time piece, carefully wrapped, was in the hotel safe, better there than in his pocket, and he had turned in the car. It had obviously become too well known and even in a city of a million cars it could be spotted. Hertz could see it back to Rome and he would take the train. He hoped the driver of the rented car wouldn't get into any trouble being mistaken for him but c'est la vie, what could he do about it? If anyone stopped him they would soon find out their mistake. He really shouldn't hang about too long though. The countess was not going to pay expenses forever and, anyway, the sooner he finished the job and headed for home the less chance there was of his doing a Mike Ayliff and coming to a very sticky end. Thornton gave a little shudder at the thought and dug a fork into his dinner. He would turn in early he decided and so have energy to explore the following day and then head for Rome. He was sure Milan, like all big cities, offered all manner of exciting prospects as far as nightlife was concerned but Thornton was in fact not much of a night bird, or an early morning one for that matter. Come to think of it, Holly was right; he was a lazy sod and no mistake. Snuggling under the bedclothes was his idea of heaven.

*   *   *

The police car pulled into the kerb and stopped outside the hotel door and Holly with a brief thank you to the driver, who happened to be Gendarme Morvan, opened the door, stepped out and said good night. Morvan sort of grunted. He was still smarting from the whole Thornton King episode and made to look an idiot in front of his peers. Holly entered the hotel through the revolving door as the car sped off. It was as though Morvan couldn't get away from her fast enough. He felt he had had enough put downs to last a lifetime and these English, so full of their own self-importance as if half the world atlas was still coloured red, invariably spelt trouble. Why he had let King slip through his fingers in the first place he really couldn't fathom. Though nothing was said, he and Guy could see on the faces in the station that they were considered incompetent beyond belief and no amount of calling anyone an arsehole was going to rectify matters. He was so intent on his thoughts he nearly slammed into the side of a van and that would have been the last straw but there was a squeal of brakes as his foot slammed down and he missed a collision by an inch, or a few centimetres depending on whether you're looking at it from an English or a Swiss point of view.

She collected her key at the reception desk (there were no messages which wasn't surprising as she had been in Geneva only a few hours) and headed for the lifts, pressed the call button and, while she waited, glance at herself in a mirror to one side that revealed not only herself but most of the area behind her. To her surprise, seated in a corner she spied the young man from the plane ostensibly reading a newspaper. Had he not noticed her go by? She turned back and advanced to where he was seated. At the last moment he looked up, smiled, and got to his feet.

'Good evening,' he said. Of course he had seen her. There was no surprise in his voice. It was if their coming together had been prearranged 'We meet again.'

Actually, Holly thought, she had somehow missed him on landing so they hadn't met in the first place let alone again but she let it pass. She thought she caught the trace of an accent although she couldn't put her finger on what it was.

'Hello,' she said, bright as a button even though, after the flight and the episode in the police station, she was feeling somewhat mucky and couldn't wait to get in the shower. 'Are you staying here?'

'Yes, as a matter of fact I am. Isn't that a remarkable coincidence? Of all the hotels in Geneva we end up in the same one.' His smile had Holly's knees all of a tremble. 'Please, allow me to introduce myself. I am Viktor Radenko.'

'And I am Holly Day.'

'Really?' Viktor raised both eyebrows and sounded most disbelieving. 'Isn't that a little, how shall I say, unusual?'

Holly was used to this reaction when meeting strangers. She had it from early school days onwards and had at times inwardly cursed her loving but unthinking parents for burdening her with a name she had for a long time actually hated. At one time she did think of changing it but as she couldn't come up with a suitable alternative, one she felt that suited her character, she decided to live with it. She thought she had long got used to people's reaction but she bridled slightly at this remark and Viktor sensed it.

'I'm so sorry,' he said, 'I didn't mean to cause offence. Please forgive me,' and once again his smile won the day. 'Please. Won't you sit down and join me for a drink?'

Holly glanced at her watch. 'I'd love to,' she said, hoping she didn't sound too gushing, 'but I'm afraid I have a dinner date to keep and have to get ready for it.'

'I understand. Some other time perhaps.'

'Of course'

"Come on, Holly", she said to herself, "get moving", but she was finding it difficult to do that.

'If you don't move,' he eventually said it for her, still with that smile, 'you'll be late for your dinner date and that will never do?'

'No, it won't, will it? I mean, yes, of course. I must look a positive fright at the moment anyway.' Shit! Why do women always come out with this old cliché? It was fishing with a long line and she knew it but was still gratified when he answered.

'No, you look very beautiful, if I may be permitted to say so.'

Holly all but sniggered she was so embarrassed at her girlish behaviour. Oh, these continentals, she thought. An Englishman would never be so bold as to say something like that on such a short acquaintance. 'Thank you,' she simpered and backed off before she turned away and before she could say anything more and make an even bigger fool of herself. Beautiful he might think her but more than likely also dumb. Remembering some of the men she had dated she knew perfectly well that beauty plus brains was often resented, especially a brain as sharp as hers. As she waited for the lift she wondered if it really was coincidence that they were staying in the same hotel. She wondered what his business in Geneva might be. She would have to ask next time she saw him.

He had remained standing, watching her all the way across the foyer. She knew it but was determined not to turn around, nor even to glance at his reflection in the mirror when she reached the lifts. Fortunately one was fairly quick in arriving.

Thornton was wondering where he would have his morning coffee before taking in the sights and indulging in that bit of culture he had promised himself before leaving. There was so much to see and do in Milan it was difficult to know where to start. He could sit in the Piazza del Duomo and admire the cathedral, reputedly one of the largest in the world. Or he could have his coffee in the Vittorio Emmanuelle Gallery, a bit like the Burlington Arcade he thought only much much, much much grander, connecting as it did two squares and with its beautiful glass roof four stories up. Was it the beginning of what the Americans call The Mall and the English call a Shopping Centre? He eventually decided on the Caffe Cova where he would break a habit and take not morning coffee, but tea like an English gentleman. Is this what it felt like for the gilded youth of England in earlier years when taking the grand tour?

The Caffe Cova in the via Montenapoleone was evidently established in 1817 by one of Napoleon's soldiers and was still there though the original was bombed during World War Two. The available pasticceria, confetteria there was as good as anything to be found at the Valerie and taking tea was a bit like the Savoy or The Ritz or even Fanny and Mary's. Sitting there and thinking of Fanny and Mary's brought Adrian Spangle to mind. Thornton smiled at the memory. He had never been a stickler for convention but he wondered where his acceptance of the non-conventional the, to many people, so-called abnormal, had come from. He had never thought there was a bench mark where normality was concerned but, after all, he was brought up in a society where men were men and women were women and there could be nothing in between and, if anything like that ever manifested itself it could only be received with a hearty put-down, or worse. He wondered if Adrian was still having his affair with Doctor Adrian of Barts. They made a handsome couple. Thinking of the Valerie conjured up visions of Holly. Dear Holly. Sometimes he could wish they were not such good friends. There were moments when he found her so attractive and felt the urge to make love but he knew in his heart of hearts that it would spoil their relationship utterly, perhaps even put an end to it and that would indeed be sad. They could never be like a hero and heroine in a *Mills and Boon* novel. It was the kind of friendship that, if they didn't see each other for twenty years and came together again, it would be as if not more than a day had gone by and they would pick up exactly where they had left off. He wondered where she was right at this moment and was she having a romantic fling? After all, why not? What's good for the gander is good for the goose. Little did he know that at the moment she had two strings to her bow though she was plucking at only one.

He was so lost in thought he hadn't at first seen the three men who had entered the café and were in fact approaching his table. Sensing their presence he looked around, taking in the number of tables vacant, but the men stopped in front of his and the elder of the three grinned down at him. Thornton noticed he had a very thin mouth, a scar on his left cheek and a couple of gold teeth. The veritable epitome of the clichéd villain. The other two, younger and looking remarkably similar to each other, brothers obviously, were regarding him intently.

'We may join you?' The older man said and without further ado sat himself down and the other two immediately followed suit.

'I am Giuseppe Fantoccini. These...' He waved a hand towards his companions... 'are the Pensotti brothers, Maurizio and Fabrizio.' At mention of their names each brother bowed his head slightly both trying to look truly threatening but in fact looking extraordinarily baby faced. Thornton realised the situation was serious or he would have been inclined to laugh their attempt at macho expressions were so ludicrous. 'They speak no English,' Giuseppe continued, 'so I am here to translate for them.'

'Really?' Thornton said. 'And what, if I may ask, is it they want to say to me that needs translation?'

'You are Mister King, I presume? Mister Thornton King of London are you not?'

'Not. 'Fraid you got the wrong feller, old chum.'

'Is that so?' He clicked middle finger and thumb together – twice, and the younger Pensotti reached in his jacket pocket and came out with a photograph that he slid across the table. Thornton glanced down at it. It was a photo of him taken in the Westbourne Grove as he left Riccoboni's shop and an image of the tourist couple he wondered about at the time flashed through his mind. So it was him they were interested in, nothing else. Fortunately the picture had been taken on a very high speed film, probably 800ASA, quite unnecessary at that time of the year, and consequently was very grainy even as a small print. That was a big mistake. Secondly the photographer was not very good at what he was doing. Even if there wasn't actual camera shake there was at least some slight out of focus blurring, enough for Thornton to be able to shake his head.

'That's not me,' he said.

Maurizio retrieved the photo and the two brothers sat staring at it, looked up at Thornton, went back to the picture, frowning, looked at each other and shook their heads in disbelief. Of course it was him. It just had to be him.

'Mister King,' Giuseppe said. His voice was low and pianissimo but there was no doubting the implied threat in it. 'I will call you that because I am sure I know who I am talking to even though you may deny it. Mister King, we don't want to cause trouble,' he spread both hands out on the table; they were quite elegant, almost feminine, hands, 'but you have something we very much want, something we are determined to get, you understand?'

'What would that be then?'

Now the other's voice held more than a threat, although still low it was positively menacing and the hands had turned palms down, flat on the tabletop. Not for the first time Thornton realised he was in real trouble and there was no way he could think of to talk himself out of it. He could not only feel his heart thumping, he could feel it running at three time's normal speed and, being the kind of guy who never took exercise unless he really had to, his heart simply was not used to doing that sort of thing.

Giuseppe Fantoccini's whole expression had somehow inexplicitly changed. Thornton couldn't quite make out how, the change was so small but it was definitely there. Was it that the scar was suddenly showing a livid white? That the lips were even thinner? He didn't know but the anger was definitely there no matter how disguised.

'Do not try to make a fool of me, Mister King. I know you are not a stupid man, stupid enough that is to have what we want on your person but you do have it somewhere and, if you take us to it, we are prepared to pay a great deal of money for it and leave it at that. You can take the next plane back to England a very rich man. You have my word.' Giuseppe smiled. 'Or we might even invite you to join our organisation. There's a lot to be said in its favour. How would you like that?'

The Pensotti brothers both turned to Giuseppe wanting to know what he had just said and when he told them they doubled up with laughter. What a joke! Giuseppe joined in, showing what could only be described as a row of yellowish fangs, two of which were more yellow than the rest, they being the gold ones. Thornton knew that Giuseppe was the kind of man who still went to an old-fashioned barber's shop to be shaved with a cut throat razor while he talked sport. He was about to ask how he could trust these three if he gave them what they wanted? What guarantees did he have that he wouldn't end up like the late Nat Berman? But that would give the game away.

'A great many people in this world give their word, Mister... Mister...'

'Fantoccini.'

'Yes. But it is too easy and in the end their word means nothing. What guarantee do I have that you will keep yours? That is providing I am the man you believe me to be and I do have this something, whatever it is, you want.'

'Mister King, we would be more than foolish to carry you out of here in broad daylight and with so many witnesses but, believe me, you will not escape us. We will be waiting for you wherever you go. Now, will you change your mind?'

Thornton knew that time and luck had run out. No amount of denial, no amount of squirming was going to wash. He also knew that to give these men what they wanted was an impossibility. Thornton had absolutely no desire to be a martyr but he knew if he was to take on a mission as dangerous as this what the end might be for him so there was, with typical British phlegm, no point in crying over spilt milk. Cry over the pain later when it comes.

Fortunately it was at that moment a voice was heard to cry out in ringing tones across the tea room.

'Charlie! Charlie Thorpe!'

Four heads swung in unison towards the sound of the voice and Thornton saw Adrian advancing on them. He was wearing his old World War Two flying jacket and, as if to compensate for the heat, beneath it a silk floral shirt decorated with some brightly coloured flower, golden shower maybe. Hanging from a chain around his neck was a small gold phallus – erect. He arrived at the table seemingly almost breathless with excitement at seeing an old friend.

'Charlie! Fancy seeing you!' He leaned forward and gave Thornton a continental kiss. In other circumstances Thornton might have felt this was going a bit too far but in the present one he welcomed it.

'Fancy,' he said when the kiss was over.

'I didn't know you were in Milan, Charlie. What are you doing here? Who are your friends? What a surprise! Introduce me won't you?' He turned simpering to take in the three gawking gangsters who had hurriedly risen from their seats and were glowering at him as well as trying to ascertain whether anyone else in the room had seen the phenomenon that was Adrian Spangle, someone who would stand out in a sports arena holding thousands and someone a straight man would not like to be acquainted with in public.

'What did you call this man?' Giuseppe barked.

'This man?' Adrian leered at Thornton who was outwardly hardly reacting at all to this new development. 'This is my dear old friend, Charlie Thorpe.' He placed a hand on Thornton's shoulder and gave it an intimate squeeze they couldn't miss. Thornton wondered for a moment if he should place his own hand on top of Adrian's but he let it pass.

'Less of the old if you don't mind, Adrian.' Thornton smiled and shrugged as the trio turned to face him and then looked back at Adrian.

'We've known each other oh for simply ages and ages. Haven't we Charlie?'

'We certainly have, Adrian, we most certainly have, and needless to say I am positively delighted to see you here. Join us. Sit down. Have some tea. Oh, I'm sorry, I have forgotten your names or I would introduce you.'

The trio had absolutely no wish to be introduced but were still not sure of the situation.

'No no no! This man is Thornton King.' For the first time Giuseppe raised his voice.

'Thornton King? Who on earth may that be when he's at home? What nonsense. My, oh my, don't talk such rubbish. Who is this Thornton King and what on earth made you believe that? Do you think I don't know my old friend, Charlie? Many's the good times we've had together, Charlie and me. Isn't that right, Charlie dear?' He was making absolutely certain they got the name. His affectionate hand on Thornton's shoulder gave vent to another squeeze and a rub.

This was too much for the macho Italians. They had obviously made a mistake. It was simply not possible a man like Thornton King would keep company with a busone, a finnochio like this one, and what must people in the tea room be thinking seeing them with him as well? With a surreptitious nudge from Giuseppe but without a word or a backward glance they started to leave, not in a hurry but swaggering as they went, especially the two Pensottis. Maurizio paused at a table to eye the young lady sitting there and help himself to a lump of sugar which he threw up in an arc to land in his mouth before crunching it loudly between beautiful strong teeth, winking, and passing on. The man with her did nothing. He knew better, even though his girl seemed quite taken with the young thug and turned her head to watch him go. There would be a row later. Adrian was also watching them go before he sat down as Thornton shook his head and heaved a breath of relief.

'I owe you, Adrian,' he said, shaking his head, 'I really owe you.'

'Nonsense, my dear. I caught on from the start something decidedly fishy was happening here and I knew you were in trouble. Thing was though, deciding when to actually interfere. Who were those horrid men?' He glanced at their departing backs. 'And what naughtiness have you been up to? Actually that one, the younger looking one is rather a dish whoever he might be.' Adrian was once again in full flow. 'Well, come on, Thornton tell me all.'

'Can't, old chum, top secret don't you know?'

'Oh.' There was no mistaking Adrian's disappointment.

'What I can say is I obviously have to get out of Milan molto prestissimo...'

Adrian shrieked which had the three gangsters, who had been

loitering somewhat, streaking for the door.

'...and head back to Rome. Obviously can't hang about here any longer. But tell me, my dear, what are you doing in Milan?'

'Oh, Thornton, you daft Ada, don't you know what this city is?'

Thornton looked blank.

'It's the fashion capital of the world, my dear! Of the entire world! I'm here to do the most fabularosa shoot for which they are paying me simply zillions of lira. Don't ask me what that is in English money; maths was ever my weak spot so a mental conversion is out.'

Thornton knew this to be one of Adrian's acts. Adrian knew to a penny exactly what he was getting.

'And I have the most adorable dishiest thing on three legs as my first assistant. That's him, over there.' Adrian waggled his fingers towards the table he had left and Thornton turned to see a comely young man indeed who smiled and Thornton returned the smile before turning back to Adrian.'

'His name is Alexander,' Adrian whispered, 'and he's twenty-four and simply heroic in bed, Thornton. That's the only word for it, heroic. Like that other Alexander, you know, the Great? Of course his family don't know about him but then continental families I have discovered seldom do know what their offspring get up to. They keep on at him about getting married to a nice Italian girl and giving them lots of grandchildren to make a fuss of. They have bambini on their minds, these people. No wonder the world is so overcrowded. But have you seen most Italian girls once they've had their bambini? It doesn't bear thinking about. Mind you, the men aren't far behind in letting themselves go once they pass twenty, I mean twenty-five, so give my Alexander another year at least.'

'Adrian,' Thornton admonished, 'you are being unfaithful to Adrian?'

'Oh, Thornton! Alas! Tragedy there, my dear. Dante couldn't do justice to it. We have split, parted, separated, divorced. We are no more an item. Fair broke my tender heart it did. Adrian found a younger, prettier, if somewhat vapid individual by the name of Brian. He would be called Brian wouldn't he? I shall hate that name forever more, not that I particularly liked it to begin with. There's something so... so... common about it. We still occasionally see each other of course, bump into each other. Who knows? One day I might have need of his medical expertise instead of having to visit that simply horrid dingy hidden away subterranean clinic at the hospital simply reeking of shame and humiliation. You would have thought by now the British would have got used to the idea that sex is a perfectly natural phenomenon to be enjoyed whichever way it comes.' Adrian smiled at the couple sitting at an adjoining table who had been listening agog to all this and who now hurriedly looked away. Then he stood up and gave Thornton a peck on the cheek. 'Well, must get back to my Alexander before some nasty chickenhawk comes in and tries to fly away with him in its ghastly talons. Good-bye Charlie Thorpe and, when we get back to London you will simply have to tell me what all this has been about. I will hold myself in patience in the meantime.'

'You'll forget all about it the moment you're back with your... Alexander? Bye, Adrian, and once again my heartfelt thanks,' and as if to prove they really were heartfelt, Thornton placed his hand on his chest. 'You don't know what a saviour you've been today.'

'So tell me about it.'

9

Holly was far from triste when she woke up. In fact she heaved a sigh of deep satisfaction and turned over to regard the still sleeping face on the pillows beside her. In sleep he seemed to her to be even more handsome than when awake He was obviously well experienced (did it matter?) pacing himself and her as though he had all the time in the world. Well, as far as Holly was concerned he did at least have all that night and possibly a couple more nights to come if she was lucky and she wasn't going to hurry him. Now, gazing at him in the light of early morning, she wondered just who he was and if she would ever see him again if those future nights were not forthcoming. She wanted to run a finger across his lips but at the same time didn't want to wake him so, after a moment, gently eased herself from the bed and headed for the shower. Viktor opened his eyes to watch her go. If Holly thought his body beautiful, that's exactly what he felt about her. He almost heaved a sigh as he felt himself stir beneath the coverlet.

Franz Lichti had been the perfect gentleman. She had been collected as promised, wined and dined in style, wondering for a moment how a policeman's pay, even an inspector's, was sufficient to foot the bill, or did it come under expenses? and returned unmolested to the hotel where she found Viktor and a memorable night awaiting her.

*   *   *

The Countess Cinelli was deeply worried and pacing her hotel suite like a caged animal was not going to alleviate her fears. There had been no word from Thornton or the palazzo for days and Holly had disappeared. Even worse than being worried, if that were possible; she was bored stiff. Most of her acquaintances seemed to be out of town and those that were left were full of their own self-importance so consequently a dull lot and in no particular favour. In fact their company would only have increased the feeling of ennui. Also the hotel during her stay this time seemed to be suffering a dearth of male staff she would consider even remotely attractive and worth secretly cultivating for off duty activities should they show an interest and now she had the greatest desire to return to Rome, the Palazzo Cinelli and handsome, willing and able young Italians. She never thought she would miss it all quite so much. Why was she getting no answer to her calls? Had the staff all gone on strike? Walked out on her? Where was Yiorgos? She hoped the Americans were comfortable; enjoying their stay in Rome and being well looked after. Maybe she ought to go back and find out for herself. After a period of dithering and more attempts to finally contact someone, anyone now, even a crashing bore, but even the bores as well seemed to have left town, she finally made up her mind and decided to return to Rome.

One lot of twinset and pearls, corduroys, deerstalker and green wellies had invited her to spend the weekend at their country cottage in the Chilterns, Friday evening to after lunch Sunday, but the countess had experienced English country life once before and didn't feel up to repeating the experience. Until midsummer the bedrooms are cold, the bathrooms even colder, it would more than likely be pouring with rain or worse just a light annoying drizzle, the earth would be muddy, the children and even the dogs undisciplined, smelly, and barbaric with a habit of jumping up all over the place, and sometimes the smell of wet horse and manure was overpowering so she gracefully declined the invitation. "Maybe next time I'm in England," she said knowing full well that was a long time away if ever. "Yes, maybe next time," her would-be hosts said, secretly pleased there was one less to cater for and less to pack up. So, her mind finally made up, danger or no danger, she would return to Italy on the first available flight. She was a Taurian and if there was one thing she hated above all else it was silence from those she expected not to be silent. It was not as though she enjoyed small talk but even small talk was better than no talk at all. It is said that no news is good news but no news at all can also drive a person totally around the bend.

Her twenty stone London bodyguard, Mickey Flynn, known to his mates as Errol and sometimes as Mister Finn, could see her to the airport from where he would be paid off. She was beginning to dislike the man intensely, not because he gave every appearance of being a monosyllabic interspersed with the occasional grunt dullard or because, as the weather was getting warmer by the day, he tended to sweat rather a lot, but because she began to think, with the ever increasing bills for food and drink, that he was taking her for granted. Next to silence, being taken for granted was something else that got right up the countess's nostrils, that and being accused of dishonesty and mendaciousness which, considering what she had been up to since her husband's death, could hardly be taken exception to. She supposed twenty stone had to receive its daily nourishment but on the other hand perhaps it was too much nourishment that led to the twenty stone in the first place and a period of abstinence wouldn't come amiss. Whichever, the expense would no longer be on her tab. Also she realised she really knew nothing about the man and trying to elicit information was like trying to get blood from a stone. The man gave off such an air of skulduggery she wondered if the agency through which he had been hired had thought to thoroughly check his references. Even if they did they could still have been bogus. All he needed to really look the part was to wear a black eye mask, carry a jemmy and have a bag over his shoulder with swag written on it. He was definitely making her feel more and more uneasy but considering the whole situation she shrugged it off as nerves. It was time to go. She looked at the trolley which had been delivered by room service on which the food she had ordered had grown cold but, having decided there was no time to eat; she would have something at the airport or on the plane if nothing else. Even if airline food was not exactly cordon bleu it was possibly better than nothing.

Mister Flynn was patiently waiting for her outside the suite, looking as vacuous as ever. For once in her life she was travelling light so it took only one hotel porter to see her luggage down and they followed, after Mickey had taken a careful look around. The vases had already been shipped back to Rome a few days previously. She hoped the staff of the removal firm in which she had put her trust knew what they were about and her precious vases had arrived safely. They always had in the past, travelling back and forth but there is a first time for everything and insurance could never compensate for their damage or loss. She was surprised customs and excise hadn't questioned their journeys but then maybe customs and excise couldn't tell one Chinese vase from another and thought the same ones were different or different ones were the same if that makes sense. Perhaps they thought they were part of a job lot and as long as duty was paid they let them pass.

In the hotel's lift the body odour made its presence well and truly felt and she wondered if she could manage the long taxi ride to the airport without heaving. She had always suffered from motion sickness anyway and the smell would make matters much worse. As with Mrs Harden an eau de cologne drenched handkerchief came into service before they hit the ground floor. The taxi was waiting for them, her baggage was neatly stowed beside the driver's cab and Mickey, having tipped the porter and hotel doorman with money she had given him for that purpose, she wouldn't dream of doing it herself, held open the door for her before, after a last look around, clambering in himself; but the cab had hardly pulled away from the kerb when it came to a stop, the door opened and Mickey got out again, standing on the pavement and looking back with a mournful expression into the cab's interior.

'I don't wish to be personal or unkind, Mister Flynn,' the countess's fruity voice, sounding rather like an Italian version of

Dame Edith in Mister Wilde's play, could be heard emanating from inside the cab, 'but it would seem to me that you are in dire need of a hot shower or a generous dab of gentleman's cologne. You could have used the hotel's public facilities you know.'

'Not my fault,' Flynn said grumpily. 'Medical condition. Had it all my life. Nothing to be done about it. Doctors haven't a clue. Tried everything. Feet are the worst. Take off shoes and even I can't stand the whiff. Phew! Take a shower, it doesn't help. It's back in five minutes.' It was the longest speech she had ever heard him make sounding exactly like Mister Jingle.

The countess wondered why she hadn't noticed it before. Maybe she just hadn't been in close enough proximity to the twenty stones or it had always been within the five minutes après shower. 'I am sorry to hear that,' the voice continued, 'but for now please call another cab and drive behind us. Make sure you do. In the meantime we will wait for you.' She gave an imperious tap on the window separating her from the driver. He slid it open. 'Wait please, cabby,' and shut it again. With his meter ticking over the cabby looked out front and smiled, seeming quite content to wait as long as she wanted though it was hardly any time at all before another cab pulled up behind them and Mickey leaned forward to address the driver.

'Follow that cab,' he said in a loud voice, carrying sufficiently to be heard in the cab in front, at the same time pointing with one hand and opening the door with the other.

'Ere, hold on a minute,' the driver said, 'wot's this all abaht then? Follow that cab? I should coco. What's this then? Bleeding candid camera? To where exactly am I supposed to follow it?'

'Heathrow.'

'You have to be kidding, mate. I want to get home for my tea.'

This is always the excuse London taxi drivers make when, for some reason or other best known only to themselves, they don't want to pick up a fare. Most Londoners who are in the habit of taking cabs have come across this phenomenon more than once, usually at the most inconvenient of times. Thornton and Holly experienced it one night in South Ken when they wanted to be taken home to the East End; the Barbican in her case, Victoria Park in his. Thornton's reaction to the cabbie led to a nasty situation which would have come to blows if Holly hadn't stepped in to end it, much to Thornton's relief.

Errol Flynn lowered his voice to just above a whisper. 'It should be worth your while, pal. See, in that cab is a very rich lady, and I do mean rich! Royalty even, foreign royalty of course, not British, and I'm sort of looking out for her, know what I mean?'

'Yeh, looking at you looking out for her means you're saying it could be dodgy, dangerous like. So, if you don't mind, matey, find yourself another cab.'

'A pony.'

'Ow much?'

'Twenty five quid.'

'Double it.'

'Okay.'

'In advance.'

'Come of it, mate. You think I got that much on me? It's her's going to pay you, innit?'

'How do I know that? I only got your word for it.'

'Strewth, what have I got here? You're a right bolshie bastard aren't you?'

"Ere, 'ere...' the cabby sniffed, 'there's no need for that kind of talk you know. Totally uncalled for that is.'

During all that uncalled for kind of talk, which was in no way actually scripted for them, Mickey occasionally threw a glance at the first cab where he hoped every word of his would be clearly heard as indeed it was and the countess had by this time grown impatient at the delay. The evening was advancing. There was after all a plane to catch and Heathrow is a long way from central London. There was no knowing what the traffic would be like, especially around Hammersmith, always a bottleneck, before hitting the Great West Way. The offside passenger door of the first cab opened and she got out. A passing car nearly slammed the open door shut again and her with it and swerved away with cursing driver just in time. She walked back towards the second cab.

'Mister Flynn, what is the delay? What is happening here?'

'I'm sorry, countess...'

'Countess is it?' The second cabby looked suitably unimpressed. He wanted to say there was no doubt in his mind that this was some sort of con trick. He'd heard about these sorts of goings on, but perhaps thought better of it.

'...but he is refusing to take me.'

'Is that so?' She now moved closer to the second cab and addressed the driver. 'My good man,' she said in her haughtiest manner, now she really was a dead ringer for Dame Edith, 'you do know that if you are showing your for hire sign it is against the law for you to refuse a fare.' This was the same mistake Thornton had made.

For answer he turned off the sign. For a long moment the countess couldn't believe anyone could treat her this way and she stood staring at the cabby who, seemingly implacable and with both hands on the wheel, looked straight ahead as if no one was standing either side his cab but there was something inordinately fascinating beyond his windscreen. Finally she gave up and addressed Mickey who, fortunately, was standing downwind of both the cab and herself. 'Find another cab,' she ordered before returning to her own, turned to look back for a moment to say 'Quickly!' and received a deep shock when she then climbed into her own cab to find a man seated in the corner there. Having learnt her lesson about opening doors without first looking, after all this time it could have been a double decker London bus, she scanned the road for passing traffic before she got in, had already closed the door and now desperately put out a hand to reopen it but he stopped her with something in her ribs she couldn't see but immediately assumed was the barrel of a gun.

'No nonsense now, countess, and no noise please.' The almost inaudible warning was totally unnecessary. Apart from an original gasp the countess was in no fit state to make a noise of any kind. In fact she thought at any moment she would pass out from sheer terror and was about to hyperventilate or suffer a horribly undignified physical reaction as the man gave a nod to the driver who was looking in his mirror waiting for a signal and the cab pulled away.

Mickey stood on the pavement and watched it go. Then he gave the second driver a fiver, at the same time winking and putting a finger to his lips, turned and walked away towards Piccadilly Circus to mingle with the milling crowds and disappear into the night. Maybe he would make a slight detour and stop off at his friend Sammy Bloom's neon lit chrome and plastic nosh bar, most popular with the girls from the strip joint next door, for a hot salt beef on rye, like Reg Venables he was most partial to salt beef on rye, then on the other hand maybe not. He couldn't wait to get home and take a shower to get rid of the stuff he had been given to spray his pits with. God, but it was rank, whatever it was! Rue gave off the scent of roses in comparison. Over his everyday smell of stale perspiration (deodorants are for poofters) like Reg with his possible reek of whisky, he couldn't imagine anyone in the underground remaining near him which was a shame because there was bound to be at least one piece of delectable totty in a mini-skirt to touch up. But, taken all in all, one had to admit it had been a consummate piece of acting by a non-actor in a short non-scripted scene. In theatrical parlance it would most likely be called an improvisation; pseuds would probably call it a happening. Non actor maybe, that is unless you count extra work in television as a sideline when available, and he wasn't even a member of Equity. Derek Blight, the lugubrious agent who only handled walk-ons, figuratively speaking, taking ten percent of their earnings, sending them from his little office just off Leicester Square out to the various studios to earn their three pounds cash in hand for a day's work, wouldn't have worried his head unduly about something like that. What would the union do about it? Extras were the dregs, hardly human, more like props though, unlike props, they could understand, well most of them could, an order from a second assistant, inflated with his own sense of importance, who yelled at them "Stand there and try not to look stupid." Then, as an afterthought, "And for Pete's sake don't try to act. None of your Stanislavski nonsense here. Got it? Good."

The cabby looked at the note in his hand, pocketed it, raised an eyebrow, shook his head, shrugged, and waited for his next fare.

*   *   *

Holly should have known better, been more aware, on her guard. As the posters admonished during the war and as her father always used to tell her, careless talk costs lives, and she had fallen into the trap of unthinkingly, blindly trusting a man she had only just met, about whom she really knew nothing and with whom she was totally besotted. Such was his charming persuasiveness she hadn't even given it any thought and realised too late that, like a punch drunk boxer, she had dropped her guard and let certain information slip, starting with her visit to Lichti and talk about the Swiss professor's murder. This may have been the reason for her being in Switzerland but it was something she really should have known nothing about and, as he had seemed fascinated it just seemed to lead on quite naturally to more detail and now she was left metaphorically chewing her fingernails to the quick as, alone in her hotel room in a strange city and obviously never going to see him again, she fretted over what she had done. With all her training, when the moment of being put to the test came, she had failed. Fortunately as she was, like everybody else, completely ignorant as to Thornton's whereabouts, that was a bit of information she couldn't divulge, but she knew she had put the countess in mortal danger and it was now up to her to try and get her out of it, that was providing it wasn't already too late. Her con-artist fly by night beautiful lover, Holly shuddered at the memory of both his love making and his perfidiousness, had already checked out of the hotel and was more than likely already on his way to England, had probably tipped off his associates there as well. She would take the next available flight to London to try and beat them to it. She had hoped to spend a couple more leisurely days enjoying Geneva before returning to England, the office, and boring routine but that was obviously now right out of the question.

Franz Lichti looked up from the paperwork he was busy with to see Morvan standing at his door.

'Yes? What is it?' He growled and scowled. Morvan was still very much in his bad books.

'I thought you wanted to know, the friend of the professor's? The Italian countess?'

'Yes? Well what about her?'

'Her name is Cinelli.'

Lichti put down his pen and stared at his subordinate. 'How do you know?' He asked.

'I used this,' Morvan replied and tapped the side of his head.

Lichti grinned. 'For once, and about time too, but good work all the same. If this is true you've certainly redeemed yourself.'

Morvan stepped forward and laid a piece of paper on Lichti's desk. 'Her details,' he said, smiling what could only be called a self-satisfied smile, turned and left. Outside the office and out of Lichti's eye line he punched the air and nodded his head like a champion tennis player who had just played a winning ace.

Lichti picked up the piece of paper and looked at it. This required a haiku before calling the Italian police. He rolled his pen across the desk as he thought of a suitable beginning which simply refused to come. This is what was called writer's block he supposed. Never mind, sooner or later inspiration would flow. In the meantime he picked up the phone to make a call to Rome. Phone… Rome… home, there was something there maybe. And maybe the elusive Thornton King and the even more elusive Nat Berman might be found in that great city.

There was no denying Thornton after his brush with the Poinsettia brothers, as he had come to call them, though they were hardly the flower of Italian youth, was just a wee bit on the jittery side. Why in the first place did he have to hire such a recognisable car, so ostentatious? It would have been much safer to have taken a little runabout such as are owned by hundreds of thousands of people, a Fiat for example. Macho showing off, that's all it was, strutting his stuff as the saying goes, as though he needed to. After all he wasn't out to impress anybody; quite the reverse in fact so what was the point of all that horse power? He had no intention of picking up nubile hitch-hikers should any have appeared on his horizon, or given twos-up to Italian speed merchants driving less swanky vehicles, so why did he do it? Flaunting your whereabouts is simply stupid and highly dangerous; being invisible is playing it safe. Why do chameleons change colour depending upon their background and why do so many creatures in nature rely on camouflage for protection, and some species for hunting it might be added? A lesson well learned and he would know better next time, always presuming there was going to be a next time. For this reason he decided he would definitely not travel first class on the train but seat himself among the hoi-polloi. In this day and age he felt pretty certain he would not have to share his journey with aged snaggle-toothed peasantry holding live squawking chickens in baskets, salami, and gorgonzola cheese as portrayed in a Fellini film. The journey would be clean, comfortable, pleasant and, although he would make sure to keep a sharp lookout for anyone resembling a Poinsettia, uneventful. He would arrive back in Rome safe and sound, his coin in the Trevi Fountain obviously having done its duty. And so it would turn out to be.

* * *

For a long while there was silence in the cab, not taking into account the countess's heavy breathing. Her mind was racing but in circles getting absolutely nowhere. There was no way she could escape from a moving cab and she wondered what the reaction would be if she pretended to faint and fell against her captor. She was quite, as has been previously noted, a hefty woman and if the young man, for she could see he was young and she hadn't fail to notice extremely good-looking, was to try and raise her up, perhaps she could get the better of him. The young man in question seemed preoccupied at the moment as he stared out of the window. The cab was heading west along Piccadilly and would at Hyde Park Corner turn left, travelling passed the back wall of Buckingham Palace heading down Grosvenor gardens towards Victoria but then a right turn into Hobart Place heading for Belgravia and beyond that, Sloane Square and Chelsea.

There was no stopping and to try and open the door and fall out of a fairly fast moving cab would without doubt result in certain, painful and possibly dire injury. Broken bones at her age were not something to be desired and, anyway, even if she surreptitiously tried it she didn't know if the driver could automatically lock the door and hadn't already done so. She was quite sure that, despite his gazing out of the window, the young man would be on the qui vive and have enough of his wits about him to suspect immediately what she might be up to.

Her breathing had quietened down somewhat and she turned to really survey her kidnapper for the first time, what she could see of him from street lights as they went by. Realising this, he in turn faced her.

'Allow me to introduce myself, countess. My name is Viktor Radenko.'

'I might have known.'

'You might have known what exactly?'

'With that name you would have come from somewhere around Transylvania. Bandits, the lot of you. Vampires. Werewolves.'

Viktor chuckled. 'Countess, you have been watching too many movies or reading too many books. Most of us in my country are peasants admittedly but we only become bandits when we are so poor we can do nothing else.'

'Nonsense, it's in the blood. You're born to it. You are delivered out of the womb with bandit written all over you.'

'What a delicate turn of phrase you have, countess. A man must eat, must feed his family.'

'You have a family?'

'I was speaking figuratively. Now you know what we want from you and you also know we intend to get it so why not be a good girl...'

'Girl? Girl?' The Dame Edith voice was back fortissimo albeit in a higher register.

'Lady then, lady! Woman if you prefer. And tell us exactly where it is. Then we can drop you off at the nearest tube station, Sloane Square is coming up I believe. We could stop there and no more need be said. Don't be stubborn. Remember what I can do to you if you persist.'

'Remember? Remember? Remember what, may I ask? I've never met you before. What's there to remember?'

'Maybe not, but you've met my handiwork.'

'I have absolutely no idea what you're talking about.'

'Oh, I think you do. The professor ... your friend? One. Your contact in London? Two. Not a pretty sight either of them by the time I had finished. That's the sort of result stubbornness can bring and I would hate to see it happen to you. The next station I believe is South Kensington. Pity it's slightly out of our way or we could have dropped you off there. We could still manage a slight detour if you change your mind.'

The countess turned to look out the window.

'Ah, well,' Viktor sighed, 'on your head be it.' And he turned away once more to look out of his.

Thornton had introduced himself at the Pension Crispi where his landlady, Elvira Mazzoni, who claimed that her deceased husband, with absolutely nothing to back her up except for the name, was a direct descendent of that famous politician, turned out to be a jolly lady who seemed to laugh almost continuously as though life was one big everlasting joke which quite obviously for her it wasn't. Her only son, Alfredo, whose ambition of being an opera singer was thwarted by the fact that not only did he have no voice; he was, like Thornton, also slightly tone deaf so that he sang just above or just below the note, never ever on it. In consequence of this frustrated ambition he was a ne'er do well in his early forties who spent most of his day either playing old seventy eight records featuring early tenore Italiani on an ancient wind-up machine with a horn; singers such as Caruso of course, Tito Schipa and Francesco Tamagra, or imbibing and playing cards in a nearby café, refused point blank to leave the comfort of his ancestral home, and was the constant bane of his long suffering mother's life and a drain on her meagre resources. It did give her something to moan about, in between the laughter, and she immediately informed Thornton how hard she was put upon, making quite a meal of it as she led him to his room. If she were not a widow who had to make her own way, she informed him, she would close the pension, sell up and go and stay with her sister in the country and what would that idle son of hers do then? Probably follow her, but her brother in law, Enrico, was a rough, tough, down to earth farmer who stood no nonsense and he would soon knock Alfredo into shape or send him packing. Thornton wondered, as Signora Mazzoni opened a door and indicated this was where he would be staying, if she ever stopped for a second to draw breath. Having shown him to his accommodation she gave no indication of leaving as she moved about the room pointing out the obvious.

The furniture was ancient, large, dark and Victorian ornate. There was a matrimonial big enough to accommodate two couples simultaneously let alone one. It was covered with a beautiful blanket of hand knitted wool squares in different colours and boasted a tall intricately carved headboard. There was an enormous wardrobe, empty except for a couple of dozen tortured wire coat hangers revealed as she opened the door, and an assortment of chairs, Mod cons the room had not. For ablutions it was still a stained slightly chipped around the edge marble topped washstand complete with basin, ewer, and soap dish, all very pretty with their decoration of flowers. A towel rail on either side complete with towels and on the shelf below a white enamel bucket with a lid, part of the enamel missing so, as far as personal hygiene went, what more could any pernickety person want? Presumably the good lady provided hot water as and when required.

There was a window of many panes, the corner panes being of stained glass, red and Bristol blue throwing different lights onto a rather threadbare patterned carpet. A large crucifix looking none too safe was suspended by a nail on the wall above the bed and Thornton wondered if it had ever fallen and given the sleeper below a rousing headache. A number of religious paintings including a bleeding heart adorned the other walls together with a large framed photograph of the Mazzoni family of about seventy years previous all very solemn, a couple even surly, as they faced the camera. A quite large plaster Madonna in her requisite blue robe stood in one corner, her halo an electrical circuit holding a number of small torch bulbs so that she could glow in the dark, perhaps so you could see her while saying your prayers. Thornton wondered if they were intermittent like those on a Christmas tree and why Mediterranean people on the whole went in for so much kitsch.

During this expedition of discovery, rediscovery on Elvira's part, the good lady crossed herself a number of times, particularly as she pointed out, quite unnecessarily, the religious items and, together with the laughter and the moaning Thornton wasn't quite certain this wouldn't get on his nerves but, having approved of his room (what else could he do? It would not be for long and he had become more or less resigned to sleeping in strange beds) he deposited his valise and headed out to catch a cab to take him to the Palazzo Cinelli.

*   *   *

There was really no point in Holly fretting more than she had been and, finally realising this, she had more or less pulled herself together by the time Lichti, after a phone call and at her request, met her at the airport as she waited for her plane. They sat down to take coffee together although this was probably the last thing Holly actually wanted to do, but it was better than a bench surrounded by noisy travellers, or pacing about. She had done enough of that whilst waiting for him to arrive.

'Well, Miss Day,' he said, placing two cups on the table between them and ripping open one of his little paper sachets of sugar, 'what may this be all about?' He sounded a bit offhand but it was only because that damned haiku hadn't yet come to mind and it was still worrying him.

'I think I may have a clue as to who your murderer is, or perhaps a part of it.'

'A part of it? A part of what? You talk in riddles.' That could be his first five syllables.

'Part of a gang.'

'A gang? A gang of what?' Four syllables more.

'A gang of gangsters for goodness sake, what else? You're not paying attention, Inspecteur.'

'Sorry, sorry.' Last four syllables. Got it! "You talk in riddles, a gang of what, sorry sorry". Hmn, thirteen syllables but it doesn't really make any sense and it needs four more syllables. Haiku don't necessarily have to make obvious sense but at least there ought to be some sort of poesy, some cohesion. He would have to think again. The "you talk in riddles" with two added syllables would be a good start but... the rest was too clumsy, didn't fit at all. He realised he was being spoken to. 'I beg your pardon, what did you say?'

'I said, do you know a man by the name of Viktor Radenko?'

'Can't say that I do offhand. Why?'

'Because I believe he is either your killer or he can lead you to him, them, whoever they are.'

'And what makes you think that?'

'I'm afraid I can't really go into details but I feel pretty sure he's your man.'

'As he was yours?'

Holly actually felt herself blushing.

'How did you know?' It came out in a whisper.

'Geneva is a big city but it is my patch, isn't that what the English police call it? And I keep tabs on as much of it as I can. You have been... rather, I believed you are hiding something from me, Miss Day, a vital piece of information that could lead me to this gang of gangsters you're so sure about and so I had you watched. You spend some time with a certain gentleman; presumably your... what did you say his name was?'

'Viktor...Viktor Radenko.'

'What? I didn't catch that. Airports are such noisy places are they not?'

'Viktor Radenko.'

'Hmn hmn. And how did you meet this Viktor Radenko?' He took his pen from his jacket pocket and scribbled the name on a paper napkin, folded it up small and put both pen and paper back in his pocket.

'He travelled on the same plane as me... I... coming here, and he was also booked into the same hotel.' She looked at her watch. Time was passing. Lichti seemed unperturbed. He wasn't the one catching a plane.

'Coincidence would you say?'

'No. In hindsight obviously not. It was a plant, of that I'm certain. Why would he disappear so suddenly and without a word? You would have thought after all that happened at least a good-bye and thank you it was good while it lasted was in order.'

'He obviously wasn't a very good buy. Sorry. Didn't somebody say one day that puns are the lowest form of wit? So I have to presume he wanted certain information from you just as I did.'

'Yes.'

'And did he get more than I got?'

There was a long silence as Holly sucked on her upper lip before heaving a deep sigh.

'In part.'

'Enough to put this friend of yours who you are protecting in some considerable danger which is why you have decided now to talk to me but you still won't tell me who it is or why. So come on, Miss Day, if you really want to help, which is why you came to Geneva in the first place, let me have the rest of it.'

'Yes. Not all of it I'm afraid; but some of it.'

*   *   *

Reg Venables was in his usual state of grouchy despondency and silently wishing his life away. Could retirement not come quick enough? Police work just wasn't the same as it used to be in the good old days when he was a young copper on the beat, when fingering a collar meant the criminal faced a proper charge and proper punishment, when prison meant being well and truly banged up, the grub was piss-poor, almost inedible, (what there was of it) and the police were there to catch burglars, protect the innocent, and help old ladies across the street and there was definitely a great deal of job satisfaction. Nowadays it was all bloody pen-pushing; never had there been so many wretched forms to fill in, enough to give a person writer's cramp. Now it was all give them a slap on the wrist time, lawyers and barristers making small fortunes and judges and magistrates saying please do not be a naughty boy again or else, and bleeding hearts telling him the buggers were merely misunderstood and should be treated with understanding and kind consideration. It would seem a truism that prison never did a blind bit of good in putting a villain on the straight and narrow but at least it kept them out of society for a while and in no position to go about indulging in their nefarious practices. That's the way he looked at it anyway. The quality of recruits had gone down as well, exemplified in his opinion by constable Roper who, after a perfunctory knock, came waltzing in, a piece of paper in his hand. How could he possibly be the daddy of twins? He didn't look a day over sixteen or was that simply because Reg was getting old? And he was far too pretty to be a boy let alone a policeman. Anyway, these days, and this was another gripe, both father and motherhood seem be getting earlier and earlier. He knew for a fact his own brats, if they were not careful would sooner or later produce a sprog or two. Rita might enjoy being a grandmother, women are like that, the old maternal instinct he supposed, but he didn't feel in the mood to be a grandfather that was for sure. How old was Juliet when she fell for that Romeo person? Thirteen was it? Still things were different in them there days of the dark ages. People didn't know any better.

'Message for you, sir.'

Reg frowned. 'Oh? Who from this time?'

Roper looked down at the paper as though he hadn't already perused it quite thoroughly. 'Inspector Lichti, (he pronounced it Likti) Geneva, Switzerland.'

'I know where Geneva is, lad. I didn't think it was in darkest Africa or over the long wall of China in the distant Orient. Well, come on then, hand it over.'

Roper stepped forward and handed Venables the paper. Then he stayed where he was.

'There was something else?'

'No.'

Then what are you standing there for looking like a spare part?'

'Might have been something else from you.'

'Well there isn't so off you go, there's a good lad.'

'Right,' and Roper turned to leave.

'By the way, how are the twins?'

'Doing very nicely thank you.'

'Good. Give your missus my best regards then.'

'Will do, sir. She's expecting again we think.' And Roper disappeared.

Expecting again? Reg shook his head in disbelief. They must go at it like rabbits he thought. Good old Roper, young Roper rather. He opened a spectacle case, its blue cotton covering well worn around the edges and put on his old fashioned National Health Service rimless glasses he should have changed years ago but never got around to it. He only wore these when he thought there was no one around to notice, although of course the whole station knew about them and there was even some graffiti in the toilets meant to be a likeness of Reg in his glasses. He started to read the message. After a quick see through he shook his head and, removing the specs in case anyone should inadvertently come in, laid the paper down on the desk. 'Well, I'll be blowed,' he said out loud and repeated it for emphasis. 'Well I'll be blowed.' Evidently that young gadabout, Miss Holly Day had been consorting, if that was the right word for it, with the Swiss police and interfering in a murder enquiry, what was more his murder enquiry, at least on this side of the channel it was his murder enquiry. Just how had she become involved? he wondered. She had evidently given this Swiss chappie a suspect, a name and full description. Here it was, right in front of him. It was possible the person concerned could currently be in England and this Swiss chappie thought it a good idea for him, Reg Venables to get on his tail, if possible. This evidently was at Holly's suggestion. Reg made a mental note to thank her for that. Life might be looking up after all. Well of course it was possible. First thing to do was contact immigration and find out if a Viktor Radenko had indeed entered the country, presumably from Switzerland, then find out where he was shacking up, if that was possible. Wouldn't be surprised mind you if he was travelling on a false passport but, if not, put out a full alert. He would get onto it straight away and maybe the papers would at last have reason to write something glowing about him. It was a pity he had ignored Thornton when he tried to involve him in rounding up the Bowmen of Essex at that club of theirs. Wasn't that what those la-di-dah villains were called? It's not just low life who dabble in crime you know, or have distinct criminal tendencies. It was the South End lot who got all the praise for nabbing that little lot of high grade toffs. In the papers for weeks they were, months even because they were mentioned again when it came to the trial. Reg sighed. He desperately wanted a last moment in the limelight before the final curtain, another fifteen minutes of fame. It seemed such a long time since the Spitskaya affair; all those beautiful girls and each one a killer. There you are, just goes to show, no one is above suspicion.

10

The Countess Paullina Cinelli had never in her life been so manhandled, that is handled by a man unless she specifically asked for it, and her fury knew no bounds. She had been bundled out of the taxi by her kidnapper on one side and the driver on the other, down some slippery area steps where she nearly did her back in as a foot slid from beneath her and she felt the spasm in the lumbar region. She was in for a painful bout of lumbago in consequence and she knew it. Thrust unceremoniously into a dark basement room with bars on the window, a window she noticed that hadn't been cleaned in many a long year, and a single light bulb (25 watt by the looks of it) hanging by ancient entwined brown flex from the ceiling. There was a small Formica topped table grimier than she cared to think about, a couple of rickety bentwood chairs and, in one corner a low divan, not looking too healthy either. A solid door obviously led into the rest of the house. Having paced a while she decided she needed to sit down

and chose what seemed to be the cleaner of the two chairs. She put
her elbows on the table and immediately withdrew them before
they either slid away on grease or got permanently stuck in muck.
What was this place they had brought her to? More important,
how could she engineer her escape or seek help? Would breaking
a pane in the window achieve anything? What could she break it
with? The heel of her shoe. Too soft. She could rap on the pane
and call for help from a passer-by but, knowing the way things
had gone, a passer-by would more than likely simply not wish
to be involved even if they chanced to look down and find out
where the noise had come from. Good Samaritans were few and
far between in this modern world. It was snouts to the tough,
keep out of trouble, and every man for himself. Oh, why did
Holly have to disappear just when she needed her most? Not
that Holly in current circumstances could have actually helped
but she could have done earlier and the countess unfairly and
illogically resented her friend's neglect.

Holly's flight was delayed. Why is there inevitably a delay
when you are in a tearing hurry to get somewhere? What was the
cause this time? It couldn't be the weather. The skies couldn't be
clearer. Well, from where she was standing the skies couldn't look
clearer. She didn't know how they looked across the channel and
over the British Isles. Could be ghastly weather there. Usually is.
Pilot a little under the weather maybe? Pilot delayed reaching the
airport? Mechanical failure possibly and there wasn't a mechanic
around to fix it? Maybe the French Air Traffic Controllers were on
a go-slow again. They seemed to be in the habit of doing that, or
was she thinking of the British? Incoming flights arriving late and
upsetting schedules? Maybe there was just too much traffic, the
skies cluttered with aircraft, like a motorway on a Bank Holiday

weekend. All very well hearing apologies for the delay, she fretted, but that didn't get her off the ground and on her way. Holly hated flying at the best of times. She thought it an utterly boring, in fact a tedious, way to travel especially if there were annoying fellow travellers on board like the seat kicking infant and, in her current state of anxiety, she couldn't even settle down with a good book to pass the time while waiting, or drink yet another cup of coffee. Her bladder was pretty full as it was and another cup would be simply asking for trouble. She would need to go to the loo just as her flight was being called or the plane for some inexplicable reason would sit on the tarmac for what seemed an eternity and she wouldn't be able to use the toilet, or the minute the plane took off and safety belts were released half the passengers would rush to the toilets before her and she would be left hopping from one leg to the other as she took her place in the queue. She was in such as state she didn't even feel like a visit to the duty free to stock up her booze cupboard if nothing else. She heaved a sigh and looked again at the nearest airport clock, checking it with her watch. No, hurtling through the skies in a metal tube was not her idea of luxury travel.

She wished she was clairvoyant so that she might know what was happening in London, four hundred and sixty five flight miles away. She mentally pictured the hotel suite where she hoped the countess was still ensconced, safe and sound; and where on earth, that's presuming he was still on earth, could Thornton have got to? Just as the abducted and fearful countess had recently felt about her, Holly knew it was ridiculous and unfair to blame Thornton for her current predicament but the fact was she wouldn't have travelled to Switzerland in the first place if, when the word murder was first mentioned, she hadn't immediately had visions of him lying on that mortuary slab and been so worried about him; was still worried about him if it came to that. She was desperately hoping he was all right wherever he might be though, if he were lying on that slab there wouldn't be any more point in worrying about him, would there? But life without Thornton around just wouldn't be the same, even with his funny and often irritating little ways. He really should never have tried to turn himself into a private eye. He just wasn't cut out for it. But then what was he cut out for? Holly couldn't imagine. It seemed the obvious thing to do to begin with when he was made redundant. Given a nine to five existence he would probably just give up and die. But then a person had to earn a living. Maybe he could be something in journalism or travel, yes, far distant places keeping him occupied, that would suit. She could never imagine how he managed to get recruited into Her Maj's secret service in the first place. He wasn't public school, he wasn't Cambridge. That Mike Ayliff now, he was a completely different character. With his background she could understand his recruitment and favour with the establishment even though he turned out to be a snake in the grass, a fly in the ointment, a possum in the wood pile, a real bad egg or a rotten apple in the barrel, whatever, you name it. Holly loved these old clichés. Why did nobody ever mention bad onion or bad tomato? The smell of a bad onion was enough to turn one's stomach and she had once as a child bitten into a bad tomato and the experience was never to be forgotten. In fact it put her off tomatoes for life.

But her mind was wandering. Yes, Mike Ayliff she could understand, he came to a sticky end, deservedly in her opinion, but Thornton? Holly shook her head as she looked around the airport lounge for signs of anything suspicious. With the delays the airport was growing more and more crowded which, if there was any danger, was possibly a good thing as far as she was concerned. She noted the gendarmes strolling about the place and surveyed her fellow travellers with a jaundiced eye. There was no one she could see who was remotely attractive. In fact they looked a regular rag tag and bobtail section of the human race, not a single attractive person among them. Maybe that was just because of the way she was feeling. Maybe it was because of the way they were all feeling; all weary, frustrated and tense. She felt sorry for those who had connections to make and who might possibly miss them. Anyway, why on earth was she looking out for something attractive? She'd made one screw-up on the outward journey (no pun intended) she had no intention of making another on the way home.

Lichti, having said his au revoirs and bon voyages, had long since left her and gone back to his office to set wheels in motion starting with that phone call to Rome and making contact with Inspector Venables in London. Maybe he would soon be able to rid himself of this tiresome and baffling case and maybe he would at last be able to compose this elusive haiku.

Holly's flight was called at last. She could hardly believe it and, as she set off for the gate, she felt a sudden desperate need to pee. Sod's law – it was bound to happen.

*   *   *

Thornton had pulled twice on the ancient bell in its brass surround and then, hearing nothing and there being no response after a quite lengthy wait, he hammered on the door of the Palazzo Cinelli with the side of his fist. Feeling highly vulnerable he took a furtive look around. It was quite possible if he were not admitted soon he could be abducted right there in the street in broad daylight, figuratively speaking as it was already dusk and he wasn't going to stand there till the light disappeared completely, that was for sure.

None of the passers by when questioned later by the police would have seen a thing. Surely the Poinsettias or whoever gave the orders would have lookouts stationed around just waiting for his return to this particular area of Rome, to this particular street, to this particular building? Any moment he expected to hear a screeching of tyres as a sedan burning rubber came hurtling around the corner, mean looking men in natty suits leaping out, grabbing and bustling him into the back seat of the car which would then speed off with another squeal of tyres, and nobody would see, hear, or smell a thing. Thornton too had watched more Hollywood movies than was good for him and was vividly anticipating this little scenario when a rather burly liveried footman opened the door, recognised him and, face expressionless, stood aside to let him pass, closing the door after them, having first given the street a quick survey. Thornton hadn't noticed this or he would no doubt have wondered why. And, if he had noticed it, he would no doubt think maybe it was a habit, something servants always did merely out of curiosity.

Once again he was struck by how cool and quiet the Palazzo Cinelli was, almost tomblike was his morbid thought. Even quiet places like libraries and churches are not completely silent. There is always some sound, a little noise, a discreet cough, the rustle of paper, a whispering, an echo, but here the silence seemed complete. Could it be the thickness of the walls and all that marble that kept the city's noise and high summer temperatures at bay? Probably cost a small fortune in heating during the winter though.

'Where's George?' He enquired of the footman, his voice echoing in the empty vaulted hall and sounding much too loud as it broke that silence.

The man, not understanding exactly, or pretending not to understand, gave a shrug but pointed up the stairs so presumably, Thornton thought, he might as well wait in the salon until the Greek or the Squirrel put in an appearance; that was if the latter was still in residence and hadn't packed up and left in a hurry for the states. The footman watched him all the way until he turned and shuffled off alongside the staircase eventually to disappear through a pass door and descend to the nether regions.

Thornton didn't have long to wait and it was Louise Anna who appeared first looking as svelte and inviting as ever in what could only be described as a shantung sheath of scintillating colours and waltzing in giving every impression of being not only delighted to see him but, for a woman who had recently lost her third husband, seemingly without a care in the world.

'Thornton! Darling!' She trilled. 'You're back!' There's nothing like stating the obvious when not knowing quite what to say.

'As you see.' His attitude was cold although she had closed in to within kissing range and obviously expected that to be the next step in the reunion but, as he gave no indication of responding to her sweetly scented proximity, she backed off, cocking her head to one side and gazing at him quizzically.

'Aren't you pleased to see your little Squirrel then?'

'Where is Yiorgos?' He asked, repressing a shudder and trying very hard to look like a man with an iron will not to be taken in by any hint of seductiveness by this siren, this Delilah, this Jezebel.

'The last I saw of him he was chatting on the phone.' She wandered over to a chair. 'That man is always on the phone. I think it's his way of getting out of the house because he hardly ever seems to go anywhere.' She was carrying a different pocketbook this time. Quite large with a shoulder strap and it looked as if it might be made of sealskin. It's amazing how many animals have their lives brutally shortened by the dictates of fashion. She had seated herself, legs crossed, and opened the bag to take out a stick of gum. Thornton almost snarled.

'Do you have to do that?'

'Do what, darling?'

'Chew gum. It's a habit almost as disgusting as smoking. I hate it.'

'Too bad, hun. You're not doing the chewing, and you're such a goody two shoes I don't think. You have no bad habits of course.' She put out her tongue and slid it back into her mouth complete with gum.

Thornton turned his back on her and moved over to one of the casements.

'The pavements of every city...' He gestured towards the world outside and it was almost as if he were seeing the pavements of Rome from where he stood... 'are littered with cigarette butts, cigarette packs, and old chewing gum that sticks to your shoes and is almost impossible to get rid of. That is, gum that hasn't been surreptitiously removed from the offending mouth and pressed under a cinema seat, chair or beneath a restaurant table top.' He turned his head to see how she was reacting to his lecture then looked out the window again. 'I believe in Singapore,' he continued while she continued to chew her gum, 'or some place like that you can be immediately arrested and thrown into jail for littering the street with chewing gum, or anything else for that matter, and a jolly good show too. I heartily agree with it.' He really had mounted his soapbox but one of the reasons for it was his feeling that something in the palazzo was terribly wrong. Nothing he could put a finger on at that moment, just a gut reaction.

'Honey, did you come all the way back to Rome to lecture me on chewing gum? Why is her Thornton being so nasty to poe l'il old me?'

That did it. Thornton closed his eyes and almost swayed on his feet. It was something else he couldn't stand at any price, the poor sweet little girl act. From a grown woman it bordered on the obscene. That deep southern accent was no longer alluring. He was fast going off the Squirrel. He was fast going off the palazzo. He would like to get the hell out of there but he needed to see the Greek, he needed to find out how the countess was. He presumed she was still in London, if not exactly swanning about, at least body and soul being kept safely together. He needed more than anything right at this moment to talk to Holly. He pictured her now. "I do not have any leave pending nor can I take time off from the department." He was strictly on his own.

'How was l'il ole Geneva anyways, hun? Did you get your rocks off with some cute l'il ole yodelling goat herding Swiss maiden or were you still incapable?' She waggled her pinkie in the air and then let it droop.

Thornton couldn't think of a put-down in answer to this and at that moment Yiorgos made a, for him, breezy entrance.

'Mister King. So sorry not to have greeted you earlier but the phone call was urgent. How are you? How was your trip? Have you a result?'

Thornton had turned at the first sound of Yiorgos's voice and now stood staring at the man, his humiliation forgotten for the moment but his feeling of unease increasing by the minute.

'Which question do you want answered first?'

The smile disappeared from Yiorgos; face. 'Whichever one you choose, Mister King.'

'All right then, the first one, I'm fine thank you, and thank you for asking.'

There was a silence. Thornton for the first time actually smiled at Louise Anna who did not smile back and the chewing gum seemed to have come to a full stop somewhere in her left cheek. He hoped it would stay there. That masticating jaw was not a pretty sight. Chewing the cud came to mind.

'The second question, Mister King.'

Thornton turned back to Yiorgos. The voice was quiet but there was nothing polite in the way the question had been put and the man's expression was stony.

The squirrel had got up from her chair and wandered off to indulge in another fantasy moment in front of her favourite Cinelli bust. She had discovered his name was Enrico and he died before the United States was even thought of and the state of Virginia was in its infancy. He was killed in a duel with a jealous lover, so the story went, though nobody really knew whether the jealousy was for him or for her as Enrico evidently played both ends of the field so it could just as well have been either. The wound was not fatal in itself, quite superficial in fact, a mere scratch, and the opponent had been held off before he could inflict a second one, honour according to the seconds supposedly having been satisfied, but unfortunately septicaemia set in and that for poor Enrico was that.

'My trip was fairly eventful, a bit hair raising at times, but that was to be expected was it not? Did you not expect it to be eventful? When we've got an hour or so to spare I'll tell you all about it and, before you ask again, the reply to the third question is yes the result is in the affirmative.' Thornton frowned, wondering why he had put it like that instead of coming straight out with the word "successful."

Louise cast a sly glance back at the two men to see Yiorgos was holding out his hand, palm uppermost. 'You have it with you?' The stony face had now given way to one of eager anticipation soon to crumble with disappointment.

Thornton noted with some satisfaction that the object of seemingly universal desire was referred to as "it". He might be mistaken of course but did this mean that George had no idea what the container was and, if that were the case, maybe no one else knew either, which gave Thornton a distinct advantage as they wouldn't know what they were looking for. It could have been a packet, a bag, a box, a tin, a valise, an old sock, anything. Who in the world would have imagined a decorated egg-timer? He shook his head.

'Of course not. You don't carry something as valuable as that around in a city like Rome, any city come to that. Pickpockets are a pretty common phenomenon, thick on the ground as it were. It is quite safe and will remain so until I am in a position to hand it over to the countess. I take it she is still in London?' Thornton was feeling smug.

'It would be much safer if you brought it here and gave it to me.' Louise had left her favourite long dead Cinelli ancestor and moved back to join those men who were still alive. Her smile did not reassure Thornton.

'I take it you know what it is,' he said.

'Of course.'

'Describe it to me.'

Louise opened her mouth but nothing came out and Yiorgos quickly stepped in.

'Enough of this. I am sure Mister King will look after it, guard it with his life I might say.' Yiorgos laughed but neither the sound of his laughter or the look on his face gave any reassurance. 'If you will excuse me for one moment, I have a phone call to make. Louise, look after Mister King for me.' He turned and walked out of the room.

What did that mean? Thornton thought. Look after. Look after had too many connotations, not all of them good.

'See what I mean?' she said, 'on the phone again and it's always a very important call.'

Thornton had the distinct feeling that this particular phone call *would* be important and was ready to make his excuses and leave, but then he remembered he still hadn't had any actual news of his employer.

'Tell me, do you know anything about the countess?'

'How do you mean, hun?'

'The status quo.'

'Status who?'

'How she is right at this very moment in time as you Americans might say.'

Louise Anna gave a little shrug and went back to her chair. She had started chewing again.

'Well, has George heard from her at all?'

Again the shrug and an even more vigorous use of the mouth.

'Right. Well I'll be on my way then.'

'What's the big hurry, Mac? You only just gotten here and I'm sure George will be able to fill you in when he gets back from his phone call. I've missed you, honey.' She got to her feet again. 'What say we slip away upstairs and take another long long look at that ceiling?'

'Somehow I don't think that's too good an idea, Louise. In fact, if you want my honest opinion, I think it's a lousy idea, Louise.'

'How come, hun?'

'Because you will remember what happened last time. You have, after all, just reminded me of it.' He waggled his pinkie in the air and let it droop.

'Oh, shucks, Thorn, happens to everyone sometime or other. Not all the time though thank the Lord. That's past tense, so come on, how about it?'

'Tense is right, little lady, and not past. Tense is like right now. So good-bye, Louise.'

'No!'

Thornton, turning away and making for the door, stopped dead in his tracks. Gone was the little girl voice, gone was the sultry seducer voice, gone was any trace of southern fried and grits, gone even was the usual nasal twang. In their place was a voice that literally did send a shiver up his spine and turn his groin into an icebox and when he looked back, sure as God made little apples as his dear mother would say, there she was, pointing her snub nose at him.

*   *   *

Because it was so damp, the basement room was beginning to feel decidedly chilly and the countess was not dressed for and

215

was not used to low temperatures. She took another look at the bed but decided, even if there were a blanket on it, it would most definitely not be advisable to wrap herself in it. The very thought created a quite violent shudder on top of the shivering. She glared at the grimy window, barred on the outside, as though her eyes like lasers could zap those bars and of course both doors would be locked and she was no expert at lock picking so the situation was pretty hopeless. A lady who has spent her whole life, well most of it, in the lap of luxury, waited on hand and foot, could hardly be expected to have at her fingertips the expertise to release herself from the current predicament. The Countess Cinelli did not, as was currently supposed, come from a long line of Italian aristocrats but in fact was Sicilian by birth who was discovered by Francesco Sebastian Sebastian when visiting the estate of relatives on that island for the purpose of hunting and whose dark beauty and flashing eyes won him heart and soul so one might say his hunting was successful. The idea that the countess had Spanish antecedents of noble blood she put about herself and nobody ever thought to question it.

She looked once more around the virtually empty room. What was she hoping for? A means of escape that would magically materialise? She had been deprived of her handbag, not that anything in it would have proved any use. She didn't carry a mace or pepper spray or lethal weapon of any sort and, even if she did, she had no doubt her handbag would have been emptied and its contents gone through for anything even slightly suspicious. She had no idea what had happened to her luggage. Was it possible that taxi driver had driven away with it, and if so where to? Neither had she any inkling of what the immediate future held for her. It was no use trying to keep unwanted thoughts away, frightening though they were. She was in serious trouble and she was well aware of it. She wasn't quite sure she even knew where she was except that it was somewhere in Chelsea. Old Father Thames must be flowing along close by and that again was not a thought to dwell on. This was all Thornton King's fault of course. How on earth could Holly have let her down so badly by recommending the man? If he had done the job she was paying him to do she would by now be safely back in the palazzo, the whole business finished and done with. Instead of which...

She was about to meditate on the possible fate of her jewellery when she heard a key turn in the inner door and it was pushed open to reveal a man bearing a tray which he placed on the table and prepared to leave without so much as a glance in her direction. Although she had for the most part only really seen the back of his head in the cab she had some time to study it and she now felt sure this was the taxi driver.

'My man!'

He stopped, turned, his face expressionless. He was a brute; she had no doubt about that. "I can see", she said to herself, "from your course features, your obviously greasy hair going a little grey at the sides, your small piggy eyes and the dark blue of your five o'clock shadow that you are an incipient murderer if not one already guilty of such heinous crimes."

'My good man...' she said aloud, though of course he was obviously not good at all but she had put on her haughtiest tone in addressing him... 'in heaven's name, what is that... thing?'

She was pointing at the tray.

'What thing might that be, your ladyship?'

'That thing ... there ... on the tray.'

'That your ladyship is a traditional English pork pie. Delicious it is. Take my word for it. You're not Jewish by any chance are you?'

'No.'

'Or Muslim?'

'No.'

'Then I'll wish you bon appetit of it as they say in France and good night.' He moved for the door.

'Wait!' She almost screamed. He stopped, turned back.

'If I were to consider it, eating it I mean... how would I go about... eating it?'

'With your mouth of course. How else?'

'Don't be ridiculous. I mean, how do I get it to my mouth?'

'With your hand of course, how else?'

'You are refusing to get my meaning.' She tapped the top of the pie with flat fingers and a look of absolute revulsion spread across her face. 'It's cold!'

'Well of course it's cold. That's the way English pork pies are eaten. And, oh yes, I do get your meaning but knife and fork you cannot have because you could do a lot of damage with knives and forks, even plastic ones. So if you're hungry, my lady, use your fingers.' Once again he turned for the door. Once again he was ordered to stop.

'Wait!'

With a sigh he turned around, his voice almost resigned. 'What is it now?'

'If I am to make an attempt at eating this revolting piece of English indigestible looking cooking, what do I wash it down with?'

He thought about this for as moment. 'Yes,' he said. 'I'll fetch you a nice drop of Adam's ale.'

Not knowing what Adam's ale was the countess thanked him and then came a further 'Wait!'

He waited.

'If I am to eat this... this...' she waved a hand over the pork pie... 'breaking it up with my fingers as you suggest, how would I wipe my hands?'

He was beginning to get rattled.

'Lady, this ain't a picnic you're on, you know. And you're not staying at the Ritz neither so get it into your head that you are in grave danger of being in a position where greasy fingers ain't going to matter all that much but, as you're so bloody finicky, here.' And he took a grimy by the look of it much used handkerchief out of his pocket and slapped it down on the table. It was all the countess could do not to hawk which made her think of something else.

'I fully realise the predicament I'm in...'

'Predicament? Is that what you call it? Is that what Marie Antoinette might have said in the Bastille? As she mounted the scaffold and saw the guillotine did she turn to the mob and say, "I realise what a predicament I'm in?"' The man laughed, a very unpleasant sound.

'But I have a further question to put to you.'

'Oh, yes? And what might that be, your ladyship?'

'Supposing I want to... need to... do things ...'

'Like what do you suppose? Like what will you need to do? Oh, yeah, of course. Hadn't thought of that. Tell you what, when I bring you your Adam's ale I'll bring a chinky as well, or something in lieu of, whatever I can find, then you can take it in and let it out all at the same time, can't you?' And with another roar of laughter he finally left. The man's attitude was intolerable and the countess lost her cool. She picked up the pork pie and hurled it at his retreating back but he was already halfway through the door which got in the way and, if it hadn't been before, the pork pie was now definitely inedible.

*   *   *

'So…' Which, in the circumstances, was all Thornton could think of to say.

'So?'

'What happens now?'

'We wait.'

'For Armageddon?'

'Arm a what?'

'Skip it.'

'Take a seat, Thornton. Be comfortable.'

'That, my dear, is the last thing I'm likely to be. I might take a chair.' He rested his hands on the nearest available chair back. 'But what I would like more than anything else is to be filled in with exactly what the situation is. I have got more of the picture but there are still a few pieces of the puzzle to fill in.'

'You do talk a load of shit, Thornton you really do.'

'What I immediately want to know is, if I make a bolt for the door, are you going to pull the trigger? Oh, having seen your handiwork, I am under no illusion about your willingness and ability to do it but if you pull the trigger and I'm as dead as your late hubby what is Yiorgos going to say when he returns and realises he can't lay his itchy fingers on the little treasure trove everyone is so keen on getting their hands on because the secret has died with me?'

Louise Anna had never heard anyone rabbit on quite like

220

this and seemed to be standing there totally mesmerised by it or, at least, so Thornton thought because, with one hand he lifted the fortunately fairly lightweight chair off the floor and threw it at her, underarm, bowling fashion. Four leg ends hit her square amidships and she staggered back completely off balance. Fortunately the safety catch was still on and the gun didn't go off. Thornton didn't wait for her to regain her balance or take off the safety but headed swiftly for the door only to be brought up short by a burly footman standing there, obviously with orders not to let him pass. He shrugged and, as if resigned to it, turned back, taking the footman off guard so that when he lunged forward again the man went arse over tip on the marble floor cracking his head with a very nasty sound. He didn't get up but Thornton did only to find it wasn't Louise's gun that threatened him but that in the hand of Yiorgos who used it to indicate Thornton should step back into the salon, which he did with a sigh but no further argument.

*   *   *

The countess was beginning to wish she had eaten earlier at the hotel when it had been ordered and was available and even that she hadn't been so rash as to destroy the heavyweight traditional English pork pie, particularly as the gesture hadn't done any good or relieved her feelings and as hunger pangs began to gnaw but, ravenous though she was, she was hardly likely to pick up any pieces of meat and leadlike pastry off that disgusting floor. Who knows what else would be picked up at the same time? The man had not returned with her Adam's ale or the promised chinky and some time had gone by, but she thought the stress must have closed her up like a clam because there was no hint of wanting to use a commode. Strange, she thought, she had always believed fright had exactly the opposite effect. She wondered how long she had been there. In being bundled out of the taxi she had lost her watch and now had no idea what the time was. Apart from hunger she was also beginning to feel somewhat tired, nearer exhaustion in fact, but still had no intention of lying down on that filthy bed. Sitting on a chair was bad enough. To occupy her mind she started to go back over the day's proceedings. To begin with nothing really suspicious or untoward happened that she could think of. After a light breakfast in her suite and a look at *The Times*, she always read *The Times* when in London, starting with the gossip: what various members of the Royal Family were up to, if anything, who was getting married to whom, who had died, who was being born, all very interesting, she made herself ready to go out and indeed, with Flynn dogging her footsteps, she found her way to the Patisserie Valerie hoping she might find Holly there but no such luck. What could have happened to that girl? Flynn sat at a different table to his employer, keeping a beady eye on her and stuffing his face with cream cakes until she was ready to leave.

The afternoon was spent at The National Gallery which bored Mickey out of his tiny mind but he dutifully kept pace with her as she wandered from room to room. It had in fact been a pleasant and uneventful day; that is it would have been had her fretful thoughts not continually flown to Rome and the Palazzo Cinelli and so she had decided her return was definitely on the cards and as quickly as possible. She would take a chance on a flight that very evening, quite sure there would be first class available. If not she would wait at the airport until there was one. With the aid of a hotel maid her bags were packed and it wasn't until she and that monster Flynn were out on the street and there was already a cab waiting that the nightmare began.

*   *   *

Louise Anna was blazing. That damned chair had hurt and she was going to be well and truly bruised because of it. She felt distinctly going for Thornton like a screaming banshee with every fingernail a lethal weapon but she was aware that it was hardly advisable in the circumstances as creating a diversion could lead to all sorts of trouble. So she angrily kicked the fallen chair out of her way, rubbed her sore spots, glowered, and tried by breathing hard to reduce the trembling in her legs. It had been a nasty moment.

The footman was beginning to come round. He sat up with a groan and a nudge with the toe of Yiorgos's highly polished shoe brought him firstly to his knees and then to his feet, though still a bit on the groggy side. He gently touched the back of his head and then gazed at the blood on his fingers as if it weren't his. Thornton was glad. He would never have been able to forgive himself if he had been the cause of the man's demise. The man would have liked to exact vengeance on his attacker as well but also thought better of it, it being neither the time nor the place whilst Yiorgos was standing there. An angry Yiorgos meanwhile was indicating with flicks of his hand holding the gun for Thornton to move back into the room which he did with no further thought of argument, wisely keeping well clear of the hellcat. She might have been tempted if he had got too close.

Having gone as far into the salon as he intended to go, Thornton turned to face the Greek. He knew for the moment at least he was perfectly safe. No one was going to do anything stupid like put a bullet through his head. That would get them absolutely nowhere except that, like poor old Nat, they would have another body to dispose of and some very angry gangsters to mollify and they knew it, so what could happen next?

'Well, old chum,' he said, 'ball's in your court. How are you going to play it?' All it needed now was for the Pensotti brothers and their interpreter to turn up. He selected a chair and settled down in it as though he hadn't a care in the world. If nothing else it irritated Yiorgos beyond words. 'I tell you what,' Thornton continued, 'as I've mentioned play and as there are four of us how about a round of bridge to pass the time?'

'Mister King, if you don't mind me saying so, I think you are an idiot.'

'You wouldn't be the first to think that, old son, but you still haven't answered my question. What happens now?'

'We wait.'

'Yes, that's what the squirrel…'

'Don't call me that!' She shrieked.

'Beg pardon but I thought you liked your nickname. All right, Mrs Berman then.'

'No! Not that either.'

'As Louise Anna said earlier, we wait, but for what? That's what I would like to know?'

'For a phone call.'

'Ah, the telephone, the blessed telephone. Where would civilisation be without it? Good old Alexander Graham Bell, what an inestimable debt of gratitude we owe him. Do you realise in five years time it will be exactly a hundred years since that very first telephone conversation that took place over a distance of two whole miles?'

'Yiorgos! Shut him up! Shut him up! I don't think I can take any more of this.'

Thornton turned his smile on her and then back to Yiorgos. 'What sort of message are you hoping to receive, apart from perhaps one giving you orders as to what to do next? Because I take it you are but a minor cog in this vast machine and are at the moment at a bit of a loss as to your next step.'

'Do you never stop talking, Mister King? You think you are so smart.'

'You've just called me an idiot. I can't be both an idiot and smart.' Thornton had crossed his legs, intertwined his fingers and sat still smiling. It was driving Yiorgos crazy. He would have liked more than anything to put an end to this but, as Thornton had so rightly surmised and like a skater on thin ice, he didn't know what his next step could be or where it would take him. Gun still in hand he took another chair. 'Mister King, why don't you play it smart and just tell us where it is then this can all be over with?'

Thornton noted it was still "it".

'We can finish the business to everyone's satisfaction.'

'No, George. I think what you mean is to your satisfaction.' He untwined his legs and released his fingers, with thumb and forefinger of his right hand making the sign at his temple of a bullet in the brain. 'Because that is what happens to me when you have got it.' He accentuated the it. 'So there is no way I am going to play this game. I have no wish to be a body floating down the Tiber thank you very much. We can sit here till the cows come home waiting for that phone call and it will get you absolutely nowhere so why don't I just get up off this chair, waddle to that door, lope down the stairs, walk out the front door and mooch all the way back to the pension and my fat landlady who talks more than I do?'

Yiorgos looked at Louise, Louise looked at Yiorgos, the footman looked at them both and no one knew what to do with this smiling seated captive who appeared to have not a worry in the world.

*   *   *

The countess did not know how much time had passed. She would have given anything for a good cigar, let alone food and drink, when once again she heard the key turn in the lock of the inner door which swung open for Viktor Radenko to smilingly enter the room. He trod on a piece of traditional English pork pie, stopped, lifted his foot and with some distaste examined the sole of his elegant shoe.

'I see you weren't hungry,' he said, lowering his leg, straightening the seam of his trousers and then looking around the dingy little room. 'Not quite what you are used to, Countess, is it? This place? Not what I am used to either I must confess. We both enjoy our creature comforts, don't we? And why not? That is what this is all about as far as I am concerned, to ensure my future creature comforts. So you see, there is really no need for you to stay here any longer than is necessary. Once we have what we want you will be free to go, no hard feelings and all this will be forgotten.'

'Like your man has forgotten to bring me my commode?' She was by now beginning to feel the need for it. 'You really are idiotic you know whatever your name is. I've forgotten it.'

'Radenko, Viktor Radenko, although there really is no need for you to remember it. In fact it would be much safer for you if you forgot it.'

'Threats threats threats. What do you hope to gain by this, Mister Radenko? I have absolutely no idea where this stuff is that you are all so anxious to lay your hands on. I sent someone to Geneva to collect it and it would appear he has failed in his task.' She would have continued but Viktor cut her off.

'No, Countess, he did not fail. He has it.'

'Oh! He is still alive then!' She could not keep the excitement from her voice.

'Alive and, for the moment, as well as can be expected. He is back in Rome and he has what we are all looking for but we don't as yet know where it is. He is, like you, refusing to cooperate.' A note of anger seemed to have entered his voice. 'Not only is he back in Rome but he is at this very moment in the Palazzo Cinelli and, if we still can't find it, we will inform him that we have you here and are willing to make an exchange. Isn't that what it's called? Making an exchange? Maybe in order to save you from any unpleasantness he will reconsider his non cooperation. You are both being extremely stubborn and, in the end, it simply will not have been worth it because in the end we will get what we want.'

'Have you quite finished?'

Viktor nodded. The countess was sincerely wishing she had never been told by her old friend the professor of his miraculous discovery or that she had been so stupid as to have put the word of its availability out to international criminality. Insane rapaciousness knows no boundaries. Now she was paying for her own greed and her folly.

'Well can I have my commode please and kindly leave the room while I use it.'

A very angry Viktor Radenko resisted the temptation to beat the living daylights out of her and stalked from the room slamming the door behind him. She hoped in his rage he would forget to lock it but no such luck. She heard the key turn once more and now, almost in despair, she sat down on the filthy chair. What she wouldn't do, because it was beneath her, was burst into tears of anguish. That was simply out of the question for a Sicilian and a Cinelli.

11

The phone rang. It seemed an age before it did so but finally here was the call Yiorgos was obviously waiting for. He left the salon with a curt order to both Louise Anna and the footman to keep a beady eye on Thornton. He needn't have bothered, this time neither of them had any intention of doing anything else, Louise with her gun, the footman guarding the door.

It wasn't too long before Yiorgos returned, shaking his head, though what that signified nobody really knew.

'Mister King, I am going to ask you for the very last time, and I mean that. We can't go on playing hide and seek for ever. Where … is … it?'

Thornton raised that eyebrow but otherwise there was no reaction.

'Whereisitwhereisitwhereisit?' Yiorgos was beginning to perspire quite noticeably and the gun in his shaking hand looked none too safe. It could go off by accident any moment. He obviously felt he was in a lot of trouble.

'Where you won't find it, old chum, so you might as well let me go.'

'No. No I don't think so.' He took a couple of deep breaths that calmed him down somewhat. 'When you hear what I have to say I believe you will see sense and change your mind.'

Thornton shrugged. This was more bluff.

'We have the countess.'

This time both eyebrows went up.

'What?'

'We have the countess.' It was said as if he had just successfully robbed the Tower of London of the crown jewels. 'That is, my friends in England have her and they will keep her until you give us what we want. Then you can have her back.' She sounded like goods found to be faulty after purchase.

'I don't believe you.'

'No?' He turned to the footman and said something in Italian Thornton didn't understand. The man left to return a moment later with a telephone that was plugged into a socket in the salon.

Thornton shook his head. 'Maybe old Alexander's invention isn't so hot after all.'

Yiorgos would really have liked to have dialled a number, taking his time about it, obviously relishing the moment, but his instructions were to wait so that is what they would do.

'If you don't want to play bridge while we're waiting, how about a round of poker?' Thornton said. There was no response. 'Strip?'

The countess had been virtually frogmarched by the cab driver from her basement cell, up to the ground floor and into a living room well furnished with antique furniture. The curtains were drawn and the room lit by occasional lamps. Viktor was seated nursing a glass and with him was a second man who turned to face her as she was pushed into the room. She didn't recognise him and she was obviously not going to be introduced. Names are not bandied about in this kind of situation but there was something about him that chilled her to the marrow. If Viktor Radenko was dangerous, this man was twice as deadly, of that there was no doubt. He was not nursing a glass but stood smiling, immaculately dressed, slender, sleek, and erect with his hands in his trouser pockets.

'Countess,' he purred with no obvious trace of an accent, 'I hear you are not behaving well and you know what happens to naughty boys and girls who do not behave themselves. Regrettably they have to be punished of course. I'm informed you have had nothing to eat or drink since you were brought to my humble abode, something that could easily be rectified, though you have I believe …' and here he laughed… 'finally managed to use your, what did you call it? Your commode. How delightfully quaint. How delightfully old fashioned. Mementoes of a forgotten age no doubt. I hope that made you feel more comfortable. I'm sorry the accommodation isn't up to your usual standard. The thing is we have only recently moved into this house, very much neglected up to now, and the basement has not yet been sorted out.'

The Countess Cinelli was worried. This man's English was too good and she didn't think he looked at all like an Englishman. With his slicked down blonde hair he looked more what? Swedish? Teutonic? He looked like someone playing a part, acting, playing the iron fist in the velvet glove. Where could he be from? She gave him her devil's eyes but it had no effect. It was more than likely, she thought, something he was used to from women.

'Now my friend Viktor here,' he continued, 'has a crude way of dealing with naughty boys and girls but I, because of my medical training...'

"Oh, so he's a doctor is he?"

'... am much more subtle and believe me I can make you talk. So tell me, where is Thornton King?'

'He's at the Palazzo in Rome, or so I am led to believe.'

'But he is not actually staying there, am I correct?'

'Yes, no, yes. He's staying at a pension I recommended, the Crispi. You may know of it.'

'I don't think so, hardly in my line. But tell me, where might he have hidden the drug do you suppose? Because that is what all this is about, no?'

'Of that I have absolutely no idea.'

'Oh, come along now, up to this point you've been very cooperative, answering my questions in all honesty. Don't spoil things now.'

'I'm afraid it's true. You must believe me. I really have no idea. Wherever Thornton has it, he is the only one who knows. I gave him no instructions other than he was to bring it to me and as I am here and he is in Rome that obviously has not happened. He was to bring it to me to dispose of. But as you seem bent on disposing of me that leaves us all... how can I put this?'

'Up shit creek, lady,' the cab driver said and was rewarded with a withering look from both Viktor and the stranger.

'Sorry,' he said, raising both hands and looking contrite.

The man claiming to be a doctor turned back to face the countess. 'All right, I believe you. But we have to find out so what we are going to do is this, we are going to make a telephone call to the palazzo and you are going to talk to Mister King, persuade him to come up with the goods in exchange for your good self. Is that understood? But there will be no hanky-panky, no attempt to do anything that can be misconstrued and that will warrant punishment. I hope you understand. Viktor?'

Viktor got to his feet, walked across to an occasional table on which sat the telephone, put down his glass, lifted the receiver and dialled.

The phone rang in the salon and, although the call was expected, it almost made the occupants jump they were all by now so jittery. Yiorgos lifted the receiver and listened for a moment then held the instrument out to Thornton who rose from his chair to take it. He looked around at the others as though he were about to perform a speciality act for their benefit and placed his hand over the mouthpiece.

'I have the distinct feeling that this is going to break up the party. Are you quite sure you don't want that round of bridge? Penny a point?'

Yiorgos turned practically puce. 'Get on with it, Mister King. Stop playing the fool and get on with it!'

Thornton smilked which in his made-up vocabulary was a cross between a smile and a smirk. He sometimes came out with odd words like this meaning to say one thing, thinking of another and coming out with an unintentional hybrid. By playing the fool as Yiorgos put it he had got them really rattled and the more rattled they became the less they were able to think clearly.

'Yo!' He said into the phone.

'Thornton, is that you?' Came the reply.

'Who else, Countess, who else? How are you? Did you know your George is a traitor? A fifth columnist? A cuckoo in the nest?' He was looking directly at Yiorgos as he said it.

Yiorgos hissed.

'A hissing snake in the grass to boot. Where are you, Countess?'

'I don't know. Somewhere in Chelsea.'

Thornton removed the phone from his ear and looked at it quizzically before turning to the others. 'Strange,' he said, 'she rang off.'

In Chelsea the phone had been wrenched none too gently out of the countess's hand and the cradle slammed down on its rest.

'Scheisse und schmutsiges frauenzimmer!' The doctor yelled. 'You were ordered not to do anything stupid!'

'Ah so! So du bist also Deutscher? How do you manage to own a house in England?'

'What has that to do with anything? And what has that to do with you? Get her out of here.'

The cab driver took her by the arm to bundle her down to the basement.

'Nothing to eat! Nothing to drink!' The doctor yelled after them, all urbane charm gone. 'And take away her commode!'

Thornton had replaced the receiver on its rest and for a moment it was as though nobody knew what to do next. It was Yiorgos who broke the silence.

'So, Mister King, you see it was not a bluff. We do have the countess and you might say she is good currency to pay you for what we want.' Yiorgos was rather pleased with himself for the way he put that, almost poetical you might think. After which it was rather mundane, 'So are you going to hand it over or are you not?'

'Not.'

'You are being very stupid.'

'I know. You've already told me that a number of times. Other people keep telling me that as well. That's just the way I am I'm afraid. When I was a kid my parents used sometimes to absolutely despair of me.'

'I have no wish to know what your parents thought of you!' Yiorgos almost screamed, 'Except perhaps they wished you had never been born. Now, you stupid Englishman, you see what I am holding here in my hand. I am going to count to ten and if by the time I reach ten you have not agreed to hand it over, you will never use your right leg again because a bullet will have shattered your kneecap. And, if I count to another ten and you are still being stupid and stubborn your left leg will suffer the same fate. Do I make myself absolutely clear?'

'Oh, absolutely. I must congratulate you though, George, your use of English is quite extraordinary. Where on earth did you learn to speak it so well?'

'One... two... three... four... five...'

Thornton's mind was racing faster than Yiorgos's counting but there seemed only one thing for it, to agree before the next five numbers were uttered. He had absolutely no wish, apart from suffering the pain, to lose the use of his legs and he knew Yiorgos had him over a barrel. Unless fate intervened time was finally up. He opened his mouth just as fate intervened by someone sounding a long insistent ring on the front doorbell. Saved by the bell was never more truly spoken.

They waited. If the bell was not answered whoever it was would go away. It was probably a couple of impecunious nuns from the nearest convent seeking donations to some charity or other, but no such luck, at least as far as Yiorgos was concerned. There was an even longer ring followed by a hammering on the door.

'See who it is,' Yiorgos hissed to the footman who duly turned and left the scene and the trio continued to wait. The silence was almost deafening and then they heard loud and clear the one word Yiorgos and Louise Anna did not want to hear... 'Police.'

*   *   *

'He's in the interview room, sir.'

'Thank you. Where did you pick him up?'

'He was just coming out of the Taj Mahal in the Whitechapel Road. Got himself a takeaway vindaloo.'

'Did he give you any trouble?'

'Came in quiet as a lamb. All I said was you wanted a word or two with him and that was that. He even made some sort of joke about it.'

'Strange,' Reg said. 'Suspicious if you ask me. He normally kicks up a hell of a fuss. Says he'll make complaint to the commissioner, have the law on us for harassing him.'

'Aren't we?'

Reg gave his sergeant an old fashioned do you mind kind of a look.

'Well in this instance definitely not. I have grounds to believe he knows something about something and he knows I know which is why he gave you no trouble and why I am so suspicious. Okay, I'll see him now.'

He made his way to the interview room where Constable Roper was seated at the table sharing a vindaloo with Mickey Flynn. Roper had the plastic knife, Flynn the fork.

'What on earth...?' Reg couldn't believe his eyes. 'Is this some kind of picnic, Roper? Get that stuff out of here. Shouldn't have brought it in in the first place. The smell of curry will hang around for days.'

'Yes, sir.' Roper had got hurriedly to his feet, collected the polystyrene containers that held the remains of the meal and was making a hasty exit. Flynn sat there, smiling.

'And get back here sharpish.'

'Yes, sir.'

'Well, Inspector Venables, long time no see,' Flynn said with a smile. 'What's on your mind this trip round?'

Reg seated himself in the chair vacated by Roper and was about to rest an elbow on the table when he noticed some spilled curry there and shook his head.

'I don't know what the world's coming to, Mickey, I really don't. No discipline these days, none at all. Don't know their bloody arses from their bloody elbows these youngsters and you can't tell them anything you know. Know it all they do or it goes in one ear, out the other. Well, how you been keeping then? Life treating you well is it?'

'Fair, Mister Venables, fair, you know. Can't grumble. Well not much anyway.' Mickey grinned.

'Hmn,' Reg nodded his head and focused on the curry on the table, curling a dark brown around the edges as it dried, before looking up again.

'Gainfully employed then are you?'

'On my life, Mister Venables, straight as a die.'

'Hmn.'

Roper returned and took a chair in the corner. He was carrying a pen and notebook. Venables ignored him for a moment so he smiled at Flynn who also ignored him.

'So, what's all this about then? All I know is you wanted to have a word with me but what about for the life of me I cannot tell.'

'Can you not?'

Flynn shook his head, the picture of innocent ignorance.

'Right. Well you realise this is only curiosity on my part because I have reason to believe you could help the police in their enquiries but let's go through the formalities, shall we?'

'No need for that Mister Venables no need at all.'

'Just to be on the safe side. Roper?'

Constable Roper, watched by his superior and adopting an air of authority, at least as far as his youthful looks allowed, recited the necessary, every word of which Mickey Flynn knew by heart he had heard it so many times. Venables finished the preamble by stating time of interview and who present. None of it meant a thing really, as Mickey pointed out, because he was not being charged with anything and he was not being represented. As far as he was concerned this was just Inspector Venables fishing.

'It's about the Countess Cinelli of course.'

'Oh, yeah. My recent employer. What about her then?'

'She seems to have disappeared, Mickey, that's what about her, and I think you might know something about it.'

'Disappeared? On my life!' Mickey was not that good a non-actor and he knew his little performance sounded as false as a forged fiver so he thought it best to continue. 'Well, whatever's happened to her, Mister Venables, it ain't got nuffink to do with me, of that you may be assured.'

'Of that I am far from being assured, Mickey. I believe you were the last person to see her?'

'Well that's where you're wrong see? She got into a taxi so it must've been the cabbie who was the last person to see her.'

'Yes. Funny but we've not been able to trace that particular cabbie but we have traced the cab, reported stolen and found abandoned near Clapham common. I'm most surprised it hadn't been torched. Hopefully forensics will come up with a lot of very interesting stuff that will put us on the tracks of whoever took her and the question is, why didn't you get in the cab with her?' He regarded Mickey carefully but the man's expression didn't change although he was silently but furiously cursing. He had been given a momentary scare. His prints were on the door handle. But, as he calmed down somewhat, he knew he could surely talk his way out of that one.

'After all said and done,' Venables continued, 'you were being paid to protect her, were you not?'

'Yeah, and I've got a legitimate beef about that because I never got my final payment, did I?'

'You haven't answered my question.'

'What question was that then?'

'Why you didn't get in the cab with her?'

'She kicked me out, that's why an' she made hurtful remarks.'

'Hurtful?'

'Extremely hurtful, Mister Venables, about my person, personal remarks about my person.'

'Really? And you such a sensitive flower. I would have thought she should have known better. So what did these hurtful remarks consist of?'

'She said I stank.'

Reg thought about this for a while, trying very hard not to laugh but he couldn't hide the smile.

'Nothing hurtful about that Mickey. She was simply telling the truth, that's all. You do stink and that's a fact. And on top of your normal stink you now stink of vindaloo as well.'

'Thanks.'

'And Roper in the corner there like little Jack Horner is in the same boat.'

Roper blushed guiltily and looked down at the pen and paper on his lap. He had been telling his missus about how Inspector Venables was mellowing and turning into quite a nice chap really but he decided maybe he had been a little premature.

'We learn from the hotel that the countess was on her way to Heathrow, due to catch a plane to her home in Rome. I don't mean the plane was going to her home... Oh, you know what I mean... and she didn't catch it. She left the hotel got into a cab, was driven off and not seen again. We have managed to trace the second cabbie, the one who refused to take you. When questioned he said there was definitely something fishy going on and he didn't like the smell of it. So what was so fishy, Mickey, apart from your body odour? Tell me?'

Mickey shrugged and scratched his over extended stomach; his shirt buttons being stretched to their limit, one about ready to pop. 'No idea, Mister Venables. That cabbie didn't want to take me for the same reason I guess the countess chucked me out her cab. And if she hadn't a done that I could have been there to protect her all the way to Heathrow, isn't that right? So she's only herself to blame if she's landed herself in hot water.'

'Roper!'

Roper, who had been dreaming of the twins, jumped so hard he dropped his pen and notebook and was scrabbling for them on the floor when Inspector Venables continued. 'See Mister Flynn off the premises, will you? We'll have another little chat, Mickey, soon.' And, with that, he got up and stalked out of the interview room.

'What did you do with the curry?'

'Tossed it out.'

'Pity. We could ha' finished it.'

*   *   *

Two members of Rome's finest, one a little on the stoutish side, the other lanky and on the skinny side plus a diminutive moustachioed detective in a shabby mac and trilby entered the salon, all giving off an air of extreme efficiency at being on an important mission.

Yiorgos and Louise Anna had quickly disposed of their guns and the threesome the policemen came across merely looked like they were being disturbed in the middle of a social get together. Thornton noticed the footman hadn't returned with them.

'Good evening, Inspector.' Yiorgos presumed this was the correct method of address. 'And what may we do for you?'

'I am looking for the Countess Cinelli. Call her please.'

'I am afraid that is not possible, Inspector. She is not here at the moment.'

'Is that so? And where might she be then?'

'She's in London.'

Thornton had understood none of this except for the words "Contessa", "Cinelli" and "London."

'Somewhere in Chelsea as a matter of fact,' he butted in.

'She's staying at the Savoy Hotel,' Yiorgos almost shrieked.

'The Ritz!' Louise Anna contradicted.

'Chelsea,' Thornton said with a smile.

The detective who name was Ettore Delmosca, turned to him.

'And who might you be?' He asked in English.

'King. Thornton King.' Was he emulating a fictional character he had read about?

'Ah, yes, Mister King.' Ettore nodded his head. 'We know about you. You have recently been in Switzerland I believe.'

Louise Anna burst into laughter and Ettore turned his attention to her.

'I have made up something funny? My English she is not so good?'

'Not at all, inspector, it's just that Thornton couldn't possibly be in two places at the same time.'

Even Thornton was a bit taken aback by this.

'I don't understand.' Ettore frowned beneath his trilby.

'I mean, he was here with me. Weren't you, darling?'

'Of course, darling. Where else could I possibly be but with you?'

Louise Anna beamed at the intruders as she slipped an arm through Thornton's. She was indeed a ravishing creature and the police, being Italian, were quite captivated by her. She knew it and was determined to play the card for all it was worth. Even the tubby one hitched up his pants and tried to look smart. Ettore turned back to Thornton and held out his hand, palm uppermost.

'We'll see about this. Your passport if you please, Mister King.'

'Sorry Inspector but I don't have it on me.' This was a lie as it lay snug in his breast pocket but he didn't think they would want to search him there and then, not in front of Louise Anna.

'Then fetch it please.'

'Can't old chum. It's at my digs.'

'Digs? Digs? What are your digs?'

'Where I'm staying.'

'You're not staying here? In the palazzo?' Ettore's eyes narrowed with suspicion.

The other two members of Rome's police who did not speak English were beginning to get a bit rattled as they didn't understand a word of what was going on and were wondering whether or not they were going to have the opportunity of doing a bit of tearing apart. It was Louise Anna who was keeping them in check and Thornton was beginning to feel he was in a Pirandello play as his mind positively buzzed in an effort to come up with a reason for not sleeping with his beloved.

'We had a bit of a tiff, Inspector, you know how it is.' Inspiration had struck. He turned to Louise. 'Isn't that right, darling?' Then back to Ettore. 'I am here this evening to try and make up.' And, as if to prove it, he gave her a kiss which had the three policemen all smiles. The skinny one even ran a lascivious tongue over his lips.

'All right then,' Ettore said, now at a loss as to what to do next. 'All right then.' He stood thinking for a while and then said, 'We will try to contact the Contessa in London. In the meantime Mister King you will not leave Rome, is that understood?'

'Perfectly. Actually, Inspector, if it's not out of your way, I would be very much obliged if you could give me a lift to the Pension Crispi perhaps? I don't really know the way very well and I need to collect my things so I can come back here to Louise Anna, now that we have made up our differences.' He gave her another kiss. It was all she could do not to shrink from it and the smile had become rather fixed, like the smile on the face of a wax doll. This was the last thing she had expected. Yiorgos too was looking extremely worried. If the inspector agreed to Thornton's request, he was about to slip through their fingers yet again.

For a moment Ettore seemed to be cogitating on it. Eventually he nodded.

'All right, Mister King. It is not our custom to assist members of the public in such a fashion but we will take you to the Pension Crispi and at the same time we will have the opportunity to look at your passport. You...' this was to Yiorgos... 'You I take it are in employment here?'

Yiorgos nodded.

'If you are in contact with the Contessa you will let her know we wish to speak with her. It is very urgent, and you will let me know you have done so. Understood?'

Yiorgos, who seemed to have lost the power of speech, nodded once more.

'Good. Come along then, Mister King.' He turned and left the salon, followed by his minions. At the door Thornton waggled his fingers at the despondent pair he was leaving behind and disappeared after the policemen.

Holly didn't want to believe what she was hearing. She hadn't even gone home but headed straight for the hotel from Heathrow via the Piccadilly line, Green Park and a short walk up Piccadilly.

'That's right, Miss Day. The Countess Cinelli left the hotel, let me see, when was it?' He pulled a register towards him but, when he looked up, Holly was already on her way out.

'How very odd,' he said. 'I do hope everything is all right.'

Thornton stood at the doorway to his room surveying the damage. He could hear the distressed wailing from down below and he felt slightly sick. The room was a shambles and they had not just ransacked the place, they had torn it apart! The damage was unbelievable. There was simply nothing left worth salvaging.

Was this really necessary? Thornton thought. Naturally they had found nothing so maybe they were venting their anger and frustration but that was what the phone call from Yiorgos was all about. "He's here with us at the palazzo," he would have told them. "We will keep him here. Search his room." And the Poinsettias or whoever it was had set about it with a vengeance. Not even the religious pictures, the holy water font or the statue of the Madonna escaped the vandalism. She had obviously been lifted off her pedestal to see if she was hollow and whether there was anything inside and, finding nothing she had at least been put back, only she was now facing the wall and her halo had slipped over her face. Thornton quite tenderly turned her around and replaced the halo, shaking his head all the while.

His valise lay on the remains of the bed. It was open and its contents strewn about, some lying on the floor. For some reason they hadn't ripped it and its contents apart, merely gone through them. He noticed his shaving cream and toothpaste were missing obviously to be inspected elsewhere but his electric razor was still intact.

He repacked, picked up the case and headed out. Behind the front door to the street he stopped. The wailing continued from somewhere in the rear of the house. He moved towards the sound and found his landlady seated weeping at her kitchen table. The weeping stopped when she saw him. There was only the occasional sob broken by a hiccup or two. Obviously she had not been hurt in any way but was mourning the loss of her precious possessions in the room Thornton had been due to sleep in. He sat at the table, placed his valise on the floor between his legs and waited for the last sobs to die away. She gazed at him with bloodshot eyes and there was a long silence broken only by a single hiccup before he found it possible to speak.

'Madame Mazzoni, I am so very very sorry,' he said 'that this should have happened to you. Did you know the men who did this?'

She continued to gaze at him but there was no reaction.

'Have you called the police?'

The howling was renewed, if possible even more violently than before. Even if she hadn't understood what he had just said, the word police is pretty universal and you do not call the police when something like this happens, not if you want to stay healthy.

'Madame Mazzoni!' It was little more than a whisper but an urgent one. Nevertheless she didn't hear it. 'Madame Mazzoni!'

He got up and went over to the kitchen sink, found a cup he filled with water and taking it to the table put it down in front of her. She ignored it. Thornton knew he had to move fast. At any moment, once information was received that he was no longer at the palazzo they would be sure to be back. He noticed there was a door leading somewhere out the back, probably to an alley, and decided this would be his exit, the front might be being watched, but first he had to try and bring Madame Mazzoni some semblance of comfort in her distress. It was right now he wished he could speak Italian. Like so many English he was quite simply useless when it came to a foreign language. As it was he stumbled along with the few words he knew interspersed with English. 'Signora Mazzoni... per favore... la Contessa... la Contessa... she will pay... pay for the damage... Tutto pagare... you understand?... La Contessa...' He made the sign of money with fingers and thumb and, at last, having gazed at him blankly for so long a look of comprehension appeared and she nodded. 'Good... good... buono.' He reached across the table and took both her hands in his, giving them a little squeeze. 'Now I must go. Bisogna ch'io vado... prestissimo,' he added for good measure, picking up his valise and getting to his feet.

If the Poinsettias weren't back soon the police might be. On the way to the pension the car radio had suddenly crackled into life and spurted forth a whole load of very rapid Italian at the end of which Ettore had turned to him and said, "We have an emergency. You are close to the pension but we must drop you off here." The car screeched to a stop and Thornton got out. Ettore leant out the window and added, "If we are not back you must deliver up your passport at the questura within the next twenty four hours. Understand? Your landlady will tell you where it is. Right now you go straight ahead, that way." He pointed down the road, withdrew his head and the car sped off. If they intended to catch anyone redhanded the noise they were making would give the miscreants plenty of time to scarper. As it was it was probably no more than a domestic punch-up. Nasty and sad as it always is in these cases but hardly an emergency unless one of the fighting duo was close to or actually being murdered.

Thornton stood in the alley for a moment getting his bearings. There was only one thing left for him to do now and that was to get back to England as quickly as possible, hopefully still in possession of the precious egg-timer; but that was easier said than done. He felt certain if they thought he was going to fly from Rome to London the airport would be closely watched and he would walk right into a trap so an alternative would have to be found and the alternative that suggested itself was to take the train once more, this time to Naples and from there fly into Luton rather than Heathrow. He hoped it wouldn't be a case of see Naples and die.

12

Louise Anna in a stylish outfit of cream linen appeared to be as cool as the proverbial cucumber but Yiorgos was in a blue funk. It was all right for her. She could more than likely slip quietly away and head back to the states to start her life all over again, presumably with another mega-rich elderly trophy seeking husband dreaming of one last great love and one last orgasm before total incapability and kicking the bucket. The last husband's slightly nibbled body, having been fished out of the Tiber, was minus its gold crucifix, Star of David and Ankh, obviously none of them having been of any use in stopping the bullet that had always been meant for him, that had his name on it from the moment of its manufacture.

Though Yiorgos was available and could have done it just as well, it was Louis Anna of course who was requested to view the remains to confirm identification and that was her only moment of apparent breakdown from which she recovered remarkably quickly once out of the building, out of sight of the corpse and ensconced in the nearest bar with a highball. In fact she had downed three and been chatted up by half a dozen macaronis, as they were once called in eighteenth century Britain, before making her way quite steadily back to the Palazzo Cinelli.

In her opinion Nat hadn't looked at all healthy; but for that moment, standing over him and until the white shroud was replaced and the rollers slid him back into the refrigerator with a tag on his toe, her weeping and her wailing and the gnashing of her pretty teeth was so convincing it had the surrounding Italians (except for one hard-bitten lady who remained highly suspicious) in floods of sympathetic tears and there was no doubt she would never be suspected of being in any way implicated in her husband's murder, not in a million years.

"Why? Why? Why?" She had sobbed. "He meant everything to me. He was my whole world!" Here there may have been the hint of reading too many agony aunt columns in cheap magazines; but in her beautiful distress no one thought to ask the obvious question, why, in that case, had his disappearance not been reported to the police?

The American Embassy was naturally informed that one of that country's citizens had unfortunately arrived at an untimely end and, when officially released, the body of Nat Berman would be returned to his home town of Chicago, no doubt to be reverently interred with a most impressive funeral. He had not achieved what he was sent out to achieve but hey, the man is dead, these things happen, no hard feelings!

For Yiorgos it was different. Italy was not only his home, it was his refuge. To go back to Greece was to commit suicide. There was a *fakelos*, an envelope with his name on it, and fraudulent politicians, maniacs, and military men who seize power do not take kindly to anyone opposing or threatening the stability of their dictatorship. Whatever their suspected opponents' outlook on life, it was just too easy to put a label on them: socialist in the most derogatory sense, anarchist, communist, whatever, and that was enough for imprisonment, torture, and even death. It happened in Italy, in Nazi Germany. The latter day Tsars did not seize power, they inherited it but it happened in Stalinist Russia and was still happening in those countries caught up in communism and when communism was no more it would more than likely continue. Why shouldn't it happen in Greece? Yiorgos had not meant to get himself into trouble with the junta but he was the kind of man who trouble seemed to follow and all he had done was enjoy the wrong kind of music in the basement clubs flourishing around Plateia Victoria. He had been seen going in, he had been seen coming out and the secret police knew that songs with subversive lyrics were sung in those places, hotbeds of rebellion that they were. He got out of trouble temporarily only by, immediately and without any conscience, implicating others as so often is the case in that sort of society. Now he was in trouble again. He had let Thornton slip through his fingers. He had not recovered "it" and he would not be forgiven. Why hadn't he just continued to do his job for the countess instead of betraying her and looking elsewhere for the promise of life ostensibly being made easier?

The Poinsettia brothers were more or less in the same boat though Fab baby prayed his brother could get them out of it which he tried to do without success, his eloquent excuses falling on deaf ears, and they were banished to an isolated farmhouse on Sicily, there to kick their heels in total boredom until it was decided what to do with them. So far so good but who knew what the future held? They too were wondering why they hadn't just remained pickpockets, in their case a lucrative profession.

Mickey Flynn, still fairly flush from his employment with the countess, despite being denied his final payment, or so he maintained, had quaffed innumerable pints of lager at various Red Lions, White Horses, Green Men, Hares and Hounds and establishments named after various other creatures: like Dukes, Earls, Marquises, Cocks, Geese, Hens, Swans and Horses; and indulged in a number of not only Indian but Chinese meals and kebabs and was finding his waistband becoming a little too tight in too short a time. But the takeaways weren't going to continue forever. There hadn't been much in the way of extra work on television, practically nothing in fact, one day's work on *Budgie*. The colour strike on Independent Television that lasted for three months, all about money of course, hadn't helped matters. No one seemed to want a twenty-one stone bodyguard or club doorman, he still owed the agency commission that he would get around to paying when he felt like it, and he was aware that Reg Venables was keeping a beady eye on him so he didn't want to step out of line. He only hoped something would turn up soon. It did, in the shape of Miss Holly Day.

Holly had not reported back to work but had called in sick. Jet lag possibly she said. Jet lag? From Switzerland? The boss said he wanted a list of expenses with appropriate invoices and a full report on how it went and she promised to let him have one. He was hardly likely to get a full report but a partial one was on the cards. She wanted to have a word with Reg Venables before possibly involving the department. The disappearance of an Italian countess and a British private eye wasn't exactly up their street unless, of course, it involved the Russians, which it didn't.

In the meantime that selfsame countess, feeling disgustingly dirty and a proper frump having not had a wash or a change of clothes for days, how many days? had lost all account of time and finally given in to nature, lain down on that disgusting bed to fall asleep in minutes. She was once again allowed her commode and had at intervals even been fed and watered while her captors debated on what to do with her. If only they knew where that damned elusive Thornton King was and could lay hands on him they might come up with some kind of solution but as it was they were floundering.

The countess appreciated the fact that the food, though hardly cordon bleu, casserole, hotpot or stew, all the same really though three different names, was a lot more edible than a traditional English pork pie but she wasn't exactly grateful either for it or her predicament.

And as for that damned elusive Thornton King, tired but not dispirited, he was on his way to Luton airport on a wing and a prayer in an ancient aircraft of doubtful vintage, possibly a Dakota from World War Two, in peacetime converted for the purpose of civil aviation, with the precious hour glass having been retrieved from one locker safely in his valise in another. He couldn't help glancing up, knowing with some satisfaction that it was there overhead.

13

The Casa Crispi was not that distant from Roma Termini, the railway station that, together with Los Angeles, must have the longest platforms of any station in the world and Thornton decided to hoof it. He didn't even feel like trusting himself to a taxi and twenty minutes or so at a fairly brisk trot would see him there if he didn't lose his way or be accosted in any way which, fortunately, he was not.

If anyone had thought to search him when first he was in Rome they would have discovered the key to the bank safety deposit box in Geneva attached to his leg, and if they had thought to search him on his return they would have discovered the key to a station left luggage locker in the same place.

Now he had enough lira left to purchase a one way ticket to Naples with a few left over and had three minutes before the departure of the next train after which there would be a wait and that was something he had no wish to do. It could just be that not only the airport but all exit points were being watched. He dashed for the lockers, retrieved his precious parcel, locked it in his valise and dashed for the platform, catching the train in the nick of time. He settled into his second class seat, heaved a sigh of relief, breathing hard and smiled at the middle aged couple sitting opposite him. They smiled back, the man bowing his head slightly in a courteous old fashioned manner and they were not carrying live chickens, salami or gorgonzola, not that he could smell or hear anyway.

The journey was uneventful. Thornton loved trains. They were for him by far the best way to travel. Ships at sea naturally but overland he would go for a train every time.

He would have enjoyed the passing scene but as it was now dark there was very little of it he could see; now and again lights as they passed by a village, at times moonlight on the sea. Under ordinary circumstances he would more than likely have fallen asleep, Thornton could catnap in almost any situation but now, with the hour glass in his valise, there was no way he would even think of doing that.

From the station in the Piazza Garibaldi, a name like that of Napoleon that seemed to haunt Thornton of late, he transferred to the airport by cab. He felt he had to put his trust in a Napoli cab driver or get lost in a city he had never before visited and he had heard as many lurid tales about Napoli as he had about Rome. He wouldn't have been at all surprised if that weren't the home base of the Poinsettias and he could be mugged before he even left the station. Fortunately that didn't happen and in a taxi the worst that could happen was for him to be taken for a ride all round the houses in order to clock up the fare, but his man must have been unique amongst the world's cabbies as Thornton was certain he drove him straight to his destination for which he deserved some sort of commendation, a medal perhaps, but was rewarded anyway with a very large tip, virtually the last of the lira. The air fare would have to be on his credit card, fortunately both within limit and final date.

*   *   *

The difference between British Rail and the Italian railways was evident from the moment he stood on the platform at Luton and surveyed the litter strewn tracks, and the carriage was no better. It was if a hundred football fans had travelled in it and it wasn't even Saturday. It was also a whole lot more expensive than Italian rail.

The streets of London were no better. As Maurizio Pensotti had so rightly remarked, Geneva was too damned clean and, after his experience of that city, Thornton was even more aware of the litter at his feet and would readily have agreed.

He had a few quid in his pocket, certainly enough and a bit more maybe to get a cab home to Hackney and, clutching his valise with its precious contents, he hailed one passing by, fortunately going in the right direction so a driver who would probably not make an excuse about going home for his tea or going off duty or sorry, not going that way, Guv.

In the cab he sat musing on what his next step should be but came up with nothing practical. Obviously the safety of the countess was paramount and somehow her whereabouts had to be discovered and the good lady rescued, but how? The cabby had tried to start a conversation but had soon given up. His fare was obviously not in talkative mood so the glass partition that was opened for a moment was now shut again.

After a good long soak in a hot bath followed by a nightcap and blessed sleep, Thornton thought maybe he would wake up in the morning with at least the germ of an idea as to what to do next. As it was he was to get neither bath nor sleep, at least not in his own bed because, as the cab approached his apartment block he noticed a car which for some reason immediately aroused his suspicious nature. Why that should have been it is difficult to tell. There were after all any number of cars parked in the street but for some reason, sixth sense if you will, this particular one seemed decidedly dodgy. He was suddenly wide awake and, leaning forward in his seat, wrapped on the glass partition which was immediately opened.

'Don't stop,' he ordered, urgency in his voice. 'Keep going.'

'But this is where…'

'Never mind. Keep going.'

They passed the car and Thornton, sitting well back in his seat, noticed there were two men sitting in it. Once passed he leaned forward again and the glass partition was slid open once more.

'Turn left at the end of the street and head back to town.'

''Ere, Guv, what's going on? You in some kind of trouble?'

The cab had turned and was now out of sight of the two men in the car. The cabby pulled up at the side of the road.

'It's a long story,' Thornton said.

'I bet and I bet it's a good one too. Where in town do you want me to take you?'

Thornton hadn't really thought about this. If his flat was being watched it was more than likely his office was as well so there was no point in going there but a sanctuary was possibly nearby. To be on the safe side he made their destination simply a drop off point from which he could walk in any direction.

'Drop me off the bottom of Tottenham Court Road. Oxford Street.'

'Maybe I should drop you off at the nearest police station.'

'If it's your fare you're concerned about, don't be. Here...' He leaned right forward and thrust his arm through the window opening, in his hand enough notes to cover both journeys. The cabby nodded his head and drove on to drop him off outside the Odeon cinema.

Thornton waited until the cab had moved some distance away before he crossed the road and set off in the direction of Fitzroy Square heading for his friend Carlotta's flat situated a few doors from his office. Outside the front door of the building he took a careful look around then rang her bell and waited. The street was deserted and he realised that if Carlotta wasn't working she would be catching up on her beauty sleep. Thornton had never actually had need of Carlotta's services. If nothing else she wasn't in the attraction stakes up his street at all, quite the reverse in fact, besides which he had never felt the need to pay for sex though he did sometimes fantasize about it; but they had become acquainted because of the proximity of her flat to his office and the fact they were continually bumping into each other, quite often when Carlotta was waiting for her Maltese terrier to do his stuff in the gutter before rubbing his paws on the pavement and being taken back inside. And now and again he saw her in his local and had even bought her a drink, port and lemon, and they chatted about inconsequential things. These occasional meetings blossomed slowly into what one might call a kind of friendship. It wasn't that Carlotta was the proverbial tart with a heart of gold but she was gregarious, she needed company other than when earning it, and Thornton was a pleasant enough chap for a chat and a bit of socialising.

It took a while for the bell to be answered and then only after his second more insistent ring.

'I'm not available,' a sleepy voice said and, before he could open his mouth she had switched off and he had to ring a third time.

'Are you fucking deaf? Didn't you hear what I said? A girl needs her sleep now and again you know. Now piss off and stop bothering me or I'll call the police.'

'Carlotta! It's me, Thornton!'

There was a Silence.

'What?'

'It's Thornton,' he hissed into the speaker. 'Let me in.'

After another moment there was a buzz, the lock was released and he pushed open the door, stepped inside and started to grope for a light switch in the passage. From somewhere above he could hear a soprano bark. Why were small dogs invariably soprano? Before he could find the switch the light was turned on from above and he mounted the stairs. She was waiting for him on the landing, wearing a pair of ancient mules and holding around her middle a skimpy blousy old kimono that had seen much better days.

'Thornton, what on earth are you up to?'

He hadn't even reached her landing when this was put to him.

The lights, which were obviously on a timer, switched off and she switched them on again. The door to her flat was open and she indicated for him to follow her in. Thornton found himself in a cramped little room that was both sitting and dining room and also kitchen. There was a cluttered nineteen thirties sideboard on top of which stood a telephone; an old leatherette sofa beneath a throw that looked like an Indian shawl, and a couple of cushions with pictures of cats. In the centre of the room was a round table covered with a green chenille cloth, four spoonback dining chairs around it and in the middle a cheap looking vase holding some even cheaper looking plastic flowers. Pictures were sentimental portrayals of children and animals including a reproduction of *Bubbles*, the famous advertisement for Pears coal tar soap.

The dog had obviously lost interest in whoever the caller might be and gone back to sleep because there was no more barking.

'Take a pew, Thornton. My but this is quite a surprise. Where have you sprung from? Haven't seen you around for a couple of days. Can I get you something? Got quite a wide range.'

Thornton placed his valise on the floor and pulled out one of the chairs to take a seat at the table.

'This might seem a bit strange, Lottie, but I could die for a cuppa rosy.'

'No trouble at all. Might even have one myself. Just pop the kettle on then you can tell me what all this is about. You've never made a house call before, Thornton, so I am intrigued. I take it you're not after my services.'

'Well, yes, I am, in a way though not that way.'

'I didn't think so.'

She had turned on a tap over the old fashioned stone sink and filled the kettle which she now put on the gas cooker and lit the burner with a Swan Vesta. This might have given her the idea but, before she joined Thornton at the table, she collected an ashtray from the sink and her cigarettes from the sideboard. She sniffed and wrapped her kimono more tightly around her ample figure as she took a cigarette from the pack. For some reason Thornton noticed the kimono was split at the armpits.

'You don't smoke do you, Thornton? Am I right in thinking that?' Thornton nodded. She lit her cigarette, waved the match about until it went out and dropped it in the ashtray, a present from Bridlington it seemed. With her free hand she fiddled with the matchbox on the table.

If there was one person in the world apart from Holly who he believed he could trust implicitly, it was Carlotta. He wondered how best to put his request because it would disrupt her business for a day or two and eventually he decided to come right out with it.

'Lottie,' he said, 'I need to ask a very big favour of you. Well, two favours in fact, though the second one is more like a job and I will make sure it's worth your while.'

She regarded him through a cloud of smoke that, after a moment, she waved away from her face with a few backward flicks of the hand. 'Go ahead. No, wait a minute.' She put down her cigarette and got up. 'Let me make that tea.' The kettle had started a gentle whistle which would soon with the pressure of the steam increase to an ear-splitting scream. She schlepped across to the stove, took a rather battered tin teapot from the draining board and a canister down from a shelf and proceeded to do just that. 'One spoon per cup and one for the pot,' she said, following the action with her words, turned off the gas, poured on the boiling water, replaced the lid on the teapot and went back to the table. 'Let it stew a while. I like my tea nice and strong.' She picked up her cigarette to take another draw and once more wrapped her kimono more tightly around her. It seemed in the habit of falling loose which was hardly surprising considering what it had to cover. 'So, Thornton, out with it as the actress said to the bishop, what is all this about?'

'Well, where to begin? The reason why you haven't seen me around recently is because I have been on a case that took me to the continent.'

'Gwan!' She said disbelievingly, her eyes opening wide.

'Yes, to Italy and Switzerland.'

'Big international stuff, huh?'

'Carlotta, you will never know how big. Anyway, I only got back here this evening and I have something in my case here that I have to guard with my life. What is more someone else's life depends on it. You won't know who she is but she's the one who I've been working for and it seems she's disappeared.'

'Gwan!'

'Not to put too fine a point on it, she's been kidnapped.'

'You're pulling my leg, Thornton.'

'No, Lottie. Believe it or not it is a matter of life or death. I believe she's being held somewhere in Chelsea and that's all I know at present.'

'Tell me about it then. No wait, let me pour the tea. How do you like it?'

'A dash of milk if you've got it. No sugar.'

'A dash of milk no sugar.'

She stubbed out her cigarette and went over to a cooler cabinet to remove a half bottle of milk. Obviously Carlotta spent her money on things other than domestic such as a refrigerator and a decent stove or the oldest profession in the world wasn't proving so lucrative of late. Thornton found himself wondering how long she had lived in this tiny apartment and what would happen when she was no longer able to work. Did she have any family? Where did she come from? He realised he really knew nothing about her but still he felt he could trust her.

She returned to the table with two cups and saucers and placed Thornton's in front of him before sitting down again and taking out another cigarette. Thornton shook his head.

'Lottie, I don't want to sound like a disapproving nanny, but if you smoke that much you're really going to regret it later on in life.'

'Thornton, I don't even think about it. The future really doesn't bother me one jot.'

There was something very sad about this statement but he persisted, trying a different tack. 'What do your clients think of you smelling like an ashtray and tasting of nicotine and tar?'

Carlotta whooped. 'Oh, Thornton you should see your face, you're so serious. What would my clients think? Most of them smoke twice as much as I do and it's really getting…' the laughter stopped and she suddenly looked serious… 'terribly expensive you know with the government putting up the tax every year. If anything makes me give it up it'll be that but Thornton carry on with what you were telling me.'

'Right. First of all, I can't go back to my flat. It's being watched and I would think the same applies to the office. I have to ensure that what is in my safekeeping stays that way and the only thing I can think of is to put it somewhere where no one will think to look.'

'In here?'

'No. That would put you in danger and there's no way I would want that. But what I would like you to do for me tomorrow morning is take the article I give you to a pawnbroker's and put it in pawn. Once you come back to me with the pawn ticket I can go back to the office and wait for what develops. In the meantime I would like to stay here if that's okay with you. I can doss down on the couch there. I mean I know it interferes with your work but, like I say I'll make it up to you. How does all that sound?'

Carlotta shrugged. 'I need a break anyway,' she said. 'You know the old saying.'

'What old saying?'

'It isn't the work that kills you, it's the stairs.' And she broke into another peal of laughter. Thornton had the grace to appreciate her little second hand joke and join in.

'Good. Now, do you have a Yellow Pages?'

'Of course.'

'Well let's look for a pawnbroker.'

Carlotta got up once more and went across to the sideboard, opened a drawer and returned to the table with the phone book. Though London was not exactly awash with pawn shops there were any number of them in fact and, after some deliberation, they decided not to use one anywhere near the city centre but chose one south of the river.'

'Right. That's it then,' Thornton said. 'That's the one we'll use.'

'Yes. And your tea is getting cold.'

14

'I would like to speak with the Countess Cinelli please.'

'Who is it calling?'

'Holly Day.'

'Ah, good morning, Miss Day. This is Yiorgos.'

'Of course. Hello Yiorgos. How are you?'

'Not too good at the moment, Miss Day, not too good I'm afraid.'

'Sorry to hear that. Nothing serious I hope.'

'It will pass. Just a fever… I believe.'

'Then see a doctor. Fevers are a symptom, indicative of something else and it could be something quite nasty, like a bug you might have picked up.'

Yiorgos was only too aware of what was giving him the shakes and it certainly was not a bug he'd picked up. 'I'll see the doctor,' he said.

'Good, don't delay. Now may I have a word with the countess

please?'

'I'm afraid that's not possible, Miss Day. She is not here at the moment.'

'Oh?'

'Yes. She is still in London.'

'Whereabouts in London? Do you know? What hotel is she staying in? Because I have been in touch with the hotel she is supposed to be staying in and they inform me she checked out some days ago. So have you any idea where she might be?'

'Checked out? Oh dear... this is news to me... I'm afraid I have no idea where she could have gone so I can't help you I'm afraid. I do hope she's all right.'

'Thank you, Yiorgos. I'll notify the police that she's a missing person.'

'Do you really think that's necessary? You know the countess, Miss Day; maybe she's having an adventure, if you know what I mean. Maybe you should leave it for a few more days.'

'I think not, Yiorgos. Like your fever I think the situation is serious and demands immediate attention.'

'As you wish.'

Holly put down her receiver. Whatever was going on that Greek had his fingers in the pie, of that she was quite sure.

*   *   *

Thornton opened his eyes and for a moment wondered where he was. The curtains across one window were still drawn so the room was in semi-darkness. A small white object could be made out sitting on the carpet facing the sofa and wagging its tail. Had it been any colour but white it would probably have been invisible.

Seeing Thornton stir it stood on its hind legs, put up its front paws and clawed at the blanket beneath which Thornton was still curled up and feeling a bit stiff even before trying to stretch out. A sofa is not exactly the best place to spend the night. He put out a hand to stroke the creature who allowed one rub behind an ear before setting up a wild incessant barking and scurrying across the room to scrabble frantically at the door which already carried tell tale signs of the same procedure.

Thornton threw off the blanket and sat up, giving a little gasp as he felt the crick in his back. He looked at his watch, wondering where Carlotta was. Unable to make out the time in the gloom he got up, limped across to the window and drew back the curtain. Light flooded into the room and to his amazement he saw it was gone eleven. He had slept like the proverbial log. The inner door was open and he trotted across in stockinged feet to peep inside, hoping to see Lottie still there but the bedroom he remembered from the previous evening when he had to cross it to use the bathroom, was empty. She had obviously already left and he was surprised her departure hadn't wakened him. She must have made some noise moving about. He was in desperate need of a pee but then so obviously was the dog and this created something of a dilemma because he did not want to set foot outside the building in case he was seen. He could use the toilet and proceeded to do so but he wondered if the dog could control itself until such times as its mistress returned.

The phone was ringing when he returned to the living room but, as Carlotta was the only inhabitant of the flat, there seemed little point in answering it. It was no doubt one of her clients. The dog was now whining and Thornton knew exactly how it felt.

He sat on the sofa and was about to put on his shoes when he had an idea. If he didn't want to leave the flat as Thornton King why didn't he go out in disguise? But the only disguise it could possibly be in this situation was as a transvestite or transsexual. He was quite sure he could get into Carlotta's clothes, no problem there, if anything just the opposite. The shoes would be difficult though, maybe he would have to stick with his own. He wondered if the dog could hold out while he made the transformation. He badly needed a shave to start with, as badly as the dog needed to go out, and no amount of face powder would cover up the obvious giveaway. Thornton was being totally unrealistic if he thought for a moment that would be the only giveaway. He had been to a couple of clubs in the company of Adrian Spangle and noted that, although there were men who could look very beautiful as women, witness Danny LaRue for example, why, he wondered, was it so often ugly men, disproportionate men, men with huge hands and feet and five o'clock shadow who dragged up and thought they could get away with it. It was really rather sad. He took his electric razor from his valise, the valise that no longer held the precious hour glass, and headed back to the bathroom and the mirror above the sink.

Having shaved and cleaned his razor over the sink and rinsed away the remains of his beard, he returned to the bedroom to see what he could find in the way of suitable clothes. There was always that old kimono of course but he didn't think it advisable to appear in public dressed in that and he would definitely need something for his head. He couldn't remember ever seeing Carlotta in a hat but there must be some form of chapeaux somewhere even if it were only a beret, or was it only French tarts who wore berets? Maybe a scarf then. Hermes?

The Maltese terrier meanwhile seemed to have given up on

being taken out and was lying silently behind the door. Thornton was all sympathy but there was nothing he could do about it until he was ready. He found what he was looking for in a rather smart suit in navy blue with a fairly lengthy skirt, but no hat. However there was a bright Liberty print scarf which would have to do. He would forget stockings and even though he looked ridiculous in his own shoes and socks he decided, once he had made up his face using Carlotta's cosmetics: eye shadow, old fashion rouge from a little container and applied with a finger, a lipstick he didn't quite like the colour off, it being a sort of off-purple but it was the only one available so he smeared it on and used a tissue and pursed lips to get rid of the surplus as he had seen women do; then he surveyed himself in a bedroom mirror turning his head from one side to the other and decided he didn't look too bad after all. He didn't feel exactly comfortable in a skirt, in fact it felt decidedly odd and unnatural and he wondered for a moment how Scotsmen felt wearing the kilt. But as it was only going to be for a few minutes while the dog did its stuff he reckoned he could put up with it. In the meantime the phone never seemed to stop ringing. If it was one client he was most persistent. If it was more than one Thornton felt he was doing Carlotta out of a whole heap of business. As the calls were definitely not for him there seemed little reason for him to answer them. He left the bedroom for the sitting room ready to go out and face the day.

The dog however didn't seem to appreciate the transformation and, had it been human, one would have said it freaked out on the spot. As it was, at sight of this apparition it set up a howl the likes of which Thornton had never heard before, leapt to its feet and fled to relative safety beneath the dining table. Thornton had to hoist up his skirt above the knees in order to bend down and drag the still hysterical dog out by its collar and then towards the door behind which he had noticed its lead was hung as the animal, no longer in control of its bladder, tried to resist, struggled for all it was worth and pissed its way all across the carpet. The pair had just reached the door and Thornton had stretched out his hand for the lead when it opened and Carlotta appeared. For one moment she stood transfixed at the figure before her and her little dog a trembling lunatic. Fortunately, on seeing its mistress, it gave up on the hysteria stakes and once more barked normally and wagged its tail at a joyous reunion but her reaction was the exact opposite. After the first brief moment of shock, seeing what appeared to be a bizarre looking creature from hell apparently about to hang her little dog by its very own collar and lead she let out a scream that practically set the walls vibrating. Then the penny dropped.

'Thornton! What the fuck are you doing to poor little Bijou? Why are you wearing my cemetery visiting suit in which I pay my respects to the dear departed and what have you done to your face? You look grotesque.'

She had closed the door behind her and now staggered across to the table on which she placed her handbag and where in front of which she sat down with a thump and tapped her lap for Bijou to jump up and be made a fuss of, an invitation he accepted with alacrity offering her a mass of wet kisses all over her face.

Thornton allowed the scene to continue for a while, waiting for the kissing to stop and Carlotta to face him which she eventually did.

'I'm sorry Carlotta. Bijou was desperate to go out and I didn't want to take him in case I was recognised so I thought I would go in disguise.'

'Disguise? Is that what you call it?'

'It wasn't such a good idea, huh?'

'Thornton, if you had set one foot outside the front door looking like that you would not only have attracted the attention of everyone around but you would have been arrested on the spot. It's just as well I got back when I did. There are a couple of bobbies parading up and down looking important for some reason best known to themselves. Normally we don't see plod for days on end. God, I could do with a cup of tea. You nearly gave me a heart attack, Thornton.'

'Sorry.'

She dropped Bijou off her lap and went to put on the kettle.

'Is everything okay? I mean with the pawnshop. No trouble?'

'No trouble at all. Ticket's in my bag. I'll give it to you in a sec.'

'How much did they give you for it?'

'Twenty quid.'

'Twenty quid! Is that all? Cheeky buggers, it's worth much more than that.' He neglected to tell her it was worth an inestimable fortune.

'You'll find the money in my bag as well.'

'No, you keep that. It's yours. You've earned it, and more besides.'

Carlotta turned away from the stove, on her way to the toilet to empty old tealeaves down the bowl but she stopped in the middle of the room and burst into laughter.

'Oh, Thornton, you do look a sight. If only I had a camera. Have you seen yourself in the mirror?'

'Yes, I have thank you.'

'Well get out of my best suit, go and wash your face and we'll have a cup of tea. I presume you'd like some breakfast as well? Or should that be brunch?'

'I would rather.'

'Good. Just let me get rid of this and I'll fix you something. How about grilled kidneys? Are you partial to kidneys?'

'Partial to anything edible at the moment. Oh by the way, I'm afraid Bijou has pissed all over your carpet. I wasn't quick enough in getting him out.'

'Oh, that's all right, Thornton. It's not the first time he's done it and that old thing needs throwing out anyway.'

At which, with another peal of laughter, she disappeared in the direction of the bathroom leaving him with make-up all over his face.

*   *   *

Viktor Radenko and Karl Diederich, the man from the Balkans and the good doctor from East Germany were at their wits end. What were they to do with the countess if Thornton didn't show up?

Although Diederich had presented himself to the Swiss as a refugee he had already been out of the communist bloc for a goodly while though remaining committed to the regime and in fact still employed, hence the current caper. He had married an English woman, a communist sympathiser true but purely a marriage of convenience, and the house in Chelsea in which they now sat deliberating was not his but hers. The question was how long would it be before she and the children realised something decidedly fishy was going on and that there was a strange woman in their basement? Mrs Diederichs would not venture down there he was sure of that. She had been down on a tour of inspection when they first bought the house, gave a big shudder and never went down again, but he didn't know about the kids, hers from a previous marriage and old enough to be curious. They didn't exactly hate him but as a stepfather figure he was not all that popular and, should they suspect anything, there was no doubt they would do something about it. So for how long could the countess's presence be kept a secret?

*   *   *

'Inspector Venables, have you no lead at all?'

This time Holly had presented herself at the station and been ushered into Reg's office where she now sat opposite him, obviously extremely agitated.

Reg shook his head. 'If you had been honest and forthcoming with me in the beginning, Miss Day, this whole situation might well have been avoided you know. Why didn't you tell me when last we met that it was the Countess Cinelli you were protecting? After all, it would appear she hasn't actually done anything illegal so why, if I may ask, the secrecy?'

'Yes, I know. I know. It was a big mistake on my part but I was just being ultra careful.'

'Ultra careful of what?'

'Of her safety of course.'

'And by being ultra careful as you put it, you have jeopardised her safety.'

'Please, Inspector, don't rub it in. I feel badly enough about it as it is.'

'Well rest assured we are doing everything we can.'

Holly knew what everything meant and was in despair.

'No trace of Mister Radenko?'

Venables shook his head.

'You've no lead as to anyone who might be connected with the case?'

'The case? You're quite convinced it is a case are you? Maybe the countess wanted to disappear for a few days. It isn't unheard of. People do you know.'

Holly was reminded of what Yiorgos had said on the telephone and she winced. There must be some way of getting through to this man who seemed on the surface to be so complacent. He suddenly leaned forward, steepling his hands, elbows on his desk, and said in a very quiet voice.

'Where does Thornton King fit into all this and where might he be at the moment?'

'I don't know where he is but, as to your first question, all I know is he was employed by the countess, probably as a bodyguard I would think.'

'Bodyguard... hmn ... There is someone you could talk to, Miss Day, if you so wish. Mind you, I have not said any of this to you but you could have a chat on the q.t. with a certain Mister Mickey Flynn and see what you come up with.'

'Mickey Finn.'

'No, Flynn. Mickey Flynn.'

He had scribbled something down on a piece of paper and slid it across the desk. She picked it up and read an address in Whitechapel. Looking up she saw the inspector nod and place a finger firstly to the side of his nose and then to his lips.

*   *   *

273

Face scrubbed clean and in his own clothes, by now pretty grimy, he really did wish he could go home for a change of outfit. Carlotta's shower wasn't exactly state of the art and if there was one thing he hated, as well as all the other things he hated, it was tepid water, and not much of it, no more than a dribble descending from a shower rose, even in summer it still gave him the shivers; goose bumps all over and made him, he always thought, look a little like a hermaphrodite. As he dried himself off he was only glad Louise Anna hadn't been in a position to see him. It would have given her something else to laugh at. He wondered how she was. Fine, he had no doubt of it. Like Luigi one of life's survivors come what may.

Pawn ticket safely in his breast pocket and valise in hand he left Carlotta's flat and sauntered out into the world, prepared to walk the few yards down to his office. He was quite sure Bijou was glad to see the back of him and had joined Carlotta who, having been up quite early to visit the pawn shop south of the river, had taken to her bed. She was determined to remain undisturbed for the remainder of the day and as a precaution left the phone off the hook and disengaged her doorbell which she could do by simply pulling out a loose wire. Then with curtains drawn and wearing her frilly pink face mask she was asleep within seconds. With what Thornton had paid her and a promise of more to come she felt she really could afford to take the day off.

Thornton on the other hand was dismayed to see two bobbies standing outside his office building and approached them with something akin to caution until he recognised them. They were constables Roper and his sidekick, the miserable looking one who never said anything if he didn't have to and whose name Thornton had completely forgotten. Shit, Thornton thought, with those two standing there no one is going to come visiting. Somehow he would have to get rid of them.

'Ullo, ullo ullo!' He said out loud, making light of it, 'What's all this goin' on 'ere then?' Thornton's Cockney accent was atrocious. 'Constable Roper isn't it?'

'That's right, sir.' Roper made a gesture towards the side of his helmet that was meant to pass for a salute. His companion squinted passed the peak of his pulled well down over his nose helmet and regarded Thornton once more with the gravest suspicion. Thornton remembered their first meeting over the corpse of that horrible old miser who allegedly had just died of a heart attack.

'And Constable Babcock,' Thornton said. The name suddenly came to mind. 'And what might you two be a doing of?'

This caused a couple of raised eyebrows and a snigger of embarrassment from Roper.

'Looking after your welfare, sir.'

'Is that so? My welfare needs looking after, does it? Now why would that be, I wonder? I suppose this was Inspector Venables' big idea, yes?'

Roper nodded. 'He thought your life might be in some danger, sir.'

'Really? I still wonder why?'

'Well, it's this case he's working on.'

'What case might that be?'

Roper was about to reveal all when a nudge from his companion put a stop to it. 'Shouldn't really say, sir. Confidential you realise. Police business. Know what I mean?'

'Of course. Yes… well then… very thoughtful of old Reg but quite unnecessary.' He really didn't know what more to say under the circumstances. He couldn't very well tell these two simply to push off so he thought he had better have words with the man himself and, with this in mind, he wished the constables a good morning and was about to enter the building when he was stopped.

'Been travelling have you, sir?' This was from Roper and when Thornton turned the constable lowered his head and raised his eyebrows to indicate the valise. Thornton glanced down at it.

'Yes. I have as matter of fact.'

'Have a good time then did you?'

'A jolly good time, Constable Roper, yes indeed. One of these days I'll buy you a drink and tell you all about it. In the meantime, if you don't mind, I need to get into my office. All right?'

'Certainly, sir. No problem. Don't let us delay you.'

Thornton mounted the stairs, walked along the passage and came to his office door which he found slightly ajar. He used his foot to push it open the full way and found, not to his surprise, that they had already been there and done the room over. There wasn't really anything that could be badly damaged, unlike at the Pension Crispi and, of course, the intruders had found nothing so he set about putting everything to right. He glanced out the window to see the two policemen were still outside so decided he really had to do something about it. He dropped down behind his desk, picked up the telephone lying on the floor, dialled the station and asked for Reg Venables.

'Thornton,' Reg called out amiably when he eventually came on line, 'how are you? Everything hunky dory is it?'

'Everything is fine. Reg, so why have you set your bloodhounds on me?'

'Bloodhounds?' There was a laugh that made Thornton

remove the phone from his ear until it was over. 'Roper's more like a poodle wouldn't you say?'

Remembering the nasty nip he had once received from another miniature, a King Charles spaniel, and still bearing the scar Thornton was disinclined to agree.

'Reg, you know what I mean and there is really no necessity for it so why not call them off? You're wasting valuable police resources. Isn't that how the papers refer to it? I'm fine, honestly, and whoever they are, they've have already been here. My office has been well and truly done over. Do you know what they're looking for, Reg?'

'No, I don't, Thornton. Why don't you tell me so we can get to the bottom of this?'

'The bottom of what, Reg?'

'We're talking in circles here. The Countess Cinelli has disappeared, I believe abducted and in great danger, and you know why so please fill me in Thornton so I can do something about it. This is police work after all.'

'Reg, call off your boys please. Whoever is behind this have been and they're not likely to come back now.' He knew this was a lie; they most definitely would be back sooner or later, most likely sooner.

'Have it your own way, Thornton but don't blame me if you land up in the shit.'

'Down I think.'

'What?

'Down in the shit, not up.'

'With you, Thornton, one never knows,' and the phone went dead. A short while later Thornton noticed Roper and his sidekick had disappeared.

Holly knew that time was running out and if the whereabouts of the countess was not discovered soon the game would be over and lost. She still had absolutely no idea where Thornton might be either: that is, if he was still anywhere, something she didn't like to think about. Neither did she think her own general practitioner would be amenable to giving her a sickness note without good cause, but she badly needed time off if she was going to be of any use, so her first port of call was Barts where she hoped to corner Doctor Adrian. He hadn't been seen at his flat for a while so she presumed he was on constant call and staying at the hospital, either that or painting the town red.

He was quite surprised to see her and greeted her affably with 'Hello, Holly, Thornton in trouble again?'

No, yes, maybe, she didn't know, but there was someone else in trouble and she desperately needed a sick note to give her a few days away from the office.

'Okay,' Adrian said, 'if it's a matter of life or death. Will a week be enough? We'll say stress and a bad back, Depression is too depressing. Bad backs are an excellent excuse, no one can gainsay them.'

'Thank you, Adrian. Thank you very much. I'm really terribly grateful.'

He shrugged. 'No problem for me, Holly, hope it helps with yours. Tell me all about it later.'

'How's Adrian by the way?'

'No idea. Haven't seen him in ages.'

'Oh! Sorry.' Seeing the look on his face she wished she hadn't asked.

His beeper went. 'Oops! Here we go again. No peace for the wicked. Bottles to the fore, bedpans to the rear!' And he was gone.

Her next port of call was no distance away at all, Turner Street, Whitechapel. She had looked it up in the A to Z so knew exactly where she was going but, not being au fait with the area, didn't know what she would find, probably just a street of old Victorian houses or shops with flats above. She discovered a pub on the corner which was only to be expected, this being the East End were pubs were once on every street corner. Now many of them had gone, often to make way for new development, but once they were the social centre of the community where mum and dad could enjoy an evening with friends while the kids stood outside in all kinds of weather munching on arrowroot biscuits. A couple of doors up from the pub, past two empty and shuttered shops, one of which had been a greengrocer's, the other a bakers, forced to close by the advent of the supermarket and Britain's shopping habits radically changing, she found a smoke filled Fred's caff where she could sit and wait, keeping an eye on a certain house further up the road for a certain person to appear while certain habitués of the caff kept an appraising eye on her. It had been a long while since Holly was last in such an establishment but she hadn't eaten that morning and her tummy was beginning to rumble alarmingly. Also she could really do with a cuppa, so she ordered sausage, egg, and chips and waited, idly toying with the bottle of Brown Sauce on the table in front of her. The café proprietor whose name actually was Fred eyed her suspiciously as he prepared her order. She was not the kind of woman to grace his portals that was for sure. He was all curiosity as to what she might be up to especially, having finished her nosh, she sat for a long while looking out the plate glass window. Slumming it, that's what she was doing and he wanted to know why so he approached her table under the pretence of wiping it down with a greasy cloth.

'Waiting for someone are you?'

'Yes, as a matter of fact.' Holly hoped the proprietor was not a pal of Mister Flynn's and flashed him a smile and her identity card which, although not for any police force in the country it did have her photograph and looked at a quick glance sufficiently authentic to pass muster. He was duly impressed. The wiping down stopped and he straightened up, so she went on, very quietly so as not to alert any of the surrounding tables. 'Do you know someone around here by the name of Mickey Flynn?'

'Oh, him is it? I might ha' known. A real bad egg that one. Lovable, you know, but a bad egg all the same.'

Holly didn't think Fred was in the habit of thinking anyone lovable, least of all a bad egg, but she let it pass.

'What's he been up to this time?'

'You do know him then.'

'From what I've just remarked that's obvious innit? Yeah, he comes in now an' again for his bangers an' mash, prefers mash to chips, or similar. Ain't been in for a while mind you. Gone all upper crust he has.'

'Is that a fact?'

'Seems like it anyhow. He's come in to a bit of dosh if you asks me or done a good job an' now my food ain't good enough for him.'

'If you see him can you point him out to me?'

'Point him out? What for? You can't hardly miss him. He's as big as a bloody barn door. He's a man mountain. Now, can I get you something else?'

'I'll have another cup of tea.'

He nodded and went off to get it from a battered tin pot sitting on top of an old-fashioned urn to keep hot. She had only said this to keep him happy. His tea was strong enough to melt a spoon if you left it in the cup long enough. God alone knew what it did to your stomach and your gullet on the way down. Probably stripped the enamel off your teeth as well. He placed the chipped cup in front of her

'On the house,' he said.

*   *   *

Thornton was still a very worried man. He wasn't at all sure his arrangement for the safety of the hour glass was sufficiently foolproof. The pawn ticket was burning a hole in his pocket where it was safe for the moment but no matter where he hid it he had a feeling it would eventually be found. Also, and this was of paramount importance, there was the safety of the countess to consider and, of even more paramount importance if that were possible, the safety of his toes. The memory of a certain shop in the Westbourne Grove and what he found there came to mind causing an involuntary shudder. He decided on a plan he felt sure was foolproof. Was any plan ever foolproof? He would pawn something else. What? What could he pawn? His watch? He doubted any pawn shop would take it for what it was worth. Ah, yes! He would pawn his electric razor, which was worth a few bob more and, if not redeemed, should be easy to sell. Watches are two a penny. Mind you, maybe electric razors are as well. There was only one way to find out and that was to visit another establishment and make sure that second ticket wouldn't be too difficult to find whilst the real one would be safely hidden away. He would explain what he had done to whoever came to collect and exchange the second ticket for the countess. More than this he felt he could not do. Was there a flaw in his plan? He couldn't think of one offhand. He picked up his Yellow Pages still lying on the floor and turned once more to pawnbrokers. This time he chose one in quite the opposite direction to the first and twice the distance away.

He found an old envelope addressed to him, one that hadn't been too obviously opened, placed the pawn ticket in a sheet of folded paper, slid it into the envelope, sealed the flap with Le Page's and, satisfied, left the office, electric razor and envelope in hand. In what was hilariously called the foyer but which in fact was merely the passage behind the front door, he dropped the envelope into his mail box and walked out into the street, took a careful look around and, seeing nothing suspicious, headed for Tottenham Court Road station.

*   *   *

'He didn't seem at all worried, sir.'

'Did he not? Doesn't mean anything, laddie. Thornton never looks worried even when he's at his most worried. I've learned that from experience.' Reg manoeuvred a metal bin with his foot into a handy position to catch the old tobacco, carefully knocked his pipe out against the corner of his desk. He still remembered what happened to his favourite pipe in the south of France when in the middle of the road and in a moment of intense anger he banged it too hard against the heel of his shoe and broke the stem. Having scraped out the last almost solid black glob with his little knife made for that purpose, he proceeded to fill the bowl with fresh tobacco from his Three Nuns tin. Roper waited. He was used to waiting. Often the silence was because Reg was trying to think of what to say next and it was slow in coming. He cleared his throat. 'Did you notice any suspicious looking characters around?'

'What's with suspicious? That part of London is swarming with suspicious characters.'

'The whole of London is swarming with suspicious characters, Roper which is why we're here.' He was tamping down the fresh tobacco with his thumb. 'What I meant was, was there anyone you noticed casing the joint?' He struck a match and held the flame to his pipe. Casing the joint? Where on earth had that one come from? Telly he supposed. Reg was not a film goer, not in the cinema, so it must have been the telly. Amazing what sort of jargon people picked up from the old telly. Such rubbish most of it. It was no wonder when watching it one fell asleep half the time. Reg let out a cloud of blue aromatic smoke.

'We nearly nabbed a couple of blokes in Oxford Street playing find the lady but they sussed us and scarpered before we could get near them.'

'Hmn...' Another cloud of smoke. 'Amazing really, how punters will fall for that old trick. All right, Roper. Get on with it.'

'Yes, sir. Get on with what?'

'Catching criminals of course, what else? That's what you're paid for. That's what's expected of you. That's what will earn you promotion in due course, providing you catch enough of them that is.'

In acknowledgement Roper's head jerked forward rather like a chicken, he stuck out his chin, turned, and left Reg's office none the wiser as to what he ought to do next so he scurried off to the canteen for a spot of lunch. He passed the desk sergeant on the way.

'If anyone asks for me,' he said, 'I'm in the canteen having a spot of lunch.'

'Who would ask for you?' The sergeant said and went chuckling on his way. He had been a sergeant for far too long and crustily realised he would never aspire to any rank higher so had somewhat reluctantly accepted his lot in life. There were chief constables he knew who should never have risen higher than inspector, if that, but there they were, big brass lording it over lesser mortals, enjoying the freebees and good things in life like municipal dinners. Life was so unfair.

He knocked on Reg's door and entered to lay the papers he was carrying on Reg's desk. Reg eyed them with distaste. 'More bloody pen-pushing,' he growled.

'That's life in the modern force,' the sergeant said. 'Need a bloody university degree these days if you want to get on.'

'Yes,' Reg agreed, 'and some of those aren't worth more than the certificate they come with.' He was hoping to rise further without benefit of a university degree. In fact he had scraped through police college by the skin of his teeth and his pretensions towards knowledge of subjects he knew little if anything about usually backfired in the most embarrassing way, which was why on the other hand if promotion was obviously not forthcoming, it was one of the reasons he couldn't wait for retirement to come soon enough.

*　　　　　　　　　*　　　　　　　　　*

The atmosphere in Chelsea was growing fraught, the situation really desperate, and among the ostensible men of steel, the steel was beginning to buckle and nerves were beginning to shatter.

It was all very well having two strange men, supposed friends of her husband's and staunch members of the party, staying as guests in her house, but Mrs Diederich was growing more and more suspicious that something not quite kosher was going on, especially when her husband quite casually over breakfast one morning, battering with a spoon the top of his boiled egg and dipping his soldier in the yolk, suggested she pay a visit to her mother in Sunderland and take the kids with her. He knew perfectly well she and her mother fought like cat and cat which is worse than cat and dog and a visit was only on the cards in a case of dire emergency, like her mother was at death's door and devoted daughter had to get up there pronto before the old bat could change her will. As the old bat was apparently in full health she couldn't understand why Karl had suggested it. "Just thought you needed a break," he added lamely which didn't help because she immediately wanted to know a break from what exactly?

The countess could only be taken from her basement prison when the three ignorant family members were out of the house as they were at this moment when the conspirators were having yet another confab.

'If there were anywhere else to move her, we would move her wouldn't we?'

This was from Gilbert, the one and one time only taxi driver. He had never driven a London cab before and he was never likely to do so again. It was in response to Diederich's bemoaning the fact that at any moment the countess's presence was going to be discovered. They were only grateful she had never set up a screaming match. Sooner or later Mrs Diederichs was going to get the decorators in to start work on the basement and it couldn't be put off much longer. She had already gone through a dozen different paint charts and reduced about four hundred shades of colour all with fancy names to half a dozen she really liked the look of. Whichever ones she finally chose, once they were on the wall they wouldn't look the same of course, they never do, but she wasn't to know that. It was only because she couldn't makeup her mind but kept dithering, "They all look so nice", that the delay had been extended. Like the surgeons' decks in Nelson's fleet, blood red would be a good colour Viktor thought, then it wouldn't matter what he got up to down there. Aloud he said, 'What about the embassy?'

'Which one? Not even the Bulgarian would be willing to take a chance on this getting out and becoming common knowledge, let alone any of the others including Moscow. Are you mad?'

'We're all mad. We're in it up to our necks and sinking fast. Failure is not part of party policy. You don't become a hero first, second, or even third class by failing but you were the one in the first place who thought it was a good idea to bring her here so there's no point in your complaining now, is there?'

'Well, I thought the whole matter would be settled overnight as it were and we could get shot of the old bag. How was I to know this Thornton King person would throw a spanner in the works?'

'Or to put it more politely,' Gilbert said, studying the well-bitten fingernails of one hand, 'fuck things up well and truly.'

'Well…' Viktor's voice was low and menacing. 'When I catch up with him he will wish he hadn't.'

'Don't you mean if you catch up with him?' Was the good doctor actually sneering? 'You haven't performed miracles so far have you?'

'All right, all right!' Gilbert tried to cool things down. 'Arguing is going to get us nowhere. She will just have to stay here, hopefully, maybe, only a day or so. Thornton King is back in London, even if we don't at the moment know exactly where. He will surface and when he does… we will get what we want.'

'I have a nasty feeling,' Diederich said, 'that if we do get what we want it will turn out to be not what we wanted.'

15

He came out of the house in his best bib and tucker and headed straight for the pub. Fred put down the cloth and the plate he was wiping, came out from behind his counter and walked over to Holly's table.

'What did I tell you? Opening time an' there he is on the dot. Who knows how many he'll knock back before closing time? A couple of hours from now an' he will be well and truly sloshed. Pissed out of his mind. Won't know his arse from his elbow if you'll pardon the expression.'

Holly turned her gaze from the window to look up at Fred and smiled. She had the feeling that Fred was quite taken with her, not that she hadn't noticed the wedding band on his fourth finger and was quite sure Mrs Fred was somewhere on the premises but men will be men. She only hoped she would have the same effect on

Mickey Flynn and have him feeling the same way. What Viktor had done to her she intended to do to Mister Flynn only in this case it would be big big promises but no satisfying the demand. The immediate question though was how much time should she give him to forget which was his arsehole and which his elbow? Despite the urgent need for speed, it would be foolish to rush in too early where angels fear to tread in cases where they were bound to make a cock-up.

'Would you mind if I stayed here a little bit longer?' She asked.

'Be my guest,' Fred said. 'You do make a refreshing difference from my usual customers if I may say so.'

So, Holly thought, romance in England wasn't quite defunct.

*   *   *

Thornton's wait was over. He was about to leave the office and head for the home he hadn't seen for a while when Viktor and Karl, the man from the Balkans and the doctor from East Germany, walked in. They were obviously in no mood for prevarication and got straight down to the nitty-gritty.

'Ah, Mister King,' Diederichs purred, 'we find you at last and this time we find you for keeps. Isn't that what you English say?'

He seated himself in the chair on the opposite side of the desk and with a lazy finger indicated over his shoulder the presence of his companion.

'I don't believe you've met my friend here, Mister Viktor Radenko.'

'I've not had that pleasure, no.'

'Oh, Mister King,' Karl chuckled, 'unless you are the masochist to end all masochists you would not find it a pleasure I can assure you so can we get straight down to business?' He laid a hand on the desk, palm uppermost. 'Where is it, Mister King? I give you ten seconds to answer.'

'It's in pawn.'

'What?'

'I said it's in pawn and you will never find it. If you care to look in Yellow Pages,' he indicated it lying on his desk, 'You will see there are quite a few pawn shops around in which to pop the weasel. Which one is it in do you suppose? Are you going to go to each and every one and ask for something you don't even know the look of? Or do you know the look of it? I don't believe you do. So, pardon me for saying so but I do believe I've got you over a barrel. Isn't that what we English say? Has all sorts of connotations that, doesn't it? Now I have a proposition to put to you and you have more than ten seconds to answer me, in fact you can take as much time as you want, within reason of course, I have something you want.'

'Yes, Mister King, but do you know what it is?'

'Of course I do. The countess Cinelli filled me in when she hired me. If it is truly what she says it is, it is without doubt worth a fortune which is why so many have shown such an interest in it.'

'So what does it look like?' This was from Viktor who up to this point had said nothing.

'Aha, there's the rub as Shakespeare might have said. You can hardly walk into a pawn shop and ask for something consisting of you have no idea what.' Thornton was aware that this was rather clumsily put but he also knew it was what he meant. 'So, speaking of the countess, you have the very thing I want and this is my proposition; in exchange for that poor woman I will give you the information you require. How about that?'

Karl looked up and over his shoulder and Viktor slowly nodded his head although his mouth was somewhat pursed indicating he felt this was not quite right though he couldn't work out why. Karl turned back to face Thornton.

'All right, Mister King. But how do we make the exchange?'

'Yes, that is a problem isn't it? You could be satisfied with your end of the bargain but I would still be left without mine, unless of course you were to hand her over first.'

'Are you crazy or what?' Viktor was losing patience.

'All right then, if you don't agree to that at least tell me where I can find her.'

'And that is just as crazy. Come on now, you're still stalling. What is the countess Cinelli to you?'

'The second half of my fee plus a whole heap of expenses.'

'That's no problem.' Viktor fished in his pocket and came out with a wad of high denomination notes he laid on the desk. 'And more if you want it.'

'Formidable!' Thornton said, using one of the few words he knew in French and then only because it was the same as in English but with a different accent. 'Hmn...' Now he appeared to be weighing up the pros and cons, eventually picking up the money and flipping through the notes. It was a not inconsiderable sum. 'Yes... well then...' He reached in his breast pocket and produced the second pawn ticket. Karl stood up so quickly he knocked the chair flying backwards as he stretched out for it and Viktor as quickly picked up the money.

'Not so fast,' Thornton said and Viktor, open mouthed, dropped the money back on the desk.

Louise Anna's snub nose Thornton had palmed, from right beneath her nose as it were, when she was concentrating so hard on the police, and which he had smuggled through airport and passed customs using the nothing to declare exit, had come in useful after all and was pointed straight at Viktor's chest.

This man Thornton King really was more than they had bargained for.

*   *   *

Holly sauntered into the pub, a real old-fashioned establishment with a saloon bar where ladies were meant to go and sit discreetly at faux leather settles sipping their stout, port and lemon or Babycham, their glasses on easily wiped down pewter topped tables and on Saturday nights join in the singing while the pianist churned out old time favourites: *I wonder who's kissing her now, You made me love you, My old man said follow the van, On mother Kelly's doorstep, Ta-ra-ra-boomdeyay.* On the other side of a wooden partition with a swing door and some fancy Edwardian etched glass was the public bar; smaller, bare and much rougher, catering for men only of course. That was where he was; holding up the bar, and that was where she couldn't get to him. Nevertheless she went up to the bar her side and stood in a position where, if he looked in the right direction, he would see her and from where she ordered a gin and tonic from a suspicious barmaid. Certainly no barmaid at the Folies Bergere, a bit too long in the tooth for that and a bit too blousy: bouffant blonde hair, bleached so often it was more like straw, Gypsy ear rings, blue eye shadow and false lashes, carmine lipstick and long blood red fingernails sharp as talons. On her feet so long she was forever complaining about her bunions but never thought to change her shoes.

'Ice?' The question was as frosty as the object mentioned.

'Yes please.'

'Lemon?' And this time as sour.

'Yes please.'

As the barmaid, whose name was Sadie, placed the requisite glass beneath the optic for a measure of gin she surveyed Holly in the mirror behind the shelves in front of her. Like Fred in his caff, she was aware that Holly was not the type of woman to haunt an East End pub and her curiosity was aroused. It was in fact this very curiosity that introduced Holly to Mickey Flynn.

Having received her drink and paid for it, there was no reason for Holly to remain standing at the bar looking conspicuous and as she really didn't know what she would say to Sadie to start a conversation she retired to a table where she hoped she might still keep an eye on Flynn even with some difficulty. It was hopeless. Because of that partition nothing in the public bar was in her eyeline. She returned briefly to order a packet of pork scratchings, not because she was hungry, she had after all sat in Fred's caff a good couple of hours or more and the bangers and chips lay heavy on her stomach, but in the hope of getting Mickey's attention. Waiting for her change she caught his eye and smiled like a true coquette before returning to her table. Hopefully that smile would be enough to pique his interest. It wasn't, probably because he was slightly short sighted and the distance between them was too far, but all was not lost. There being no one in the saloon at that moment to serve or chat up Sadie limped around to the public bar and engaged Mickey Flynn in conversation. It started off as a moaning session about her feet but it soon became clear that what she really wanted to talk about was that strange woman in the saloon bar. She kept looking over her shoulder, not to see if there were customers waiting but to see what Holly was up to which actually amounted to no more than sitting demurely behind her dimpled pewter topped table, her drink in front of her and her pork scratchings unopened.

'A bit of a goer, that one, if you was to ask me,' Sadie said in what she thought was a confidential but knowing manner. 'Get my drift?'

Mickey nodded and ordered another pint of draft Guinness which Sadie duly started to pull.

'Have one yourself, love,' Mickey said.

'Don't mind if I do,' she replied coyly. 'Got one on the go round the corner so I'll save it for later, love. Gin it will be if that's all right. Is it?' She knew perfectly well that, even if he resented the fact that she was on the spirits he was unlikely to back down in front of other customers and earn the reputation of being a cheapskate so he nodded and paid for the drinks. There would actually be no gin. Sadie, when she went around to the cash register, would simply pocket the money, adding it to anything else she had collected. The drink she had on the go around the corner was like a theatrical prop, a glass of soda water.

'Yes, I know her sort.' This was said as she pushed his glass across the bar. 'Can tell 'em a mile off I can. Don't know though what she'd be doing in a place like this. Looks a bit more high class to me. Know what I mean? Smashing looker though I have to admit.'

It was this last observation that did the trick. If there was an available bit of delectable totty sitting next door he wanted to at least take a good butcher's at it. With a 'Watch this for me, there's a girl. Got to see man about an' orse,' he left his drink on the counter, squeezed through the partition door and floated across the saloon; that is if twenty-one stone can be said to float. It is a well known fact though that truly heavy people can be extremely light on their feet. His excuse for so doing as he had told Sadie was his need to go the toilet that happened to be situated off the saloon bar. He stopped in front of Holly's table. 'Well well well, an' what have we here then? Ain't never seen you in here before. New to the neighbourhood are you?'

'You could say that,' Holly replied.

'Could I?' He pulled out a chair and sat down. 'Mickey, Mickey Flynn,' he said, extending a paw which reluctantly she took and eventually he reluctantly let go her hand. 'So what's yours then?'

'Gin and tonic actually.'

For a while Mickey rolled about with laughter, everything undulating like a heavy swell of the sea and then, having recovered, he continued with, 'No, I wasn't asking that. I was asking you what's your name?'

'Oh. Holly.'

'Holly. Well, Holly, I don't see why I shouldn't oblige you with another gin and tonic.' He looked around for Sadie who was still serving in the public bar. It was early days and trade was still a bit lax. When the pub grew somewhat busier the guv'nor would deign to join her and help out.

'No, please!' Holly blurted out. 'Look, I've hardly touched this one. I really don't need another, thank you all the same.'

Going to play hard to get, Mickey thought.

Going to try and get me pie-eyed, Holly thought. Fat chance.

'So what is it you do, Holly?'

'Do?'

'Yeah, do. Like what is it you do for a living, if anything? You're not a bricky or anything like that, I can see that.' This was intended to pass as wit and she dutifully smiled.

'I'm a secretary, what else? In a bank.'

'Oh. Anybody ever try to rob it?' And again the fat rippled quite alarmingly.

'Fortunately not.'

'Well, there's a first time for everything so they say. Do you agree?' And he gave her a big wink.

'So what do you do?... What did you say your name was?'

'Mickey Flynn.'

He got up and moved away. Holly thought she had lost him but he only went up to the bar and asked Sadie to pass him his drink which he took back to the table and sat down again.

'Cheers!' He said, lifting his glass.

'Bottoms up,' she replied smiling.

'Ere, tell you what, when we've had our drink what say we mosey on somewhere for a bite to eat?'

'Thanks, no. I've already eaten.'

'Pity.'

'You still haven't told me what you do, Mister Flynn.'

'Mickey.'

'Mickey.'

'Oh, a bit of this and a bit of that. You know.'

'Mainly that, huh?' And they both laughed.

* * *

In another bar close by the station, Inspector Venables was sipping his half and half and wondering what he would say if the papers got hold of the Countess Cinelli story. Someone at the hotel was bound to give the game away, especially if they could persuade a rag to pay out some money for information and a possible big story.

'You look worried, Reg. What's eating you?' The Guv'nor said, standing close by behind his bar polishing glasses. He held the one in hand up to the light to inspect it before hanging it by its stem in an overhead rack made specifically for the purpose. He didn't always bother with this but customers were few so it helped to pass the time between serving. When things were busy a quick rinse and drain was enough.

Reg dipped his fingers into his bag of crisps and brought out the last few which he stuffed into his mouth, surveying the writing on the bag before crumpling it up and dropping it into an ashtray.

'I dunno, Bert. Now and again a case comes along that you would give your eye teeth to figure out but nothing comes your way. You ever feel like that?'

'Not my scene, Reg. The only things I've got to look out for are hooligans bent on mischief...'

'And God knows there's plenty of them about.'

'That's true. And dud notes.'

'You've had some of those of late have you?'

In answer, Bert turned to the shelves behind him and took a note from a pint mug. 'Take a gander at that,' he said, passing it over.

Reg took it and held it up to the light. It was a forged twenty and a very good one.

'My my, that's a beaut that is. Whoever made this knew what he was doing. Bank of England would have difficulty sussing this one out.'

'Got by my barman it did. I could ha' killed him 'cept he's new at the game so I just gave him a good ticking off. The bugger who gave him that not only got a free drink he got the change for a twenty an' all. I tell you, Reg, you can't trust anybody these days. The country's really going to the dogs.'

'Been doing it for a long time, Bert, for a long time. Here, I'll have another for the road then I must be on my way before the lady wife starts to worry.'

Bert took the empty glass and started to pull the ale.

'Why haven't you reported this, Bert?' He was studying the note still in his hands.

'Only happened lunchtime and I've been that busy since. Been having a bit of a ding-dong with the brewers. Mean bastards. I tell you, Reg, keeping a pub these days? Not worth the candle.'

'Not worth being a copper either, Bert.'

*   *   *

Holly, after a few more drinks, had Mickey virtually eating out of her hand and she decided to cut it short and get to the point. Time really was running out. Her questioning had got as far as the fact that at the moment, despite having earned a fair amount fairly recently, he was stony broke. It wasn't just the day to day living that had drained his resources but the gee-gees and the dogs had taken most of it and right now he was in dead shtuk. He owed his bookmaker and unless he could come up with the readies pretty soon life wouldn't be worth living. In fact life most probably wouldn't even be.

'How much do you owe?' She asked.

'A hundred quid. Not much is it for a man's life, or at least his kneecaps? Fifty quid each knee.' This time the laugh was bitter. 'Baseball bats can hurt like hell if you know what I mean.' He saw the look on her face. 'I know I know. More fool me but that's all there is to it. What's done's done.' He sniffed and took another mouthful of Guinness. She regarded him steadily and then came right out with a proposal. She had to take the chance.

'What if I were to give you the money? Or lend it to you, just to get you off the hook as it were?'

'Here, what's your little game?' His piggy eyes narrowed. 'Why would you want to do that for me? We've only just met. What's in it for you?'

'Why should there be anything in it for me?'

'Because nobody in this world does anything for nuffink, that is why.'

'All right, I'll level with you.'

'Why don't you do that?'

'I need some information and I need it fast. I believe you can give it to me.'

Mickey got to his feet and picked up his glass. No point in wasting good beer. 'Good-bye, Holly.'

'Two hundred!'

Mickey sat down again.

'And no one need ever know where the information came from.'

'You serious? Two hundred?'

Holly nodded.

Mickey took a look around the bar. It had filled up a bit but there was nobody he knew. Only Sadie could say he had talked with Holly and he didn't think she would put two and two together. As far as she was concerned he was just a randy polecat chatting up a bird. 'It's about her isn't it?'

Holly nodded.

'What is it you want to know?'

'Where she is of course.'

'Two hundred?'

It was Holly's turn to nod.

'How do I collect?'

'Fifty in advance, like right now, this very minute, it's all I have on me. If you tell me true then I will be here same time tomorrow with the rest. That's a promise and I never break a promise. You'll just have to trust me.'

Mickey thought about this for a moment. Even if she never turned up with the rest and he felt sure she would, fifty quid and a promise for the rest would get his bookie off his back and the lads wouldn't be coming around with the baseball bats. He picked up a coaster and put it down in front of him. 'Got a pen?' he asked and she produced one.

Reg finished his one for the road and thought he'd best be getting back to the station. Getting to his feet he went over to a corner to retrieve his hat from the stand, before walking in the opposite direction towards the street door. He hadn't taken off his coat. It was lucky for him that he made that little detour for his hat because the guv'nor's missus appeared from behind the bar and called out to him.

'Oh, Inspector Venables, phone call for you. It's back here.'

'It's not the lady wife is it?'

'I don't think so, but it is a lady, young by the sound of it, and she says it's terribly urgent. Evidently Constable Roper said where to find you. The message is she has the address.'

'What!' Reg's bellow practically shook the pub to its foundations as he went to pick up the telephone.

16

Having been sent on a wild goose chase, Viktor and Karl were, to put it mildly, hopping mad. They couldn't get back to Thornton's office fast enough to confront him with his duplicity and throw his razor in his face. Viktor in particular knew exactly what he was going to do with it and it wasn't Thornton's face he was thinking of. He was almost salivating with anticipation. He would show Mister King what over a barrel, or in this case desk, really meant. He would have him screaming in no time and finally telling them the truth.

They were rather surprised then to find the office unlocked and no sign of the private eye, but there was an envelope taped to the door and addressed, "To Whom It May Concern." Both of them knew immediately who the whom were and Karl pulled away the envelope and ripped it opened with hands that were almost trembling. The note inside read,

Dear Sirs – By now you will no doubt realise that I am not to be trifled with and that if you still want what is in my possession (I am about to depart for the right pawn shop to redeem it so henceforth it will be on my person) you will without fail bring the Countess Cinelli to me in exchange. The exchange will be made this evening at say nine o'clock on Chelsea Bridge. You will no doubt approach it from the north so I will be waiting closer to the south. If the countess is not produced I can assure you you will never receive what you are after. I remain, yours faithfully Thornton King.

So it had finally come to this. They were at last close to ending the whole episode. They would get rid of both the countess and Mister King at one and the same time and finally have the drug and the formula in their hands. For the moment though they would just have to be patient for a few more hours. It was back to that little house in Chelsea and then… Karl crumpled up the note and shoved it into a pocket as they set out on the penultimate leg of what had been a very long journey.

The quiet little road in Chelsea was at the moment far from quiet but a hotbed of activity with a number of police cars in evidence. The team was led by the intrepid Inspector Venables. No one was going to do him out of what was rightfully his. A constable had been sent down the area stairs, peered through the barred window, looked up at Venables looking down and given the thumbs up.

'Right, lads,' Venables said to the men standing with him at the front door and rubbing his hands together, 'she's here so let's get on with it.'

It was the intrepid Constable Roper who, ignoring the bell, hammered on the door with his fist and yelled, 'Police! Open Up!' He had wanted to do that ever since he had joined the force. He could just imagine how proud of him Blodwen would be at that moment. There being no answer to his hammering he glanced at Reg who gave him the nod so he repeated his performance and this time the door was opened by a quivering Mrs Diederichs who stared at the men at her front door and could only gasp out one word.

'Yes?'

The children, a skinny boy of about fourteen with acne and asthma, he was using his inhaler, and a girl perhaps a little older who didn't seem at all put out by what was going on. She had always suspected her stepfather of nefarious goings on and that this day would be coming. She thought Constable Roper rather cute and was disappointed to see the wedding ring on his left hand. He was rubbing the right one that had got slightly bruised from his vigorous knocking.

Reg stepped forward, flashed his identity, and started his spiel which began with 'We have reason to believe...'

Mrs Diederichs hardly believed a word he was saying. She felt she was about to faint. Her legs were buckling anyway.

*   *   *

And so the Countess, at last breaking down and sobbing with relief, was rescued, assisted out of her basement prison and passed, days worth of accumulated muck and all, into the welcoming arms of a police woman. Venables was most disappointed though that Mrs Diederich and children, apart from a man named Gilbert who he had never heard of but who would be arrested on suspicion anyway, particularly as he had tried to scarper over the back garden wall, appeared to be the only people in the house. It had been gone through top to bottom and definitely no one else was found hiding there. So where was this Viktor Radenko then and where was Mrs Diederich's husband? He needed to have a face to face with both those gentlemen.

Both those gentlemen, on turning the corner at the bottom of the street and seeing what was going on immediately turned on their heels and walked away as fast as they could go.

*   *   *

Thornton was waiting. He had the precious little hour glass safely in his pocket. It wasn't too much to imagine that in the wrong hands it could change the whole history of the world. He looked at his watch. Five to nine. Traffic came and went over the bridge but there was no sign yet of Viktor and Karl and the Countess Cinelli. He had no reason to suspect anything could go wrong at this stage of the game. The only thing that worried him was, once the countess had reached him and safety, what would he do with "it" and, once the men had "it" in their hands what would they think of doing to him and the Countess? Well, there was no sign of them yet so he would just have to wait and see. He turned to look down at the river and when he looked back across the bridge he was somewhat startled to see Viktor approaching on his own. No sign of the other two. What kind of a double cross was this? For a second he closed his fingers around the butt of Louise's gun in a jacket pocket to reassure himself somewhat and waited. Viktor arrived to within talking distance. He more than likely would have got even closer had Thornton not raised his hand like a traffic cop ordering him to stop.

'Where is the Countess Cinelli?' Thornton asked.

'Safe. Quite safe I'm sure you will be pleased to hear.'

'No, I won't be pleased at all. That statement could imply anything. Safe could even mean dead. Where is she?'

'She's been rescued so you don't have to do anything more. Now...'

'Rescued? Rescued by who?'

'The police of course. Somehow they found out where she was being kept and they've arrested Gilbert...'

'Who is Gilbert?'

'Never mind. Let's get on with the business.'

'Where is your sidekick?'

'My what?'

'The good doctor.'

Viktor shrugged. 'Who knows? We went back to the house but left in a hurry when we saw the police. I went one way he went another. I haven't seen him since. Now give me what I've come for. We've talked enough.' He glanced nervously around beginning to suspect a trap and suddenly withdrew a gun. Holding it in one hand, with the fingers of the other he gestured for Thornton to hand over what he had come for.

Thornton reached in his pocket and came out with the egg timer, holding it up in front of him almost as if it were a talisman that would protect him from a bullet. He looked at it, head cocked to one side, looked back at Viktor. 'Pretty little bauble isn't it?'

Viktor Radenko could hardly believe his eyes. 'That... that is it?'

Thornton nodded and studied it once more as though he had never really looked at it before. 'This is it.'

'You have got to be joking.'

Thornton shook his head. 'No joke, Viktor, no joke. This really is it. It's got writing on it, here.' He indicated the undersides top and bottom, or bottom and top depending on which way it was standing. 'I don't know much about chemistry but I can recognise a formula when I see one.'

'All right, I believe you. Hand it over.' He stretched out an eager arm and open hand.

Thornton stretched out his own arm, holding his hand over the side of the bridge and Viktor visibly blanched.

'You wouldn't do that, Mister King. You wouldn't be so stupid. If you do I will shoot you. Believe me I will have nothing to lose now and it would give me the greatest satisfaction.'

'Better than roasting toes I suppose. Quick anyway.'

'Give it to me!' Viktor almost screamed and raised the gun higher.

'Hello, Viktor.'

He swung around to face the voice that seemingly had come out of nowhere and took a fist in the face that sent him reeling. She moved in fast and without breaking his arm but getting pretty close to it, she had his gun in her hand and let him go. Hell might not have fury like a woman scorned but it was as nothing compared to a woman used, abused, and abandoned.

'Left it a bit late, didn't you Holly?'

'I made it in time didn't I? And that's what matters. Where's the stuff?'

'Stuff? What stuff?'

'The stuff he came for.' She prodded the recumbent Viktor with the toe of her boot. 'The stuff that started this whole business. The stuff that got a number of people killed and the poor countess incarcerated in a disgusting smelly old cellar. Now where is it, Thornton?'

Thornton looked down at the river and then back to Holly.

'Gosh,' he said, 'in all the excitement I must have dropped it. If the glass breaks there are going to be some quite happy fishies down there.'

The police car came careering over the bridge, blue light flashing.

*   *   *

Thornton had one more duty to perform, duty as he saw it that is and he waltzed breezily into Reg's office.

'Hello, Thornton. I don't want to come out with that old chestnut about turning up like a bad penny but what is it I can do for you this time?'

'More than a penny involved here, Reg, about fifty thousand nicker at a guess.'

'What?'

Thornton dropped Viktor's packet of notes onto Reg's desk and took a chair. 'Something for the Police Benevolent Fund, Reg.'

Reg picked up the packet took out a note, then another, then another.'

'Where did you get this?'

'Viktor gave it to me. Now I'm giving it to you.'

'No point, old son, they're duds… forgeries.'

*   *   *

And so, in the manner of that old Russian tale, *Peter and the Wolf,* to sum up: Carlotta was delighted to have received enough from the countess's treasure chest to pay for a week's holiday in

Torquay on the English Riviera. She didn't go to a continental Riviera because it would mean Bijou having to go into quarantine and kennels on their return and she wasn't going to have that. He could go to Torquay with her. She found a hotel that welcomed pets. Bijou was delighted to have a new carpet to piss on. Mickey Flynn aka Errol aka Finn was only too pleased to be able to pay off his bookmaker and have a hundred quid to put on the gee gees or the dogs. You never know, his luck could change. It didn't: but he still thought Holly was just the most wonderful woman alive and got all tearful whenever he thought about her which was often; and Holly? Well she was only too happy that the Countess was safe and the whole business over and done with. The Countess Cinelli too was happy, happy to be back in her palazzo where she was keeping a sharp protective eye on Yiorgos. He was too much of a treasure to lose and knowing now that much more about him, she felt he would make sure she in turn was well protected rather than betray her again.

Louise Anna returned to the good ole U.S. of A. where she eventually married an aging oil tycoon, stayed with him for a year and then divorced him on the grounds of non consummation and walked away with a few million dollars thanks to a good ole rather biased judge with stars, or rather the vision of Louise Anna, in his eyes. She still had fond memories of Thornton King but that was all they would ever be, memories. Nat was never given a second's thought.

Karl Diederichs fled back to East Germany and wished he hadn't when interrogated by the Stasi and Viktor Radenko, indicted for murder, was being held in custody in London until his trial came up. Mrs Diederichs tore up her party card and wanted nothing more to do with it. She also sued for divorce and put the Chelsea house up for sale. As property values were increasing in leaps and bounds she made a sizable profit and no longer worried about whether she was in her mother's will or not.

Constable Roper was very happy at the birth of an addition to his household. They called the little girl Ceridwen Gwyneth and Reg Venables in his usual way asked "how Welsh can you get?" Well what could you expect from a girl like Blodwen Roper who came from the valleys or Cardiff or Swansea or Aberystwyth or llanfairpwilgwyngyllgogarychwyrndrobwllliuantysillogogogoch or wherever? He was quite chuffed when Roper asked him to be Godfather and turned up at the church in full uniform and carrying a swagger stick and with the lady wife in tow in her best bib and tucker, mutton dressed as lamb, bless her.

More important and to his intense satisfaction, the media were having a field day. This was more than his fifteen minutes. This would last him a lifetime, the hero of the day, the man of the hour even, the brilliant cop who rescued a kidnapped foreign dignitary, arrested a mass murderer and saved the country from being swamped with forged twenty pound notes. There was no doubt, no doubt at all that chief constable was on the cards in the not too distant future.

Inspector Lichti was happy that at last he had almost found his haiku, *Only to the clouds does the high mountain give up her mystic secrets.* He wasn't sure whether it was the obligatory three lines or not but it could be divided five, seven, five, it did consist of seventeen syllables and it did have a sort of poetic ring to it so he heaved a sigh of relief and admired it on the paper lying on the desk in front of him, repeating it to himself a number of times.

> *Only to the clouds*
> *Does the high mountain give up*

Her mystic secrets

Five, seven, five. Yes, he was very pleased with it.

And Thornton? Well, he was only too happy to collect his expenses and final cheque and have his bank manager almost bowing and scraping to him but more, much more than that, he sat in his apartment and admired the Cinelli vases – the gift of a grateful countess.